SOUND ON SOUND

SOUND ON SOUND

A NOVEL BY

CHRISTOPHER SORRENTINO

DALKEY ARCHIVE PRESS

A portion of this work appeared, in slightly different form, in *Private Arts* #7.

Library of Congress Cataloging-in-Publication Data

Sorrentino, Christopher, 1963-
    Sound on sound : a novel / by Christopher Sorrentino. —1st ed.
    I. Title.
PS3569.O697S68   1995   813'.54—dc20   94-37596
ISBN 1-56478-073-2

Partially funded by grants from the National Endowment for the Arts and the Illinois Arts Council.

NATIONAL
ENDOWMENT
FOR 🌱 THE
ARTS

Dalkey Archive Press
Campus Box 4241
Normal, IL 61790-4241

Printed on permanent/durable acid-free paper and bound in the United States of America.

To Josh Milder

CONTENTS

"Objectivity" is in spite of itself a willful program for the stacking of perceptions; facts emerge not from life but from revelation, gnarled as always by ancient disharmonies and charged with libidinous energy.

—Robert Coover

. . . rock and roll at its core is merely a bunch of raving shit . . .

—Lester Bangs

SOUND
ON
SOUND

FOUNDATION
(Basic Rhythm)

One disadvantage to sound-on-sound recording is that as the process is repeated, and successive layers of sound are placed atop previously recorded material . . . [this older] material has a tendency to lose clarity. Thus, if multiple "overdubs" are anticipated, it is prudent to first lay a foundation, typically consisting of a recorded performance by the band's rhythm section, over which the remaining elements of the music can be laid. . . .

—Perkin Gifford, *Sound Recording: Its Methods and Applications* (New York: Cronus, 1959), chap. 9, "Popular Music," 147

Tuesday, January 20, 1981

Motionless except for his long coat, unbuttoned on what has been an unseasonably warm day and flapping gently in the wind, the figure stands with his back to the late-afternoon sun so that his expression, his features, the very color of his clothing, are obscured from those approaching from the east. The equipment sits before him, blocking the sidewalk in front of the building in which the band rehearses. The dwindling light, reflected by the melting snow all around, strikes the equipment in odd, unexpected places, affecting the matte black of the guitar cases and amplifier covers with a dull sheen. The snow is the product of a small storm two nights before. The sidewalk has a filthy path worn into its approximate center, but is broad enough to allow a thin margin of pure white on either side. The figure stares at one of these margins, its dazzling brilliance, then looks away, following the hazy grey afterimage floating across his field of vision, imposing the perspective of this old perception upon the buildings, parked cars, and the lines of the street. The afterimage passes, and is gone. The manifest neutrality of the setting hangs suspended for a moment—black, white, black, grey, white—until a new figure intrudes upon the scene, changing its values. The two shift about as they speak; shades of grey, now white, and now black replace each other as they move.

After a while, the other departs. Figure 1 cracks his knuckles, listens to the car horns cutting cleanly through the colder evening air. A man comes out of the building with a broom and dustpan and begins to sweep the shards of a shattered flowerpot into a pile. He mutters to himself as he sweeps the fragments, yanking the broom with short, loud strokes. A voice calls to Figure 1 and he enters the building to stand in the vestibule between propped-open inner and outer doors. Here his own responding voice takes on a reverberant quality, losing the muffled flatness with which the enveloping snow had imbued it. The sweeper pushes past him, carrying the broom and the dustpan full of broken clay up the stairs.

He waits in here, facing the street, keeping an eye on the equipment. He turns toward the sound of an approaching couple and for an instant they come into view as they pass, framed in the doorway, their soft conversation and laughter unintelligible to him, moving down the block with them. A door slams upstairs. He studies the vestibule. A framed inspection certificate hangs on the wall, last signed in June 1980 by A. Oso. In the opposite wall, a row of mailboxes is recessed. A label on the first mailbox reads "R. Bobtak." The second has written on its metal surface, in elegant calligraphy, the names "Clifton / Sweet." On the third, a card is taped:

ZOUNDS
* Rehearsal *
* Eight Track Recording & Mixing *
* Late-Nite Hours *

The fourth is stenciled "INT'L BROTHERHOOD OF HOUSE-WRECKERS," beneath which is affixed a decal depicting an attractive, partially clad young woman, with oddly misshapen breasts, straddling the seat of what appears to be a bulldozer or tractor of some kind. Above and to the right of the mailboxes is a small graffito, which says, "Mo Eats Scum." Under it, a feminine hand has written "Only Nat's." Figure 1 smiles at this, caressing the rough plaster applied sloppily to one of the large cracks in the wall, sliding his fingers into the crack itself and absently working them, loosening chunks of plaster that fall at his feet, until he feels the wooden strips of lathing beneath. He hears the three other band members as they begin to descend the staircase, the rhythmic creaking of the steps tapering off at the landings and then starting again, growing louder with each successive flight of stairs. The first of the three lands heavily on the ground floor, just before the vestibule, and reaches to zip his tight motorcycle jacket, the stiff, new leather resisting. After two attempts, he grasps the jacket firmly at the hem and pulls hard at the zipper, tossing his head to free his shoulder-length blond hair from beneath his collar. Behind him, a tall, endomorphic young man stands on the bottom stair, running his left hand along the banister and slapping his thigh with the palm of his right. The third peels the wrapper from a candy bar and begins to eat it hungrily. Figure 1 lights a cigarette. The smoke irritates his throat and he bends slightly at the waist, the hard cough rising from within him and shaking his body. He finishes coughing and sharply, involuntarily, inhales, his face burning. Figure 4 speaks to him and he responds.

The mild temperatures prevailing today have disappeared with the sun and a stiff wind has come up. The soft snow is hardening to ice. Soon it will be bitter cold. Despite the open doors, it is warm and comfortable in the building, and the band members linger for a moment, talking. Presently, Figure 2 puts on a pair of work gloves and goes behind the staircase, where several items are more or less permanently stored. These include an old pair of wooden skis, a large Styrofoam cooler, a broken air-hockey game, a plastic snowman, whose hat serves as a hopper of some kind and whose abdomen houses a crank, and a dolly, which latter item Figure 2 retrieves, pulling it by a piece of stout rope tied to one of its carpet-covered wooden crosspieces. He drags it out of the building and into the cold. Figures 3 and 4 follow him. Figure 1 takes a long drag on his cigarette and then drops it to the cracked mosaic of the floor, grinding it out under his left foot. He shuts the inner door and, kicking the stop from under the outer door, steps out onto the sidewalk, allowing the door to slam behind him and checking to make sure it is locked.

The four work quickly in the cold, preparing the equipment for travel. Figure 1 squats with Figure 4 and the two of them gently turn one of the amplifiers upside down so that its four metal casters are pointed skyward and place it on top of the dolly that way. The other amplifier is placed next to it and a bungee cord is wrapped around the dolly's frame and the amplifiers, securing them. Most of the drum equipment—the floor and aerial toms, stands, pedals, cymbals, and throne—has already been placed in a reinforced trap case, but the bass and snare drums have to be balanced on top, along with Figure 2's second guitar. Figures 2 and 3 discuss this briefly. Now, the equipment is distributed among the four of them: Figure 1 carries two guitars, Figures 3 and 4 maneuver the trap case, and Figure 2 pulls the dolly.

Figures 1, 2, 3, and 4 are here identified as Nathanael Spielvogel, aka Nat Phenomenon; David McCall; Richard Poindexter; and Jay Lustig. The name of the band is Hi-Fi.

It is warm and brightly lit inside the empty club. A man behind the bar pours pretzels into the small wooden bowls set at regular intervals upon its surface, occasionally glancing at the television suspended from the ceiling at the front of the barroom. He takes no discernible notice of Hi-Fi's arrival, turning to stand before his reflection in the mirror behind the bar, checking the rows of bottles there. At one of four tables against the wood-paneled wall opposite the bar, a cigarette sits burning in an ashtray before a shapeless gold lamé handbag. Arc lights near the back of the club are directed toward a small platform, raised approximately a foot above the floor, which serves as the stage. Save for three old gooseneck microphone stands, the stage is bare. Figure 5 turns toward the band again, and begins wiping the bar down with a rag, lifting bowls, ashtrays, and stacks of cardboard coasters out of his arm's elliptical path as he moves along the bar. When he reaches the point at which the bar begins to curve toward the wall, he throws the rag down and leans on his arms against the bar, studying the television. He laughs as Redd Foxx explains something to Demond Wilson. Jay approaches him to say something and as he does an obese middle-aged woman wearing a gold lamé dress which matches the handbag emerges from behind a door marked PRIVATE located in an alcove of sorts that divides the barroom from the rest of the club. She speaks to Jay as she walks, moving past him to seat herself before the burning cigarette and the handbag, so that Jay instinctively turns to follow the sound of her voice. She falls silent, staring with the bartender at the television, dragging heavily on the cigarette, the coal glowing brightly. A grey cylinder of ash falls to the polished surface of the table.

Figures 5 and 6 are here identified as Don McOral and Mona Barron.

Spanning the wall behind the stage is a mural depicting a flat rendering of a radio-era microphone. Two parallel diagonal stripes run from stage right, at floor level, to stage left, where they disappear near the molding at the edge of the ceiling, diverging in the middle of the wall to form the microphone's outer contours. Lettering between the stripes spells out C H E A—mouthpiece—T E R S, the name of the club. The stage is constructed of sheets of plywood nailed to a rectangular frame of two-by-fours and raised sixteen inches above the floor by a means of support concealed behind the pleated white fabric that has been affixed around the frame's perimeter. It is small, thrusting out from the wall a total of eight feet and measuring twelve feet from side to side. The drummer is situated on the same level as the rest of the stage, obscuring him behind the musicians standing in front of him. Off stage left is a dressing area, hidden from view behind folding screens, which area the musicians share with cases of empty beer bottles. There are a few feet of free space just before the stage, and then commence two columns of tables and chairs against the walls on either side, with a narrow aisle between, leading to the barroom at the front of the club, where Mona's cigarette flares in the darkness, some sixty feet distant, now that the lights there have been dimmed.

Framed by the microphone's gigantic mouthpiece is Richard, who adjusts the height of his cymbals and hi-hat, the positions of which skeletally suggest the final configuration of the drum set. Richard employs a common drum arrangement, keeping the hi-hat close by his left foot, just beyond the snare. Flanking the bass drum will be the crash and ride cymbals. The crash is maintained high enough to permit it to move freely after it has been struck. Attached to the bass drum are the two aerial toms, and to Richard's right is the big floor tom.

Nat, Jay, and Dave sit at a card table in the cramped dressing area while Richard sets up his drums on the stage. They say little, listening to Richard assembling the set. Occasionally, the sound of the television in the barroom reaches them. The surface of the card table is thinly padded and covered with a quilted plastic material. Nat absently pokes the surface with his finger, watching it yield and then regain its shape. In places, the surface contains small, regular holes, the result of cigarette burns. Nat adds to their number with his own cigarette, the plastic jaggedly curling and receding as it melts to form perfectly round holes. Dave says something to Jay, who shrugs in response and then abruptly rises and leaves the dressing area, leaving Richard's startled question hanging unanswered in the air as he passes.

Words are exchanged in the barroom. Jay asks Mona a question and she and Don divert their attention from the television to look at him. In the subdued light here, Mona appears completely golden; her dress, her hair, even her skin. She sits with her chair turned slightly from the table, her left elbow resting on the tabletop, a cigarette dangling from her right hand. Her legs are crossed and the upper one rocks slightly. The shoe at the end of it is gold as well. The words, mostly Jay's, rise and fall. In the silences between them the sound from the television seems to swell and dominate in the closeness of the room. There is surprisingly little modulation or variance between the sounds it emits. It is the hour of the evening news. Mona gestures angrily toward the alcove off the bar.

The drums are now scattered across the stage, waiting for Richard to finish adjusting the hi-hat and cymbals. They must be perfect. Richard is somewhat distracted from his efforts by the events in the barroom. The enormous woman has risen from her seat and stands near the bar, talking to Don, who leans across the bar to hear her quiet words. Although he cannot see him, Richard can hear Jay's voice coming from somewhere at the front of the club. His words are clearly independent of the conversation between the woman and the bartender. Jay emerges from the alcove, entering Richard's line of sight. Mona says something to him and he answers with his back to her, moving quickly toward the stage down the aisle between the columns of tables and chairs.

It has become very cold. The street on which Cheaters is situated is a corridor through which the icy wind off the Hudson rushes. It takes loose snow from the freezing piles at the edge of the sidewalk and blows it, in swirling gusts, down the street so that it seems as if it has begun to snow again. At the corner, on the avenue, Jay and Nat climb into a taxi. First in, Nat settles into the lumpy rear seat, on the driver's side, as Jay leans forward, giving the driver directions through the open partition separating them, an Upper West Side address. He reclines into the seat, pulling the door shut, and the soft glow of the dome light is extinguished. For a few moments, as the two of them silently recover from the cold, there is only the muted clicking of the turn indicator as the cab pulls out into the traffic, the quiet fanfare from the radio as the station begins its top of the hour report on news, traffic, and weather. Nat listens as he reads, once again, the notices and caveats affixed to the partition. Jay begins to speak to him after a while, looking through the window on his side. Nat stares ahead, memorizing the driver's name from the hack license mounted on the right-hand side of the dash.

Nat looks at Jay now as Jay speaks to him. Beyond him, the sylvan darkness of the park, set behind the low fieldstone wall, streaks by. Jay's voice is the low monotone that it often becomes when he is tired or upset. Nat has to lean toward him, his right hand sinking into the upholstery of the seat, his left braced against the front seatback, in order to understand him. The driver turns the cab into a broad residential street, and Nat is thrown against Jay. The conversation is ended now as Jay directs the driver to stop before a building on the block; Nat removes a five dollar bill from his wallet with which to pay the fare. The cab slows to a stop parallel to their destination. Jay says a few words to Nat, who replaces the money and wallet, and then substantially repeats the phrase to the driver. He gets out of the cab and walks quickly toward the entry of the building. The doorman admits him and he disappears into the mirrored recesses of the lobby. Nat crosses his legs and throws his right arm over the back of the seat. He turns to look through the rear window at a large, Gothic apartment building further down the block, at the corner. Hanging from the wrought iron fence surrounding the building are flowers, photographs, and signs, and affixed here and there to it are candles. Although he has never seen them before, Nat stares at these things with recognition.

After several minutes, Jay emerges from the building accompanied by a young man. Together they are carrying a speaker column: a long plywood box covered with black vinyl in which are set two heavy-duty speakers. They set it on the sidewalk in front of the building and return to retrieve its twin from inside, along with an amplifier and various coiled electrical cords. The driver leaves the cab, and Nat uncrosses his legs to join the other three on the street. Before the cab's open trunk, Jay, the driver, and Figure 7 are discussing something. Money changes hands to end the discussion, and presently the driver and Nat are placing one column in the trunk while Jay and Figure 7 wait with the second. When the trunk contains both columns and the amp, its lid, which now cannot be closed completely, is secured by wrapping a bungee cord around the latch on the underside of its curving lip and the corresponding part on the inside of the trunk itself. The driver climbs back into the cab, where he is joined in the front seat by Jay. Nat returns to the back seat with Figure 7. The cab immediately pulls into traffic.

Figure 7 is here identified as Paul Marzio, lead guitarist for a band called the Identical Strangers and former bassist for Hi-Fi.

The two speaker columns flank the stage on either side. They are turned so that they are at an oblique angle to the line formed by the apron of the stage, speakers directed toward both the columns of tables and chairs leading to the barroom and, to a lesser degree, the stage. This configuration has been devised to allow the band to monitor its vocals while minimally affecting the volume and quality of the sound reaching the audience. On the stage, from left to right as viewed from the audience, are the bass amp; floor tom; ride cymbal; bass drum, with aerial toms attached; crash cymbal; snare; hi-hat; and guitar amp. Arranged in a row parallel to the edge of the stage are the three microphone stands, to which microphones have been attached, their cords wound around the telescopic chrome shafts of the stands. The slack lengths of cord extending from the bases of the stands have been drawn together and taped, and follow five parallel serpentine trails leading to the first table of the left-hand column (again, from the audience's perspective), on which the amplifier sits. Jay mounts the stage and removes the microphone from the middle stand, unwinding the cord from around the shaft.

Nat and Richard come into Cheaters from outside. They pass through the barroom, in which a couple and two solitary drinkers are now seated. Nat carries a large paper bag. As they start down the aisle between the columns of tables and chairs, Mona emerges from the alcove, staring after them from the dimness of the barroom. Nat sets the bag down on one of the tables and proceeds to remove from it four sandwiches wrapped in white butcher paper, a large bag of potato chips, a small bag of pretzels, a package of cupcakes, a pack of cigarettes, and two quart bottles of Pepsi. Jay sits on the edge of the stage to eat as Nat distributes the food. Mona approaches the stage, speaking to them as she moves down the aisle. The conversation is short and confusing: she has addressed none of them in particular, and all of them respond simultaneously.

Nat is in a phone booth in the alcove off the bar. It is an actual, enclosed booth; equipped with hinged sliding door and a small wooden seat. Two tattered directories sit on the triangular chrome shelf beneath the phone, but Nat does not avail himself of these. Instead he dials—it is a dial phone—a number from memory. While waiting for someone to answer, he stares furiously at a small graffito scratched into the wall beside the phone.

Jay waits at the bar to talk to Don, who stands with his back to him as he checks the rows of bottles in place before the mirror. Jay yawns, then draws one of the bowls of pretzels before him and begins to eat from it.

In the dressing area, Dave removes a small mirror from his guitar case and carefully examines his reflection. He bites the flesh on the inside of both cheeks and flares his nostrils. He places the mirror on the card table to fluff his hair with both hands and then studies his image again, clenching his teeth so that his jawbone bulges.

Richard stands before a chair over which he has draped his coat. He carefully arranges several items so that they protrude from his coat pocket in such a way that they are clearly visible to anyone who passes, and backs away to examine his work.

As Nat speaks into the phone, he studies the portion of the barroom visible to him from the alcove: he can see enough of the street door to discern when it opens and closes, and a flash of the clothing of whomever it admits or releases (although this does not occur while he is in the phone booth); he can see the shoulder, upper arm, and part of the forearm of someone sitting at the bar before a gin and tonic mixed in a tall, slender tumbler and garnished with two minuscule wedges of lime; and he can see that part of the bar that curves toward the wall. He notices now that this section of the bar is hinged, so that the bartender can come and go from behind it without having to walk all the way to the opening at its opposite end, near the plate glass window. Directly opposite the sliding glass-paneled door of the phone booth, which Nat now shuts, is the door to the men's rest room, distinguished both by the word MEN and the symbol ♂. Adjacent to the men's room door, and behind Nat's left shoulder as he peers into the barroom, is the women's restroom, similarly labeled with the word LADIES and the symbol ♀. As he talks, Nat creates an imaginary barrier opposite the women's room door, forming, in his mind, a perfectly realized set of right angles composing a square.

Don stoops to retrieve a large plastic bag of pretzels and begins to move along the length of the bar, refilling the bowls upon its surface. Before he reaches where Jay is standing, he returns to the end of the bar near the plate glass window, where he replaces the bag of pretzels and starts to wipe the bar with a rag, working his arm in a regular, elliptical motion as he moves down the bar. Jay looks first at Don, then at the empty bowl of pretzels before him, shrugs, and then walks back down the aisle between the columns of tables, at the end of which he moves Richard's coat aside to sit in the chair over which it had been draped. Dave sits opposite him and Jay reaches out to muss his hair as he turns to ask Paul, who sits before the amplifier, a question.

Nat hangs up and exits the booth, coming face to face with Don, entering the alcove. The bartender has come from behind the bar via its outlet near the plate glass window. For a moment they look at one another, and then Don edges past him and disappears behind the door marked PRIVATE. As Nat moves down the aisle between the columns of tables he looks over his shoulder to watch Don push a small lectern, to which a hand-printed sign is attached, through the barroom, positioning it directly in front of the street door.

Nat sits on the edge of the stage, eating the remnants from the large bag of potato chips. Across his lap is his bass, which is plugged into an electronic guitar tuner. Wiping greasy crumbs from his right hand onto his pants leg, he plucks the instrument's E string and studies the fluctuations of the tuner's needle. He selects the corresponding tuning peg and makes a slight adjustment without moving his eyes from the needle. Placing his fore- and middle fingers beneath the string, he lifts them so that the string arcs just behind the pickup, angling steeply toward the bridge, and then slides the fingers along the underside of the string, maintaining the tautness, until the space between fretboard and string becomes too narrow to permit his fingers any further movement. He plucks the string again, watching the needle and adjusting the peg. He repeats the process with the three remaining strings.

Behind him, Jay moves from microphone to microphone, speaking single syllables into each while Paul adjusts volume and tone from the table on which the amplifier sits. Jay lingers over the middle microphone, repeating the same syllable over and over while extending his right hand, palm up, and making what appears to be a beckoning motion. He steps away from the microphone to discuss something with Paul, and then begins to turn the columns so that the speakers are directed more toward the stage. Paul and Richard both offer their comments. Jay returns to the middle microphone and resumes speaking monosyllables into it, making a different hand gesture this time. There is a sharp screech of feedback and Paul hurriedly adjusts the volume.

In the dressing area, Dave removes his T-shirt, peers out onto the stage, comes entirely from behind the folding screens for a moment, and then withdraws, sitting down and beginning to read a copy of *New York Rocker*.

Nat plugs the bass into his amp and leans it against the bass drum, on the other side of which Richard is just settling into the throne. As Nat dismounts the stage to retrieve the two empty Pepsi bottles standing on the table opposite the one on which the amplifier sits, he hears the simultaneous sounds of the bass hitting the stage, landing first on one of the cutaways and then flat, fretboard down; Richard's voice; and the muted sound of the crash cymbal which has been struck by Richard's outstretched arm. Nat and Richard speak for a moment, as the others suspend their activities to watch, Dave appearing from behind the folding screens, still shirtless, arms akimbo, the copy of *New York Rocker* tucked into his pants waist. Richard stands and comes from behind the drum set, pushing past Dave to retrieve his coat from where he has placed it in the dressing area and then dismounting the stage, moving up the aisle between the columns of tables, through the barroom, and out onto the street. Shrugging, Nat grabs the bass by one of the cutaways and overturns it, leaving it like that on the stage floor. He takes the bottles from the table and carries them with him to the men's room.

At nine o'clock Don glances at the three people at the bar—the couple and one of the solitary drinkers remain—and switches the channels on the television, stopping at a hockey game. Checking the patrons again, he comes from behind the bar, draws one of the empty stools to the lectern, and sits there.

Jay, Nat, and Dave are standing on the stage, positioned as they will be when they perform. The drummer's throne is still unoccupied. Nat and Dave wear their instruments hanging from straps that run over their left shoulders and across their backs. Jay drinks lukewarm water from one of the Pepsi bottles. No one speaks, and all three of them look toward the street door as it opens and two people enter. They are met at the entry by Don, with whom they briefly converse. Nat removes his bass, dismounts the stage, and moves up the aisle between the columns of tables to join them in the barroom. He talks to Don for a moment and then he and the two new arrivals cross through the barroom and down the aisle between the columns of tables. Figure 8 is led by Nat behind the folding screens. Figure 9 places the canvas bag that he is carrying on the table behind that on which the amplifier sits and removes from it a camera and related equipment. After a moment, Dave removes his guitar and pulls a chair out from under the table on which the amplifier sits, turning it around and then straddling it, arms folded across the seatback, to begin talking with Figure 9. Jay sits on the edge of the stage, attentive to this conversation.

Figures 8 and 9 are here identified as Maureen Ferret and Miles Miller.

Maureen perches uncomfortably on Nat's right knee as he peers at Jay across the table where they are seated, opposite the one on which the amplifier sits. They are composing the set list, and discussing a few minor changes that have been made to some of the songs. Jay is working on a large piece of paper, and near to it is a piece of paper of identical size, which has been folded into four equal sections. The finished set list will be copied onto each section, and the paper will then be torn down the creases formed by the folding of the paper. One section will then be taped to each microphone stand and to one of the cymbal stands. With Dave's assent, it is agreed that two of the songs to which changes have been made will be tested during the sound check.

Don turns from the hockey game toward the opening door, which first admits Paul and then, immediately after him, Richard. They are both red-cheeked and exhale clouds of condensed water vapor in the cold air coming through the open door. The bartender questions them as they attempt to sidestep the lectern and Richard responds while miming the action of executing a drum roll with his gloved hands, what appears to be a look of disgust crossing his face—a slight curl of the lip, the subtlest suggestion of a rolled eyeball. Whatever it is, it passes swiftly as his eyeglasses begin to steam up in the warmth and he lifts his left hand from out of its downward stroke to remove them and wave them at his side.

On the stage now are the four members of the band. Richard is behind the drum set and Nat, Jay, and Dave stand before the three microphones. Maureen sits at the table where Miles had been, smoking a cigarette and reading Dave's copy of *New York Rocker*. Paul is at the table on which the amplifier sits, which he has temporarily moved into the middle of the aisle in order to be more precisely located between the two speaker columns. Miles moves from place to place seeking advantageous positions from which to photograph the band. After some desultory and uncoordinated tuning up, most of which has to be repeated because of the tendency of one instrument to drown out another, Dave counts off the first song. It is to be the first song of the set, and the change made to it consists of the addition of a scream, to be vocalized by

Jay and Nat, to the fourth bar of the intro. Dave counts the song off too quickly, and although the intro, and the scream, are executed flawlessly, Nat stumbles as the song enters the verse and he attempts to play somewhat more complicated bass figures. The band stops playing and a brief discussion is held between Nat and Dave. Dave counts off, more slowly this time, and the song is played through.

Richard prepares to join Nat and Dave, who are posing for Miles's camera. As he starts forward, placing his left foot before him, Jay reaches out and grabs his left shirtsleeve just above the elbow, pulling sharply at it and speaking to him. Richard turns to look at Jay's face as Jay recoils from his own sudden act, water splashing onto his shirtfront from the Pepsi bottle he holds near to it.

Against the wood-paneled wall opposite the bar are four small round tables. The tabletops are constructed of several joined pieces of imperfectly matched pine. An attempt has been made to disguise the inconsistencies in the grain via the sloppy application of a dark stain. Each tabletop is supported by a twenty-seven and one-half inch length of four-by-four, similarly stained, attached beneath its direct center. This in turn is balanced at its bottom by a pair of wooden crosspieces, similar to those that come with Christmas trees, which are notched where they are joined so that the two pieces rest evenly on the floor. On each tabletop is an ashtray, a bowl of pretzels, and, in amounts and combinations that vary from table to table, empty and full glasses, bottles, purses, packs of cigarettes, matches, lighters, and change. Several of the stools at the bar opposite are occupied, and a few people move about in the space intervening between bar and tables. Some of the tables forming the two parallel columns leading to the stage have people seated at them. Now that the lights in that section of the club have been extinguished, except for a small light directed toward the stage, it is darker there than in the barroom. From the table nearest to the street door, the coal at the end of a cigarette can be seen as it flares, some sixty feet distant.

Nat and Maureen sit talking at the table nearest to the street door. Nat faces Maureen and, beyond her, the door, looking up from her face to glance at the door whenever it opens. Maureen sits with her chair turned slightly from the table, right elbow resting upon the tabletop, a cigarette dangling from her left hand. Her legs

are crossed and the upper one rocks slightly. Now and then someone will stop at the table, standing beside it and chatting with the
two of them for a few moments before moving on. Each time the
couple is left alone again, they begin to talk to each other as before.

Seated as she is, Maureen looks at the bar, sometimes glancing
obliquely at Nat, but for the most part watching the motions of
those who pass directly in front of her. Suddenly, she takes her
purse from the table, stands, and exits through the street door. In
a moment she can be seen walking past the plate glass window,
heading east. Nat remains alone at the table for a few moments and
then, with equal suddenness, stands and leaves as well.

A man enters the club and says a few words to Don, who responds,
sliding off the barstool behind the lectern. Figure 10 promptly replaces him there, and Don crosses through the barroom, into the
alcove, and enters the room behind the door marked PRIVATE.

Jay, Dave, Paul, Miles, and a young woman are seated in the
darkness behind the folding screens. Before them, on the card
table, are three beer bottles; Jay's water-filled Pepsi bottle; a pack
of cigarettes, on which rests a book of matches; and Miles's canvas
bag. Figure 11 shares a marijuana cigarette with Dave. She hands
the joint to him and reaches for the bottle before her on the table,
glancing at him as she drinks from it. As she replaces the bottle,
swallowing, she raises her hand, signifying that she has something
to say, and turns slightly to her left, bending to retrieve a plastic
bag from the floor beside her. Placing the bag in her lap, she
undoes its top, which is secured by a drawstring, and removes
from it four white T-shirts, putting these on the table and then
holding each, in turn, up to her chest to model it. Each shirtfront
is decorated with a different design confined within the boundaries
of a square formed by four red lines of approximately ten inches in
length. The designs have been executed by hand in black paint.
Only two of the designs utilize the white of the shirts as a means of
contrasting values: one, the silhouette of a turret, rising above an
unseen castle, in which a small rectangular patch of white suggests
a single lighted window; the other, two black half-circles separated
by an inch-wide diagonal swath of white, which swath is continued
beyond opposite sides of the circumference of the ovoid realized
by the two half-circles and the space between them and defined by
two parallel diagonal lines of black which at a length of two inches

begin to taper until they meet, the overall shape of which is somewhat reminiscent of the planet Saturn and its encircling rings. The other two designs are somewhat simpler: the stylized silhouette of a bat, depicted with outspread wings and huge ears, curved and pointed like horns; and a jagged arrow, point downward. Comments and laughter accompany each shirt's display, and when they have all been shown Jay selects the shirt picturing Saturn, while Dave takes the one with the lighted tower.

Figures 10 and 11 are here identified as Jed Solowicz and Girl Bovary.

Jed has come from behind the lectern and stands blocking the doorway, talking loudly to someone in the street. Maureen stands in the alcove with another young woman, who is embracing her. Her face is red and swollen, a bruise beginning to form under her right eye. Maureen starts to cry, evidently not for the first time this evening, and Figure 12 guides her out of sight toward the women's room. Someone approaches Jed, coming from one of the tables, and speaks quietly to him for a few moments. Jed turns to face him, shouting, but the other gingerly places his hand on Jed's shoulder and continues to talk. After a moment, he backs away slightly, still talking, making conciliatory gestures with his hands. Jed shrugs, turns back to face the street, and says one final thing to the figure waiting there before standing aside to let him pass.

Figure 12 is here identified as Mimi Miller.

Mimi and Maureen enter the women's room and there encounter one of the members of the band, bent over the sink, inhaling the cocaine that is laid out in four lines upon a small mirror resting on the sink's edge. A safety-razor blade lies on the edge of the sink as well. He raises himself upright, sniffling, and looks at their images reflected in the mirror over the sink as they stand in the doorway. Mimi, who still has one arm tightly around Maureen's shoulder, speaks sharply to him. He replies with a shrug and few words. These four events occur simultaneously: as Mimi begins to respond, he kicks the door shut in her face, Maureen breaks loose from Mimi's embrace, and Don emerges from behind the door marked PRIVATE.

On the television, a man announces the day's noteworthy events against a mutating backdrop of graphics. As he glances to his left, the picture shifts to a woman who also delivers the news, in identical fashion, except that she occupies the right hand side of the screen, where he had occupied the left, and the graphics appear beyond her right shoulder, where they had appeared beyond his left. This shifting from male to female occurs regularly, with a discernible rhythm, broken only by the appearance of a taped report or the inevitable commercial.

Behind the folding screens, Nat is offered his pick of the remaining T-shirts by Girl. He walks out onto the stage with them, examining them under the stronger light there, and is offered suggestions as to the better choice by Jay, Dave, and Paul, who are seated around the table on which the amplifier sits. He selects the shirt depicting the bat, steps back behind the folding screens, and removes his sweater and light blue T-shirt, placing these in his instrument case. He puts on the new T-shirt and turns to model it for Girl, but she has already gone to rejoin the others at the table.

An imperfect silence fills Cheaters as the members of Hi-Fi step out onto the stage, coming from behind the folding screens where they have been sequestered for ten minutes. The brief quiet is bordered by the ordinary din of a reasonably busy nightclub and by a round of applause, raucous cheers, drunkenly shouted song titles, etc. The silence has been imperfect because it has isolated, briefly, elements of the former and latter conditions: the hurried last line of a conversation, the sound of a chair scraping across the floor as its occupant moves closer to the table, a door opening in the alcove, the sound of water running through pipes, glass against glass as an empty beer bottle is thrown into a plastic garbage can reserved for them, three loud handclaps, a shouted exclamation that most likely has been prompted by the appearance of the band on the stage, which is completely lighted now. Jay makes a few introductory remarks to the audience while Dave and Nat quickly check to see whether they are still in tune with one another. As Dave reaches to dampen the strings of his guitar in order to stop their tuneless droning, Richard abruptly counts off the first song, setting a fast tempo. Jay turns to look toward Richard, Nat and Dave crash into the opening bars of the song, and for a moment all three instrumentalists are out of time. Nat must dash to his microphone to contribute his part in the vocalized scream, and in so doing drops his pick. He flails at the open E string with his thumb as he screams, and then steps back to grope for one of the extra picks he has tucked between the plastic pickguard and the body of the bass. Richard drums with a radiant smile on his face as Dave stands, his back to the audience, staring at him for a moment before turning away.

From their vantage point, the members of the band can clearly discern only the faces of those seated at the two tables nearest the stage. On one side, Paul sits before the amplifier, one hand resting on it. He looks at the band, unresponsive to the words that Maureen, who is seated beside him, shouts into his ear. On the other side sit Girl, whose eyes follow Dave, and Mimi, whose chair is pushed up against the wall and who might be mistaken for someone who is asleep, or unconscious, if she didn't raise a cigarette to her lips every now and then. Miles squats beside their table, blocking the aisle, focusing his camera and talking to them. Girl looks at him and nods, smiling, although it is doubtful that she can understand what he says, but Mimi only repeats the mechanical gesture of raising the cigarette to her lips, inhaling, and limply dropping the arm down at her side again, even as long segments of ash drop onto her sweater and, sometimes, her skirt. Beyond these two tables, all is indistinct. Occasionally the memory of who had been sitting in a particular spot, or area, will aid in identifying the movements and gestures of one of the shadowy figures there; but it is an educated guess, at best, as to who is making them. Beyond the tables, in the barroom, only the movements themselves can be detected.

Nat has managed to slow the song's breakneck tempo by playing it an octave lower than he usually does on the first verse and dragging out the simple triad figure that he employs to actually alter the time signature from 4/4 to 3/4. When he, Richard, and Dave are in sync on the downbeat, he brings the song back. The conclusion of the song is greeted by the audience with a round of applause, raucous cheers, drunkenly shouted song titles, and the buzz of indifferent conversation. Jay says a few words to Nat, who begins addressing the audience as Jay turns to speak with Richard, covering the microphone he holds in his hand as he does so.

A ballad is begun. Jay counts it off himself, bringing his hand down in an exaggerated boxing referee's gesture on each count while

mugging for the audience. Dave hunches over his guitar as he plays
the simple arpeggios, accented by single strokes to the crash cymbal, that open the song. As the intro is completed, he straightens
and backs into a far corner of the stage while strumming the chords
of the verse, emphasizing each chord's tonic note on the first two
beats of every bar. Because this song calls for Jay to sing notes
outside of his vocal range, it poses a problem that he has custom-
arily solved by singing parts of the song in falsetto and by adding
backing vocals sung by Nat and Dave to the chorus. As the chorus
nears, he automatically looks at the microphones flanking him on
either side; first to his right, where Nat has just positioned himself,
legs astride and bent slightly at the knee, and then to his left, where
the other microphone remains unoccupied. Dave still stands at the
far corner of the stage, apparently oblivious to his role in the
performance of the song beyond the guitar part. While singing, Jay
backs into that corner of the stage and grabs at Dave, pulling him
by the guitar strap toward the free microphone and leaving him
there as he moves back to center stage. Dave sings his part, remains
at the microphone and repeats it for the second chorus, and then,
glaring at Jay, forsakes the minor chord progression of the coda for
major power chords, pointing his guitar toward his amp to create
screeching feedback that drones through the first part of Jay's
between-song banter, ceasing only when Jay kicks at him.

Nat looks toward the table on which the amplifier sits. Paul sits
there alone, in almost precisely the same position he has maintained since the start of the set. At the table across the aisle, Girl
sits talking to a couple who, judging from their red cheeks, tousled
hair, and the way in which they alternately look at Girl and glance
curiously around the club, have only just arrived. Mimi and Miles
are no longer at the table, and are nowhere evident in the audience
as Nat ascertains when he steps forward beyond the blinding stage
lights to look. Also absent is the regular burst of Miles's flash that
has punctuated the set so far.

Figures 13 and 14 are here identified as Susan and Sean Dennis.

After a false start—Jay breaks one of the hoary rules of show
business by aborting the song after it has begun, in order to avoid
the type of fiasco that opened the set—this song, a twelve-bar
rocker, finally engenders the sort of reaction from the audience
that the band has been seeking: a couple of people get up to dance,

after a fashion, in the aisle; a few members of the audience clap in time; and Sean Dennis leaps onto the stage, grabbing Jay's hand and attempting to swing him in as wide an arc as possible given the stage's confines. The members of the band warm to the attention and play up their cornball parts: Nat struts around the stage in time to his walking bass line; Jay, holding his microphone by its cord, swings it in a circle over his head; Dave attempts a duckwalk; and Richard freezes, sticks poised high over the drums, during rests. Dave plays a solo consisting of artfully blended scraps from other songs, and the band even manages to pull off a false ending, reprising the song in the midst of the hearty applause that greets its apparent end.

Nat takes a drink from the water-filled Pepsi bottle offered him by Jay and wipes the sweat from his forehead with a hand towel kept atop his amp. Looking into the audience, he sees a figure, ultimately identifiable as Mimi's, moving down the aisle between the two columns of tables and reclaiming her seat near the stage. She holds a fresh drink, a gin and tonic mixed in a tall, slender tumbler and garnished with two minuscule wedges of lime. She is alone.

For the intro to this song, Dave exercises his demonstrated penchant for power chording, while Jay stands with his feet close together, bending and unbending his knees, bending slightly forward at the waist while arching his back, bringing his arms up over his head as he throws out his chest, and then repeating the entire process in reverse. He then forsakes this vaguely undulatory motion to twitch and shake his arms, legs, and head, staggering from side to side on the stage, colliding with Dave and Nat, as if an electrical current is passing through his body. Nat, tightly gripping the neck of his bass, glances into the audience at Girl, and sees what appears to be a look of disgust cross her face—a slight curl of the lip, the subtlest suggestion of a rolled eyeball—as she watches Jay's display. Whatever it is that he believes he has discerned, it passes swiftly and her eyes shift, inevitably, to Dave. Nat peers deeper into the audience, looking past the people he knows in the first rows, past the recognizable faces he can assemble from amongst the shadows and lit cigarettes and dark movement, toward the nebulous blur of the barroom; trying above the chaos of sound to hear the clinking of glass against glass, the squealing hinges of the telephone booth door, the shouted conversations. For a moment he stops playing altogether, standing with an air of frozen confusion. Jay immediately notices the vacuum in the overlay of sound upon sound and walks, while singing, to the bass amp to check it for Nat. Nat begins to play again and Jay walks back to center stage, punching him gently in the shoulder.

This song, with its lilting rhythm, quirky changes, and fairly complex vocal counterpoint, requires the full concentration of the band members. Jay draws Nat and Dave together before the bass drum, the three of them huddled there, leaning toward Richard so that he can hear. As the conference breaks up and each band member assumes his normal place on the tiny stage, Nat looks once again into the audience, its component faces plain, now that the stage has been darkened for the hiatus between songs, all the way to the mysterious darkness in the barroom. The audience is growing rather restless, and this restlessness is made manifest in its actions, which have less and less to do with paying attention to the band on stage. Nat and Dave go through the motions of checking to see whether their instruments are in tune; Richard executes a couple of muffled drum rolls, pounding on the pedals of the bass drum and hi-hat; and Jay walks from microphone to microphone, speaking monosyllables into each. Jay then signals to Paul, still seated at the table on which the amplifier sits, who leans forward and rotates a dimmer switch on the wall, brightly lighting the stage again. Jay makes some apologetic but upbeat remarks to the audience, and the band is off again.

Jed watches the television over the bar, alternately drinking from a bottle of club soda and eating from a bowl of pretzels that he has placed on the lectern. The volume of the television has been turned so low that it would be barely audible even without the crashing noise of the band. On-screen, Jack Klugman argues silently with Al Molinaro. Mona emerges from behind the door marked PRIVATE and leans over the bar, shouting over the noise. Don stares at her for a moment and then places a bottle of beer on the bar before her. She takes this with her back into the room behind the door marked PRIVATE. Now the barroom is empty except for Jed and Don, who glance at each other. Don shrugs and then wipes the spot on the bar where the sweating bottle had been. Now and then someone outside stops and looks in through the plate glass window, then moves along the street. Don comes from behind the bar and crosses to the tables against the wood-paneled wall opposite. He moves from table to table, clearing them, wiping them with a rag, and emptying the ashtrays. With the rag draped over his left forearm, he carries three glasses, two bottles, a crushed cigarette pack, and one ashtray into which he has emptied the contents of the others and places them on the bar. He tosses the cigarette pack into a garbage can and empties the ashtray after it. He places the beer bottles in another garbage can marked EMPTIES ONLY. He pushes the glasses down the bar and dips each in turn into a basin filled with soapy water, rinses them in a basin filled with clear water, and then places them upside down on an adjacent drainboard to dry.

Don and Jed simultaneously look toward the street door as it opens. Miles and Maureen enter Cheaters. Jed gives them a glance and, with a nod, allows them to pass the lectern. They pass through the barroom, stopping just before the aisle between the two columns of tables. Maureen speaks to Miles, who shrugs and begins down the aisle alone, the shadows moving down his body as he walks. Maureen goes through the alcove and into the women's room.

Inside, she places her purse on the edge of the sink. Then she removes her coat and scarf and, checking to see that the toilet stall is unoccupied, drapes them over the top of the partition. Removing her hairband, she takes a hairbrush from her purse and very carefully brushes her hair, watching her bangs in the mirror as they flip back into place over her forehead. Replacing the hairband, sweeping the bangs back under it so that her forehead is bared, she thoroughly washes her hands and face in the sink, patting her face dry with rough brown paper towels from the dispenser and then wiping her hands. She removes from her purse foundation, lipstick, mascara, eyeliner, powder, and blush.

Jay relinquishes center stage, replacing his microphone in its stand and introducing Nat to the audience, just as Miles reclaims his seat at the table opposite the one on which the amplifier sits. Nat steps up to the microphone and, after a moment's silence, begins to address the audience. For an instant, his eyes lock on Miles's, then break off again. A light ripple of laughter passes through the audience.

Maureen removes the cap from the tube of foundation and lays it on the edge of the sink. She stands there for a moment; the tube in her left hand poised over her right index finger. She smiles, fleetingly, at her image in the mirror.

Don begins to pour pretzels into the small wooden bowls set at regular intervals along the bar, turning to check the rows of bottles behind the bar, and then commences to wipe the bar down with the rag, lifting the bowls, ashtrays, and coasters out of his way, working his arm in a big, regular, elliptical motion, moving down the bar toward where it curves into the wall, near the alcove. He stops there and leans against the bar, looking at the television. In the relative quiet he can, after all, hear Klugman explaining something to Tony Randall.

Maureen very carefully applies the cosmetics. She runs the brush through her hair again and then replaces the brush and makeup in her purse. From her coat pocket she takes a roll of mints and places two of the candies in her mouth. She puts on her coat, glances again in the mirror, and leaves the women's room, carrying her scarf in her hand. She goes to the bar, sits under the television set, near the plate glass window, and orders a gin and tonic. It arrives in a tall, slender tumbler and is garnished with two minuscule wedges of lime.

Maureen looks down at the remains of her drink; the melting ice cubes and crushed wedges of lime gathered at the bottom of her glass. She picks up the glass, shakes it to mix what is left, and then raises it to her lips for a final sip.

By now the hot lights and concentrated activity have taken their toll and each member of the band drips sweat; their hair plastered to their foreheads, the T-shirts soaked through. The resumption of the regular bursts of Miles's camera flash exaggerates these aspects of the band's appearance, capturing for an instant the glistening veins standing out in relief on Nat's neck as he plucks a note far up on the neck of the bass, the corona of sweat surrounding Dave's head as he shakes it, the complete obscuring of Richard's features by the reflection of the lights on his dripping face as he throws his head back, Jay's expression of fatigue when, for a moment during which he is not required to sing, he half-crouches, hands resting on his knees.

Maureen moves down the aisle between the two columns of tables and seats herself beside Paul at the table on which the amplifier sits. She glances at Nat, and sees what appears to be a look of disgust cross his face—a slight curl of the lip, the subtlest suggestion of a rolled eyeball—as he watches her. Whatever it is that she believes she has discerned, it passes swiftly and her eyes shift, inevitably, to Miles, who leans toward Mimi, nodding his head at what she shouts into his ear. Miles looks back at Maureen and for a long moment they stare at one another. Suddenly, she takes her purse from the table, stands, and walks back up the aisle between the two columns of tables, through the barroom, and out into the street. Miles remains seated for a few moments and then, with equal suddenness, stands and leaves as well.

At the completion of the twelfth song of the set, Jay says a few parting words to the audience and replaces his microphone in its stand while Nat and Dave unplug the cords from their instruments and Richard rises from the drummer's throne. Hi-Fi then withdraws to the dressing area behind the folding screens and Paul dims the lights on the stage. The diffuse applause subsides quickly and the band is not recalled for an encore. Soon, the members of the audience begin to leave, moving in twos and threes up the aisle between the two columns of tables, through the barroom, and out into the street. Some of them can be seen through the plate glass window, milling in small groups, hands thrust deep in pockets, stamping their feet and moving about in the cold. Presently they begin to disperse, moving east along the street toward the avenue.

When the club has nearly emptied, Jed gets up from his stool, stretches, and takes his coat and hat from where he has draped them over the lectern. He crosses to the bar where he and Don exchange a few words and then the bartender turns to the cash register and opens it, reaching under the tray and counting out a few bills before handing them to Jed. Jed pockets the money, puts on his hat and coat, throws Don a salute, and leaves. Don comes from behind the bar, moves the stool behind the lectern back to its place at the bar, and then wheels the lectern into the alcove to the door marked PRIVATE, through which he momentarily disappears with it.

Richard stands before the reinforced trap case, which has been drawn close to the apron of the stage. He places the cymbals, stands, pedals, throne, and the three tom-toms in it and fastens the lid. He balances the bass and snare drums on top, and then pushes the unit, its wheels wavering and causing it to fishtail awkwardly, up the aisle between the two columns of tables and through the barroom to where the rest of the equipment sits near the plate glass window. Jay waits at the bar to talk to Don. Nat, Dave, and Paul sit crowded around one of the tables against the wood-paneled wall opposite the bar. Don gestures toward the door marked PRIVATE and Jay leans against the bar, staring at the door until it opens. Mona emerges, crossing slowly and unsteadily to one of the tables opposite the bar, on which she lays her handbag and a large snifter half-filled with brandy. She hands Jay an unsealed envelope which he opens, examining its contents with great care. He says something to the woman, slapping the envelope with the back of his hand. What appears to be a look of disgust crosses her face. This passes swiftly as her eyes move to Don, who watches the two of them carefully, his hands out of sight under the bar. He responds to Jay as Mona turns on her heel and walks slowly through the barroom and down the aisle between the two columns of tables, stopping before the stage. With some difficulty she mounts the stage and turns to face the columns of tables leading to the barroom. Don stares after her, shakes his head, and then turns away. Jay looks at the others in silence, and then tosses the envelope onto the table before them. After a moment, Dave reaches for the envelope and removes its contents, a few bills. Richard, who stands by the trap case before the plate glass window, leans forward, squinting, and then begins to laugh. Jay snatches one of the bills out of Dave's hand and thrusts it at Richard, talking to him. Richard makes no move to take the money, so Jay stuffs it into his pants pocket. Richard stands frozen for an instant, and then relaxes, leaning back against the trap case. Nat rises suddenly and exits through the street door. Don begins pouring pretzels into the small wooden bowls set at regular intervals along the bar, occasionally glancing at the television hanging suspended from the ceiling at the front of the bar, near the plate glass window. He takes no discernible notice of Hi-Fi's presence, turning to stand before his reflection in the mirror behind the bar, checking the rows of bottles there. The gold lamé handbag sits beside the snifter filled with rich amber liquid. The bartender begins wiping the bar down again.

Motionless except for his long coat, wrapped tightly around him on what has become an unspeakably cold night and whipped violently by the wind, Nat stands with his back to the window so that his expression, his features, the very color of his clothing, are obscured from those on the other side of the glass. He looks east, toward the avenue, where the cars proceed with abnormal care through the icy intersection, and then west, at the silent dark blocks leading toward the river's edge. He turns, and through the window he can see the bartender wiping the bar, lifting objects out of the way of the arm moving in ever-widening ellipses as he walks the length of the straightaway portion of the bar, stopping near to where it curves toward the wall and turning. Over his left shoulder, some sixty feet beyond him at the end of the aisle between the two columns of tables, the coal at the end of the woman's cigarette flares brightly in the darkness.

DUB I
(Secondary Percussion, etc.)

Allowances should be made, of course, when recording jump, rhythm and blues, and "rock and roll" music, each of which derives its visceral effect from the preponderance of its heavy, ritual beat. Many producers and engineers recording music of this sort take that into account and choose as their first "overdub" a recording of what is frequently referred to as "secondary percussion," although it is by no means limited to that, consisting of pointed musical "comments," thereby accentuating the material recorded earlier by the rhythm section and reinforcing it against its inevitable erosion as the layers of sound mount.

—Gifford, supra, at 151

[1]Dour, blunt, olive drab, and black.

[2]One Roland Jazz Chorus amplifier; one Peavey TNT 100 amplifier; one Fender Telecaster guitar (pre-CBS); one Gibson SG guitar with DiMarzio Super Distortion pickup in rhythm position; one Rickenbacker 4001 bass guitar; one Tama drum set with twenty-two-inch bass drum, eighteen-inch floor tom, three aerial toms, six-inch snare; K. Zildjian cymbal set (crash, ride, hi-hat).

[3]Current thoughts having little or nothing to do with concatenation of instant meteorological and optical phenomena. "Latent Heat of Fusion" is a concept that gains wary and brief admittance to consciousness; Miss Rosenberg would be proud.

[4]Possible Suspects: Miles Miller, Jed Solowicz, Susan Dennis.

[5]A young woman's unfaithfulness. News of an impending ouster. Catholic repression. Social inadequacy. The possibility of gaining complimentary admission to a musical performance. The new blonde waitress at Leshko's. Folk dancing. Homosexuality and its place in contemporary society. The potential ramifications of a new political administration. Nuances of fashion. Petty theft and its consequences. The unseasonably warm weather. The exact wording of a promotional bio.

[6] Key of F.

[7]"OK, yeah, hurry, it's getting fuckin cold."

8

144 Prince
NOTES

A Quarterly Newsletter By and For
The Tenants of 144 Prince Street

Bob Bobtak certainly has a lot of irons in the fire, and he hasn't let that little trip to **St. Vincent's** emergency room after visiting one of his favorite **West Street** haunts slow him down any! Buoyed by sales of six of his "Aspidistra" series at the **Washington Square Outdoor Art Exhibit**, he took the proceeds - after a run to **Sam Flax** for more **Fredrix Canvas Boards** - and put them back into 144 Prince and now holds a whopping 32.543% equity!!!! **Bob** also reports that he's formed three ad hoc committees that we'll be hearing more about in the future - tenants interested in working to preserve the zesty ambience of our area should contact him directly for more info. We're also happy to report that **Bob's** Color Xerography scam appears to be profiting handsomely! . . . . . Not much news from **Joseph Clifton**, but we can report that he is still **Black** and **Angry** and that he will be more than happy to tell you about the time that he nearly got into a fistfight with **Ishmael Reed**!!! His belief that **Jimi Hendrix** was assassinated by a conspiracy of Jewish entertainment executives remains firm, and brisk sales of his book on the subject, *Click-Bang, What A Hang!*, have attracted an offer from a major Hollywood studio. **Joseph** rolled his windfall over into 144 Prince to raise his equity level to 23.089%!!! **Joseph** relates the news that his son, **Kenyatta**, is doing quite well at **NYU**, an institution he laughingly characterizes as a "racist, fascist slumlord." He anticipates that between *Click-Bang's* movie sale and profits from the perennially successful Stolen Art dodge, he should be able to continue to finance **Kenyatta's** higher education! . . . . . Also circumspect is **Joseph's** housemate, **Darlene Sweet**. We hear that she's been quite busy falsifying evidence in furtherance of the wrongful death suit filed on behalf of her daughter **Mary's** estate, and apparently her recent trip to **Greymoor** to take the cure didn't quite work out as hoped. Sources report that **Darlene** is still in the habit of playing **Barbara Cook** records at excessive volume on her cheap stereo, and remains afraid of paper matches! If **Darlene** would come clean with **Joseph** and tell him about all the money she has invested in **DeBeers**, he might conceivably overlook his ideological and moral revulsion toward **Apartheid** since divestiture and reinvestment in 144 Prince could bring them well over the 50% equity level!!! Well, it's possible that this moral dilemma can be postponed indefinitely, since early indicators show that **Darlene's** Self-Mutilation con stands a very good chance of hitting big! Good Luck! . . . . . **Zounds** still seems bent on violating as many **Board** rules as possible, some old, some new, and some created especially for them!!! Well, we can perhaps disregard the "Quiet Enjoyment" clause since there's no actual evidence that they're lowering property values, and, after all, they have an overwhelming 72% equity!!!! Still, we should all remember that the **South Bronx** became a burnt-out shell precisely because inconsiderate tenants failed to respect the needs and rights of others, and we would hate to see the same thing happen in our vibrant little neighborhood! Here's hoping their rock 'n' roll swindle works out. . . . .The International Brotherhood of Housewreckers denies any liability for the recent break-ins, and reports that four of its high officials remain incarcerated in federal facilities. Hopefully, the art and craft resources there will help to prepare them for full re-integration into our exciting community!!! Meanwhile, thrilling times were had by all when the police department was summoned to the **Brotherhood's** sixth annual **Beer, Wine, and Sangria Fest**, and stairway conversations were fueled for weeks by the intriguing news that two **Brotherhood** members fell to their accidental deaths from the roof within three days of one another!!! Let's not forget that the **Brotherhood's** fifteen-year lease is up for renewal next year - the scuttlebutt is that they're in for a whopping 1000% increase!!!

[9]She was the "other kind" of girl.

[10]Patently untrue.

[11] **Warning: The Surgeon General Has
Determined That Cigarette Smoking
Is Dangerous To Your Health.**

[12]The salient differences between punk rock and new wave, between British punk and American punk, between West Coast punk and East Coast punk, between East Coast hardcore punk and East Coast classic punk, between East Coast hardcore punk and new heavy metal, between new heavy metal and old heavy metal, between old heavy metal and hard rock, between hard rock and blues rock, between blues rock and rhythm and blues, between rhythm and blues and rockabilly, between rockabilly and country and western, between country and western and pub rock, between pub rock and new wave, between new wave and punk rock. The apparent tendency toward universal entropy.

[13]Formerly owned by Ms. Sweet's daughter; Jay has always associated them with the terrifying screams he heard on the night that Ms. Sweet received the news of her accidental death.

[14]Its otherwise undistinguished record of service is colored by one moment in its history: for the better part of one afternoon and evening in 1969 it had held 280 clams dug at low tide from the shore of Portsmouth Bay. A magnificent soup was prepared. Jay asked for a cheeseburger; which he then refused to eat because of the presence of a bottle of Hunt's Catsup on the picnic table. Its image lingers to this day.

[15]Bobbys Hull and Orr both report it to be remarkably satisfying and realistic.

[16]*"Who's the kid with all the friends hangin' 'round?"*

[17]"Fuckin scrubby trap case. Pain in the fuckin ass."
   "Ah, watch your guitar there, never know, might fall off by accident."
   "You're a fuckin scrub, you know that?"
   "Oops."

[18]A Whiter Shade of Pale, I'm Telling You Now, Trash, Damaged Goods, Macho Man, Dedicated Follower of Fashion, Hungry, On the Road Again. (Dawning of a) New Era.

[19]Prince to Thompson. Thompson to West Houston. West Houston to Sixth. Sixth to West 38th. West 38th to Eighth. Eighth to West 40th. Various stops en route as enumerated below.

[20]At *M&O Foods*: regular coffee (Nat); small bag oil and vinegar potato chips (Dave); ham and Swiss hero with everything (Jay).

[21]Devotion uttered thereat by Jay:

> *O M&O Foods, your kitchen and larder,*
> *great in calories and rich in Miracle Whip,*
> *to you I have recourse in my hour of feed.*

[22]At *Golden Pizza*: Calzone (Jay). At *McDonald's*: Chicken McNuggets (Jay); black coffee (Richard). At *Blimpie's*: medium number 4 (Dave); giant number 6 (Jay). At *B&B Deli*: small bag barbecue potato chips (Nat); onion bagel and cream cheese (Jay). At *House O' Weenies Stand*: knish (Jay). At *Ali's Food Mart*: large

bag barbecue potato chips (Jay); small bag barbecue potato chips (Nat). *At Siciliano Pizza*: Sicilian slice (Jay). *At Sabrett's Stand*: frank with mustard and onions (Jay).

[23]Formerly a franchise outlet of a chain of bars operating under the name "Patsy's Irish Rose." The limited partnership that had been formed to purchase it in 1976 dissolved in the midst of spiraling litigation between its members (representative causes of action: fraud; breach of contract; breach of covenant of good faith and fair dealing; negligent and intentional misrepresentation; false imprisonment; violation of RICO act and related statutes). As a result, the parent corporation and mortgagee was not uneager to relinquish what had ceased to be a lucrative franchise and foreclosed, selling the lease to the premises and all fixtures therein to Mona Barron and her common-law husband, Don McOral, in September 1980. Ms. Barron and Mr. McOral began operating the facility, d/b/a "Cheaters," that November after effecting minor repairs and renovations. New name derived from advertising motif used by one T. J. Eckleburg, O.D., an upstairs neighbor. Dr. Eckleburg subsequently effected service of process upon Ms. Barron and Mr. McOral (representative cause of action: conversion).

[24]It's the "Rashomon" episode, in which each of the regular characters offer their differing versions of an event experienced in common.

[25]An examination of the blueprints reveals that the platform was supported by twelve-inch lengths of two-by-four toenailed where the sections comprising its wooden frame intersected.

[26] Two (2) steel desks, one (1) Western Electric rotary dial phone, one (1) four-drawer file cabinet, one (1) swivel chair, one (1) straight chair, one (1) portable lectern, two (2) wastepaper baskets, one (1) portable black-and-white television set, one (1) three-foot by five-foot cork bulletin board, two (2) tensor lamps, one (1) metal storage cabinet, one (1) drafting table to which a set of blueprints is pinned, one (1) Slingerland bass drum, with two (2) aerial toms attached, one (1) rusted snack rack to which a bag of Wise potato chips and a bag of Quinlan pretzels remained affixed, one (1) broken Wurlitzer jukebox.

[27]"We want you on at eleven o'clock Jay. No bullshit, hmm?"

[28]

NOT TO SCALE

[29] Proposed epitaphs for these dead soldiers: The kind you first loved? For those occasions when you're having more than one? For nights that are kinda special? Refreshing, not sweet—the extra dry treat, in fact? If you had had the time, they would have had this? There goes the King? Tasted as good as its name?

[30]Richard also employed what was referred to by Jay as "The Mercy! Beat."

[31]"They mike the instruments here?"
"..."
"What's going on?"
"..."

[32]I saw the figure six in gold.

[33]The hostages are released, their 444-day ordeal ending just moments after Ronald Reagan is inaugurated as the fortieth president of the United States. At his inauguration, President Reagan promises an "era of national renewal." A surprise offer by media baron Rupert Murdoch. A prosecution witness is grilled by the defense at the ongoing Harris trial. A thirteen-year-old is arrested and charged with setting a fire that killed six in a Jersey City tenement. Cleanup is underway in that big Brooklyn oil spill.

[34]"I want you to keep your eyes and ears peeled tonight. I think these guys are trouble."

[35]A brief inquiry as to whether capricious providence had chanced to smile upon him, the rejoinder to which was framed as conjecture anent her illicit reproductive activities with sundry blood relations.

[36]5 West 72nd Street.

[37]You give us twenty-two minutes—we'll give you the world!

[38]Kumar Pati.

[39]Dr. Pati, a dentist in his native Hindustan, sought and obtained employment from the Sunshine Cab Company, Inc., upon his inability to obtain board certification to practice his profession in the United States. He insisted upon three completions of what he thought of as his "cycle" during each shift behind the wheel, and would summarily dismiss passengers from his cab if their destinations interrupted the cycle once it was in progress, or rudely offer to take them to that point at which the route would require him to take a tangent, and no farther. Careful study of his trip sheets and logs indicated that his cycle consisted of tracing on the streets of Manhattan the contours of the Hindu goddess Kali.

[40]I hate to break it to his fans, but Johnny Ace is dead.

[41]The size of the speaker columns relative to the capacity of the trunk; specifically the width of the trunk as compared to the length of the columns. There was a considerable, visible discrepancy between the two measurements.

[42]This is arguably not in the audience's best interests.

[43]"You can not bring food in from outside!"
   "We gotta eat!"
   "Fuck the hell off!"
   "What chickenshit!"
   "This is not 'food.'"

[44]"Mo Eats Scum." No ameliorative rebuttal.

[45]To Maureen Ferret? To the Girl on the Phone? To Hoodwink's? To the A&R department of a small but nationally distributed record

label? To Mimi Miller? To Night Owl? To the Apology Line? To Sean Dennis? To Page Six? To respond to an ad in the *Voice*? To the twenty-four-hour Anheuser-Busch switchboard? To Miles Miller? To Aaron Cohen? To score some Canadian Brown? To hang up on Beth Rabinowitz? To 634-5789, or, failing that, to 736-5000? To Mrs. Louise Ashby? To heckle an acquaintance by singing "The Bubba Song" or "Chinese Nigger"?

[46]
$2.00 Dollar Cover
After 9 PM
<u>No Minumum</u>

[47]The efficacy of this technique is doubtful, but it looks good.

[48]"I can't hear this, man."
"It's gonna feed back on you."
"Oh yeah, can't do that, it's gonna feed back."

[49]FIVE YEARS AFTER: WHERE ARE THEY NOW?/*an oral history*

[50]   1/20/81 "Inauguration Bash," Cheaters Nightclub, NYC Associate (R. Poindexter) willfully, maliciously, and intentionally sought to damage equipment (Ricken-backer 4001 Bass Guitar) while offering loud and abusive verbal harassment. Poindexter exacerbated said damage by taking flight after speciously counter-claiming that occurrence had arisen as a result of alleged tampering with his property (Tama 22" Bass Drum).

[51]Islanders v. Calgary

[52]Maureen plus one.

[53]Bad Moon Rising, Turn Me Loose, Down the Aisle of Love, I Heard It Through the Grapevine, Catch Us If You Can, Cretin Hop. A Hard Day's Night.

[54]   ALL ABOUT H.
         GODDESS
         I WISH

BITE
THINGS WE WANT
F U CN RD THS
KID WITH THE SNOWMAN
ROCK THE DELI
DOLL'S HOUSE
TWITCH AND JUMP
ALONE ON THE BEACH
BEDTIME STORY

[55]A paradiddle, actually.

[57]"I've asked you like a million times you in a hurry or what?"
"You're a fuckin scrub you know that?"

[58]LUSTIG EFFECTS CHECKS—POINDEXTER VEXED AS NAT, DAVE FLEX

[59]A single Capezio toe shoe, a box containing a deck of erotic playing cards, labeled "54 Oriental Models," a partially consumed tube of Ortho-Gynol contraceptive jelly, a paperback book entitled *How to Get Out of a Losing Relationship*, a number 8 Grumbacher Bristle China paintbrush, a copy of *The Guitar Case Chord Book*, a Xerox copy of a typescript stamped "UNCLAIMED—VIRGIN AIRLINES 04.11.80," a bronze statuette of the Hindu goddess Kali, a small black missal, stamped "First Greek Orthodox Church, Oradell, New Jersey," a small painted box, a small-caliber foreign made pistol (unloaded), a small talisman known as a "toby," a torn flier describing one of "Four Fagbashers": white male, approximately twenty years old, short, wiry, wearing a dark blue ski parka and a black concert-type T-shirt with the words "The Who Kids Are Alright Tour 1979" on its front, a Kodak Hawkeye Instamatic camera, a copy of the *New York Post*, a small glassine envelope filled with cocaine, a booklet of food stamps, a pack of Ernie Ball Super Slinky guitar strings, a copy of the Minnesota Multiphasic

Personality Inventory, a portable device known as a "pocket pal," a Square Deal brand composition book labeled "P.M.," a brochure describing home security systems, a broadside whose rubric reads, "They're removed violently from their native habitat, imprisoned in overcrowded tanks of stagnant water, and then boiled alive. Bon Appétit!," a package of "Old Forester" brand Cheroots, the stem left over from what had been a bunch of white grapes, two plastic wallet inserts.

[60]"I am sick of this *sick of this* you are *crazy* and you're making me crazy too I'm leaving. Good-bye."

[61]"There's some crazy punk rock asshole knocking the bejeezus out of some frail out there thought you ought to know."
  "They're all crazy."

[62]Symbols, clearly.

[63]Contemporaneous notes, attributed to Dave McCall:
  Well I gave you the shirt off my back girl
  but you would'nt beleive me when I said
  I Love You
  Well this time I'm gonna take one more crack girl
  but please do'nt decieve me cause you know
  I Love You

[64]Possible suspects: Peter Dimitri, Michael Bachmann, B. J. Hornbeck.

[65]Street Fightin' Man, Take Me to the River, The No-No Song, Mirror in the Bathroom, Respect, No Feelings, Oh Bondage Up Yours!, Break on Through. Waiting for the End of the World.

[66]For those who waited, the yellow ribbons come down at last. The nation's capital plays host to an evening of gala celebrations welcoming President Ronald Reagan into office. A delay in the Abscam trial. A prosecution witness challenges Private Robert C. Garwood's insanity plea. Ten inmates at Nassau County Jail slash their wrists in protest over conditions there. A motive is sought in the senseless shooting death of a thirteen-year-old girl at the hands of a fourteen-year-old boy in Williamsburg. Police determine that

the woman found dead in Van Cortland Park was murdered. A surprise request is made of former Beatle Paul McCartney.

[67]Shape up for summer!

[68]"And you know fuckin-A well they're gonna kick him out after this one!"
  Paul was so drunk that he upset all three gin and tonics.
  Don emerges from the men's room, bearing a mop.
  Where have you gone, Chris Schenkel?
  "Venus!"

[69]Must to Avoid, The Look of Love, Lipstick Traces, Freeze-Frame, She's Not There, Voodoo Chile (Slight Return), Going Underground, Silhouettes. The Eve of Destruction.

[70]"Ayy!"
  "Ven-*US!!!*"
  "Deli Rock!"
  "Style Pile!"
  ". . . like he's going to get us in on the guest list but it doesn't work out, you know, so we're waiting and waiting at fucking *Phebe's* . . . reading comprehension has *got* to go down under Reagan . . . so Fagel writes him up in 'Bad,' and his shit don't stink anymore, right . . . anything to *eat* around here? . . . in the men's room at Hurrah's and there's blood like all over the place . . . are the first amphibious combat boots issued to U.S. ground troops . . . right on 8th Street screaming out Oh My God Oh My God There's Joe Strummer into Electric *Lady*? Yeah right . . . if I put maybe Dippity-Doo in my hair? . . . he goes No Really I Buy the Speedies' Cereal . . . loaf a French bread that's just a little bit stale so it's kinda crunchy and slice it in half the long way and load on like a mountain a ham swiss lettuce tomato and spread mayo and mustard on toppa everything . . . some hippie dive, the University of the Streets, and they unplug the PA on them and some hippie guy starts going, Yo Man Yo Man It's Time To Share The Space, and they just keep going . . . *know* I'm being followed. . . .
    Well, off to another rollicking start. Thanks for coming down to the Inauguration Bash and remember we wanna be seeing a lot more of you over the next four hope-filled years. . . .

don't do that again!"

[71]What, it may be enquired, was the music of this threne? What at least, it may be demanded, did the boy soprano sing?

[72]Contemporaneous notes, attributed to Dave McCall:
    You got the ring in my nose,
    and then you dragged me around.
    Well, now that chapter is closed,
    and I'll be standin my ground—
    It's Your Turn
    (to tow the line, girl)
    It's Your Turn
    (vengince is mine, girl)

[73]Apparently a sufficient quantity of heartwarming memories had been captured.

[74]"Hang on to your diaphragms with both hands, ladies—this one's for the Good Old Days!" (We all tittered and voted Republican)

[75]
        I had a fight with my baby
        and it hurt me to my soul
        Well, I had a fight with my baby
        and it took an awful toll
        Well, I know what'll fix it
        and it comes on a seeded roll.

        Well, gimme a bagel, gimme some lox
        gimme a cream soda—on the rocks
        gimme some slaw, come on, pile it up high
        slap some pastrami on that Jewish rye
        Now you know how to rock that deli rock!

        Rock the Deli Rock
        Rock the Deli Rock
        Rock the Deli Rock
        Rock the Deli Rock
        Without one near, I would surely go ferkach'

        Well, my baby came back,

she said, "please can I come home?
I didn't mean to leave you,
can't stand being all alone."
I said, "you're just in time for dinner,
but you'll have to get your own."

Well, a sour garlic pickle, soaked in the brine
took care of that sick old heart o' mine
Take it from me, when your love life gets rough,
eat your heart out, and do it on the cuff
Now you know how to rock that deli rock!

(repeat chorus)

[76]An unwitting performance of a dance, briefly popular in the 1960s, known as the "Jerk."

[77]Whole Lotta Shakin' Goin' On, Too Much Monkey Business, People Are Strange, Sonic Reducer, Sleepwalk, Bewildered, He Hit Me (and It Felt Like a Kiss). Oh, What a Night.

[78]   1/20/81 - "Inauguration Bash," cont.
       Physically assaulted onstage by associate (J. Lustig) as
       a result of proper and timely complaint re: his tamper-
       ing with amplification equipment. Suffered painful and
       debilitating injury to right deltoid, and sustained dam-
       age in an unspecified amount to Peavey TNT 100 Bass
       Amplifier; as well as loss of stature and good will in the
       community as a result of this humiliation.

[79]"I need you guys to be like awake here. Is this too much for you? Have we had like a rough day at the office honey? The thing of it is is I ain't got the excess charisma to schlep you through the set. Right? Good."

[80]Plans are being made to go to Glancy's, the Dublin House, the Holiday, and the Park Inn. To Irving Plaza, Hurrah, Danceteria, and Tier 3. To private residences on West 81st St., Charles St., Greene St., and St. Marks Place. To Kiev, Homer's, Dave's Cor-ner, and the Triumph.

[81]It's the "Rashomon" episode, in which each of the regular characters offer their differing versions of an event experienced in common.

[82]" 'm hot. M'whole body'sh hot. Gim' a beer."

[83]Hello, Fresh Face! Why don't you just turn your pantyhose inside out?

[84]"This next one's for my dearest faithful Maureen who doesn't seem to be around right at the moment. Could someone here possibly know where she's been and what she's been up to Miles?"

[85]I have been faithful to thee, singer. In my fashion.

[86]

[87]You get the impression he's done this kind of thing before.

[88]You've Lost That Lovin' Feelin', Substitute, Little Sister, Can't Take My Eyes off of You, Just One Look, She's Gone, Next to You. Is That All There Is?

[89]

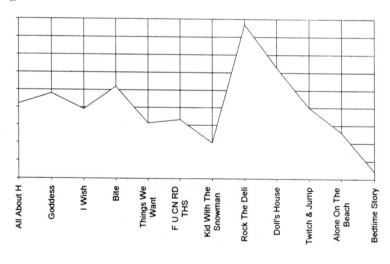

[90]$30.00

[91]$17.00

[92]"You're lucky. We get the bar you get the door. You said you'd bring people down and you didn't mention that they'd all be on the guest list or that they'd all be underage and look it. You're lucky."

[93]Ascending: Astor Home, Calvert's, Carnaby's, Gilbey's, Gordon's, Tanqueray, Beefeater.

[94]Current thoughts having absolutely nothing to do with concatenation of instant meteorological and optical phenomena.

[95] Information confirming this data is readily available through levels of research familiar even to Physical Education majors. It was not obtained.

DUB 2
(Solo)

So we find that the solo is generally improvised and . . . governed only by the sensibility of the music itself, and by elementary theoretical rules concerning key, time, and tempo . . . relatively unburdened by the constraints defining the performance as a whole. As such, it is often an example of unbridled self-indulgence, but that is beyond our concerns here.

—Gifford, supra, at 152

The introduction of descriptions of photographs into a work of prose is always a questionable proposition. Illustrated books are certainly nothing new—why not simply insert the photographs themselves? You might in that event look at the pictures, allow them to enhance or otherwise affect your reading experience, or pass over them entirely, breathing a sigh of relief that their presence eliminates the necessity of reading yet another massed block of type. That is none of my business, however. My business is to imagine these events and other bits and pieces—for it's bits and pieces we're dealing with now—and then to execute them in prose. For this purpose I have developed the most pedestrian story I could conceive, although it may as well have been another. The idea of a rock and roll band going through its paces seemed to parallel the form I have selected. A themeless, plotless story, with nothing to recommend it but its own intransigent shape. Each section of the book attempts to address the fictional possibilities suggested by this story, which, as you can imagine, are endless. A daunting task, you are no doubt thinking. The story itself took four months to compose. But the problems posed by it were merely technical, familiar to writers everywhere. Try it sometime; get out a sheet of paper and try to get a few people seated at a table. It makes me nervous simply to think about it. If you have manners, you'll allow the women, if any are present, to be seated first. If you're dealing with a certain milieu—perhaps the one we're concerned about here—you may choose to have the men turn the chairs around and then straddle them, arms folded across the seatbacks. The idea of three or four men doing this simultaneously is somewhat hilarious to me. But I digress. The "idea" here is to examine rock and roll utilizing the same tools as its critics, and although I use the term "critics" advisedly I do so with some hesitation because what passes as critical theory is really only the thinly disguised chronicling of visceral reaction, and is betrayed at every turn by its willful ignorance of the thing's place in music, in history, and in commerce. Where else is the substance of the artist's output so completely overshadowed by the circumstances of his or her life? What others are perceived in heroic terms so absolutely at odds with their sophisticated reckoning of the marketplace? The importance of a comprehensive theory of rock and roll; as art, as event, as commodity, becomes plain. Saddled as it is with the dual burden of embodying both youthful rebellion and shrewd capitalism, its validity reposes in the hands of the intelligentsia, who have, so far, constructed their various dissertations out of anecdotes, present and contemporaneous political and social attitudes, myth, posed photographs, and sales figures; so that in furtherance of his effort to understand, the student is led not to the artifact itself, but instead to the various shards lying near to it: these disconnected anecdotes, photographs, and sociopolitical interconnections. Because these are common to all rock and roll bands, differing only in terms of the scale of their dissemination, it is as instructive to study any one band as it is any other. But to return to the photographs I implicitly promised you. There'll be a few of them, although not right on top of one another. We'll begin with one that is both archetypal and redolent of self-consciousness, which is not to say that the two conditions are somehow incompatible. The poses, attitudes, and setting are virtually encoded in both its subjects and its photographer as a result of exposure to hundreds, if not thousands, of similar images. The band is posed on an unused section of the elevated railroad track which runs north and south along the West Side. The exact street, perpendicular to the track, at which the photo was taken is difficult to ascertain from the picture itself, and the memories of those who were there are not to be relied upon. It is possible that the street is somewhere in the mid-twenties. In the background of the picture, the facades of two buildings, facing each other from opposite sides of the street, sweep eastward toward a horizon defined by the enclosed walkway that appears to span the space between the two buildings, linking them. The roof of the walkway forms a horizontal line roughly equidistant between the upper and lower boundaries of the photograph. The line is broken in places by the intrusion of the figures in the foreground of the picture, and in any event would not have reached the left- and right-hand margins of the photo since it ceases where it meets the two buildings, but it serves as a horizon. The architecture and approximate location of the two buildings would seem to indicate that they have a definite commercial purpose; most likely they are warehouses or light industrial buildings. Beyond the walkway, to the east, a corner of the roof and upper story of another building, on the northern side of the street, can be seen. It is much shorter than the buildings linked by the walkway. East of that, at the corner, on the avenue, looms a tall building, perhaps twelve or thirteen stories.

In the foreground of the picture, Jay stands before a concrete platform approximately five and a half feet high, his back against it. He is between two lengths of wood, each of which is nailed at a diagonal angle to vertical lengths of wood that project several feet above the platform. These vertical lengths of wood serve as the left- and right-hand margins of the bottom half of the picture, while Jay is its center. He stares directly into the camera, his closed lips forming a slight smile. His right shoulder is slightly lower than his left, so it can be assumed that he is resting most of his weight on his right leg (the photograph is cut off below the level of his chest) even though he leans against the platform for support. He wears a collarless leather jacket which is open and which is too small for him. Atop the platform behind him are Dave, standing to his right; Nat, seated directly above him; and Richard, standing to his left. Dave is coatless, and stands with his right leg slightly advanced so that the toe of his shoe protrudes an inch or so beyond the edge of the platform. Like Jay, he is supporting most of his weight on one leg, his left. From a strap running over his left shoulder and across his back hangs an electric guitar, a Fender Jaguar, which he mimics strumming and fretting with his gloved hands. He looks beyond the camera, face in three-quarter profile, mouth defined by the two parallel straight lines where the shadows of his upper and lower lips fall. Nat sits turned slightly to his left from the edge of the platform. His right leg is tucked beneath his left, and his left foot and ankle stick out past the platform's edge. His right hand is underneath his left thigh, as if to keep the leg from slipping further over the edge—he might kick Jay in the shoulder in that event— and his left hand rests on his knee. He is wearing a U.S. Army field jacket, the hood removed from its zippered pouch on the outside of the collar and bunched between his shoulders. On his head is a dark beret, several sizes too small, and from beneath it his eyes stare directly into the camera. His face, like Dave's, is viewed in three-quarters, although Dave's pose is calculated to turn his face away from the camera, while Nat turns his toward it. Richard leans against the vertical length of wood that serves as the right-hand margin of the photo so that he faces Dave, who is approximately five feet distant. His left leg is bent, and his right leg is thrust out straight at an angle designed to compensate and keep him on balance. His hands are in the pockets of his jeans; the tweed overcoat that he wears is open. He has on a pair of earmuffs manufactured from artificial sheepskin and connected by an adjustable plastic headpiece. He looks directly at Dave, his lips parted as if he is in the middle of saying something to him.

Beyond the four members of the band grouped together in the foreground of the picture, a figure, hands thrust deep into the pockets of his jacket, walks among the weeds sprouting thickly from between the railroad ties. He is heading in a southerly direction. His features are hidden behind Richard's right shoulder, but the creasing and dimpling of the skin on that portion of his face that is visible indicates that he is smiling, possibly at the knowledge that his presence has ruined the picture.

So we begin to try to knit these people together. They're young, they're native New Yorkers, children of that cosmopolitan middle-class dwelling at the periphery of the art world. None of that proletarian shit for me! Very sophisticated families, these parents had their kids badly beaten in terms of discovering sex, drugs, rock and roll, and *la vie bohème*. It is enough to say that their parents nearly drove them to distraction by encouraging their interest in rock and roll, urging them to play their new records for the family at dinnertime, buying their expensive instruments for them. This is important to note because it draws attention to the essential fakery of it all. Another thing: none of them is talented, musically, in the least. They are members of that generation that took guitar, silkscreening, and judo lessons just as their parents had joined the Boy Scouts and Little League. They were "good students" and they extended this outlook, so antithetical to creativity, to rock and roll, so that they came to regard it the way its critics do, as the faithful repetition of certain prescribed poses and attitudes, augmenting these with their own special trademark—that is, gimmick. If you begin to see rock and roll as merely another contorted expression of fashionability, you can understand why thousands of kids in New York who attended St. Ann's, Friends, Stuyvesant and Elizabeth Irwin walked around extolling the virtues of Anarchy™ absolutely oblivious to any sense of irony. Tribal people, tribal. A network emerges, slowly but surely, its interlacings forming a relief upon the surface of red clay and batik. If Nat sits at the table with his father and condemns him as a hideous bourgeois deserving of death, Dad will likely pull out *The Theory of the Leisure Class* and proceed patiently and understandingly to bludgeon his son into silence. Out of these woods comes Hi-Fi. They felt cheated, of course: they wanted to rebel and here were these embarrassing old farts helping them with their lyrics, loudly applauding at gigs, letting them store equipment in their lofts and apartments, reminiscing about the Fugs and the Velvet Underground. Maybe if they'd exploited all that, labeled themselves a kind of "second generation," they wouldn't have been quite so hopelessly lost, but about a million reams of PR massed against them, thousands of sets of crooked English teeth. Perhaps it was because of this that Jay dropped by the other day to let me know that he thought I hadn't really devoted enough space to Hi-Fi's concept of itself. I advised him that I intended, through the construction of an intricate literary mosaic, to subtly limn all components of the band's existence, and that the reader would then be capable of drawing his or her own inferences about Hi-Fi's self-image. He wasn't having any of that literary hyperbole, as he put it, and suggested that I include a press release or promotional letter in the text. I countered by telling him that, in my opinion, such things were merely cheap devices engineered to obfuscate, rather than to clarify, as are all types of advertising. He pointed out to me that if I were at all serious about examining popular culture (a mistaken inference on both counts) I would realize that a band's public image is the self-myth that lies at the heart of its aspirations. It went back and forth like that for a while, during which time Jay consumed three large bunches of white grapes that lay in a bowl on the table. I finally conceded, just to get rid of him, but decided that the piece of fluff I would write—precisely the term I used, angrily, with him—would do nothing more than accentuate the sheer amateurism of the outfit, and that not only would I sign Jay's name to it, but I would disguise it via a clumsy anagram, easily deciphered by a reasonably close reader, for whom the idea of Jay's vapidity would then be cemented.

`HI-FI` is a seasoned club band which has spent the past year honing it's act to a sharp edge. It's **ALL ORIGINAL** reportoir consists of songs running the gauntlet from hard rock to ballads. On-Stage the band combines a sense of intimacy with it's continually growing number of fans with an energetic fire-breathing set guaranteed to leave them shouting for more.

What with all the boys constantly generating new material to the **ALL ORIGINAL** reportoire, **HI-FI** offers a creative, refreshing break from New wave monotony and punk posing that has already begun to wear thin.

HI-FI has performed at such New York venues as, **CBGB'S**, **MAXS' KANSAS CITY**, **STUDIO 10**, and the **PRYAMID CLUB** opening for such headliners as **VERTICAL MADNESS** and **THE CONTRADICTIONS**.

HI-FI is:

JAY LUSTIG *(lead vocals, percussion)*

Jay, former singer for Sandwiches, Again?, is the centerpeice of the band. His unique vocal style, versatile enough to handle hard rockers as well as ballads with equal sensitivity, has been compared to **PAUL ROGERS**.

DAVE McCALL *(lead guitar, vocals)*

Dave used to play with SpeedStick and quickly aquired a reputation as one of the fastest axe-handlers in town. His new role allows him to showcase the sort of firey lead guitar work, reminisent of **TED NUGENT**, for which he is known, as well as delicate finger-picking that shows a whole new side of this talented Artist.

NAT PHENOMENON *(bass, vocals)*

Nat was hand picked by Jay for **HI-FI** after Jay caught his act as a member of the Lab Rats. No mere thumper, Nat's basslines provide a fluid, yet rock solid foundation to the **HI-FI** sound. A Self described **McARTNEY** "freak", Nat emulates his heroes vocal abilities as well as his dextrous fretwork, providing the upper half of **HI-FI's** rich vocal harmonies.

RICHARD POINDEXTER *(drums, percussion)*

Richard, formally trained at the High School Of Music And Art, was persuaded by Jay to swap his timpanis for a Tama drum set. Combining **KEITH MOON'S** virtuousness with **CHARLIE WATTSES** careful attention to the backbeat, he has set a whole new standard for rock drummers.

HI-FI is represented exclusively by:

Zounds Entertainment Group
144 Prince Street, 3d Floor
New York, New York, 10012

— J. Slugit

I'm back in New York now, and unable to afford even simple luxuries, like grapes, so Jay will have to retreat back into the page and once again be what I make of him. From this standpoint, of course, I can afford to be kind, although without resorting to the sort of ridiculous comparisons above—Jay sounds, or sounded, *nothing* like Paul Rodgers, unless of course he'd broken into song across the table from me that day: "I CAN'T GET ENOUGH OF YOUR GRAPES!" I don't know why those grapes bother me so much. Perhaps it's because I thought of the oppressed people laboring in the sun to pick them for him, while he prattled on about his public image, the fascist. He was, to say the least, a connoisseur of rock and roll, but was caught in the paradox presented by it: he understood that its strength and vitality were unable to transcend the ability to tap them, and had come to grips with the fact that successful attempts at that sort of thing, e.g., the Monkees, the Archies, Bobby Sherman, et al., were ultimately indistinguishable from the sources that had inspired their creation. If Jay were more literary, the image that might occur to him is that familiar one of the serpent eating its own tail. This goes all the way back to rock and roll's roots, which have been discussed many times. The problem is that once the rock and roll critic has managed to dispose of the roots in four or five pages, he announces that an "embryonic" "new" form of "art" was then "born," going on to extend the unwieldy metaphor by throwing in a few gratuitous comments about illegitimacy, adolescence, and maturity. No critic ever states that rock and roll's entire history has been a process of rendering itself more palatable. Better he should give you first choice of backstage passes, or his seat on the chartered jet. Yes, yes, I know all about punk rock, "breaking free of the stagnating morass into which rock had plunged during the seventies." Zzzz. Malcolm McLaren certainly had his cake and ate it too. The Chronicles fall silent regarding Adam and the Ants and Bow Wow Wow. So Jay, then, was a connoisseur of shlock, and increasingly aware of it. The inherent shlockiness of his field of interest never bothered him, but it did prevent him from forming a coherent vision of what the perfect rock and roll band would consist of, although it existed, in bits and pieces, in his mind. They were fixed there, these bits and pieces, flashing at him so hauntingly and persistently that at night it would cause him to cry. I use the image "at night" to suggest a cliché, to wit, Jay alone in his bed, his room starkly furnished—perhaps his guitar leans against a chair or a staff book is open to a new song he's composing. Add a few crumpled, empty bags of Cheez Doodles and we'll have gotten it about right. Jay crying, alone, "at night," wiping the tears from his cheeks with orange-stained fingers. The fact is that he should never have played, never have been anything more than a dedicated and knowledgeable fan. He did play, though, and played comparatively difficult pop during a time increasingly dominated by I-IV-V progressions and much posing. He also taught himself to write songs; to engineer and mix sixteen-track recordings; to harmonize with other voices; to organize groups of musicians utterly disparate both in ambition and in giftedness; to arrange for bookings, and for demo tapes to be played on college radio stations; to see to the pressing and distribution of independent 45s; and to double his vocal range from one to two shaky octaves. By the time that he was twenty years old he was a seasoned professional, thought of the band and its sustenance as a job, and doggedly pursued his self-imposed and single-minded task of tinkering with whatever things lay at his disposal in an effort to create the fluid machine he sought.

So, what, then? To have Jay encapsulate himself—in the form of a personal ad. The shorthand of love. The irreducible distillation of one's public face, since he's so into that.

SWJM, 20, Loves Beatles, Disco, Ramones, Impressions, seeks SWF, 14-35, similar interests, for Chinese food, trips to

Canal St., lots of sex. Middle-class girls with suburban roots given preference. Photo, please. Reply Box 1234.

The astute reader will note that Jay's gluttony is beginning to serve as a rather gratuitous "motif." Actually, it has no purpose other than to signify his abiding vigor. Jay's quite a healthy guy; the hero, really, of this evasive tale. We won't find him brooding over the contours of his abdominal muscles, or holding condoms up to the light, or having an epiphany just before he goes under the knife to have his deviated septum repaired. I can see it now, the cramped hand laboriously forming the letters, the classifieds worker at the *Voice* offering to correct the spelling, out of pity. Jay doesn't care—that way lie StairMasters. What Jay wants are afternoons browsing amongst piles of cheap electronic equipment, frequent orgasms, and, most especially, the dollar egg rolls and chow fun at Wo Hop's.

What about that "**ALL ORIGINAL** reportoire"? I thought that it might be amusing to compose some of the songs performed in the first section. I considered having lead sheets made up, but was vaguely embarrassed by the idea of bringing the songs to some professional musician, telling him that they were the work of "a friend." Besides, none of the boys reads notation, upholding another proud tradition. It is even rumored that Dave has said "I don't know what syncopation is and I don't want to know," and that he refers to minor chords as "the scary chords." I choose to believe this.

"All About Heartache"
by Dave McCall

Ahhhhhhhhhhhhhhhhhhhhhhhhhhhhh!
I know—all about heartache
I felt it for your sake,
but, where—were—you?

Now you—want to cry on my shoulder
well, I'm a thousand years older
so here's what you do:

Girl, all you need
to stop feeling blue
is come back to me
and feel—my love—so true

I saw—you girl with others
I went back to Mother's
and cried—for—you!

Now life—has burst that big bubble
so you're back on the double
well, baby—we're—through

Once I was freed
I went and did what you said you'd do
it made me forget
and now—I'm with—someone new!

I'll allow myself only the slightest criticism of the song, given the fact that I'm operating without the benefit of having heard its music, which may well ameliorate what I perceive as its lyrical inadequacies. It's typical of all Dave's work in its bungling of the clichés that inform it. Narrative songs like this usually adhere to a specific format, wherein (a) the singer bemoans the loss of Girl,[1] (b) begs her to return to him, (c) discovers love anew, and (d) rejects Girl, who has belatedly seen the error of her ways. This song crackles with acrimony from the get-go, except for the first chorus with its oddly conciliatory message. Now, is the rhyme scheme formed by those nineteen words the delicate balance on which the rest of the song is poised? Is there some other aspect to those nineteen words, grouped precisely as they are, which render them indispensable to the song? Not really—Dave thought the words were fine; they served their purpose, which was to propel the song back into the verse. He would gladly record it for national consumption tomorrow. Dave was a hack. Rock and roll is hackwork.

The song was written in 1979, inspired by a comment made by Maureen, Dave's girlfriend at the time, when she was at her most boringly world-weary, to wit, "I know all about heartache." Even Dave, in the grips of adolescent hysteria, of which the argument they were then having was a part, grasped the utter absurdity of the remark. She was no more than fifteen years old at the time. Her allusion was to the painful fact that the man to whom she had lost her virginity, a young Soviet recording engineer who had fucked her on top of a mixing board and in a fit of onanism spilled semen onto her suede go-go boots ("I'll never wash them again!"), had

[1]This word is a trope common to rock and roll. Take it to mean, "You who are breaking my balls."

just been deported. She had not known the young man prior to the incident, nor had she seen him subsequently, but cherished the memory in a way that might have been more understandable had she in any sense cared about her virginity, its loss, or the man who had taken it. This is a problem for her therapist to explore, not us. Her function within these pages is as a sort of prop on which Nat can drape his innate misogyny. Once written and rehearsed, the song became Hi-Fi's traditional opening number, if for no other reason than because it was fast and relatively easy to play.

The young man, incidentally, was promptly sentenced to twenty-five years at hard labor in a Soviet gulag, only three of which years he survived; perishing from the gangrene that had begun one winter in his inadequately protected feet. His own sense of heartache was not discussed.

Back to the photos. I have a nine-by-twelve manila envelope stuffed with them which Nat was kind enough to lend me when I told him the specific nature of my research. Actually, I lied to him, but he never would have let me have them if I'd told him the truth. So I said that I was undertaking the compilation of an oral history of the post-punk New York club scene. Possible release, on a small but nationally distributed label, of a companion CD containing digitally remastered demo tapes and independent 45s. Would he help? He laughed casually, chatted a bit about the old days, and then told me that he'd "see what he could do." After we hung up I thought about how far he'd traveled from his own old days, days in which he manifested himself as a violent, borderline psychotic. I preferred him then, but. The next day I received, via Federal Express, the photographs accompanied by a fifteen-page diatribe, typed by his secretary, which began: "Just wanted to make sure my side of things is represented accurately." What a memory! What a paranoiac! He even went so far as to list individual bum notes that he'd played, and who, of course, to blame for them. Had he been keeping records all those years, while I frittered them away, sans notebook, and am now forced to invent all this nonsense? I took his memorandum and filed it under "Objectivity," no sarcasm intended. One man's reality is as good as any other's, and if I ever decide to use it I'll just change everything around anyway. The photographs are before me on the desk. Most of them I'm not interested in, others we'll come to soon, but there is a third category worth mentioning: several photos, apparently taken on the same day and at the same location, depict a stranger along with Jay, Nat, and Dave, whose identity is an utter mystery to me. The drumsticks protruding from his back pocket can only suggest that at one point Hi-Fi had someone else drumming for them. There is nothing in the record about who this person is or what became of him. Perhaps he left the band for bigger and better things.

This photo is one that the reader has had the opportunity to see "in the making" back in the first section. It came out pretty poorly, as most of Miles Miller's photos do, but I thought that I'd include it for the stunning contrast it provides to the mean, moody, magnificence evinced by those figures on the abandoned railroad track. Jay was talking about the self-myth that lies at the heart of the band's aspirations, but this pretty accurately represents the truth that lies at the core of its inadequacies. It is underexposed, so that even though the lightest of its values appear as shades of grey, they stand in stark contrast to the darker hues, which are black and dark grey, moving into one another and losing distinction. In the foreground of the picture, Nat and Dave smile into the camera. Nat's arms reach behind his neck, as if he is flexing his biceps or about to remove his T-shirt, whose fabric forms parallel diagonal creases running from the network of seams near the shoulders and armpits. The triangle formed by his eyes, their dark pupils centered in the whites, and his teeth, is the focal point of the picture. His expression reveals little or nothing, since it is instantly recognizable as one of the meaningless faces one is expected to assume when confronted with a camera. His skin glistens with a light coat of sweat, worked up under the hot lights during the sound check, which concluded moments before the picture was taken. It may be said that Nat and his eyes and teeth are the photo's focal point by default, since the photographer has succeeded in capturing Dave in the process of shutting his eyes against the flash. He stands slightly in front of Nat, nearer to the camera. With his blond hair, small teeth, and pale skin (he is shirtless), he is a greyly luminous blob in the picture.

After the observer's eye has passed over the two dominant figures, he may find more interesting the activity in the background. Jay, the corona of his hair indistinguishable from the shadow it casts on the wall behind him, appears between Nat and Dave's heads, his left arm reaching toward Richard, at the left-hand side of the photograph. His hand can be seen in the space between Nat's bent right arm and his head. The spatulate fingers seem to be emerging from Nat's ear. Jay's own right arm holds a quart Pepsi bottle, filled with a clear, colorless liquid which does not appear to be Pepsi, close to his chest. The interesting activity seems to be centered around Jay's outstretched hand and Richard's reaction to it. Jay's fingers are splayed, and bent at the first and second joints: arrested this way it looks as if he is mimicking an unfortunate deformity. Richard's right shoulder, visible behind Nat's upraised right elbow, dips away from the hand; his head follows the shoulder, but his eyes remain on the camera, or at least they remain pointed toward the camera—the light from the flash is reflected by and spread across the convex surface of his eyeglass lenses. His maneuver appears sudden and uncomfortable, reactive: a slight doubling of the chin is apparent, his cheeks are slightly puffed, his lips are separated. But his eyes, it appears, remain on the camera.

None of the members of the band has ever liked this photograph. Sean Dennis obtained a print of it from Miles, and hung it on his bulletin board, where it remained until its edges curled and the paper began to yellow.

You must understand that that photo was taken, that the events from which this novel purports to have evolved occurred, near the end of the line. I suppose that any venture undertaken by two or more organic components is destined ultimately to run down, or, more precisely, to reach an impasse at which a decision must then be made either to remain static and move inexorably toward entropy, or to split cleanly from the core and attempt a new direction. In either case, disintegration of the matrix is certain. It is strange to me that in view of this tendency, no less constant in the field of human endeavor, people actually hold out hope, believe that there is a point. But what an extrapolation from a photograph of loutish boys! None of *them* ever thinks about the universe's constant squandering of itself, although I must say, punk rock certainly made its mark by adopting nihilism as its stock in trade. So long as nihilism brought with it Big Checks and Cock Sucking Groupies. But we're onto another digression, an interesting one which I think I'll pursue, regarding punk (and its immediate descendants), "that most vibrant and valid form of rock and roll!," as some of you no doubt bristled when I slammed it a while back. If rock and roll's central paradox is its exponential co-opting of itself, where does that leave punk—which set itself up as the debunker of rock—

artistically? Take a band like the Clash, for instance, whose musical goal was to pose, suggest, or inspire practical answers to political problems in Great Britain and the world at large. In this respect they probably had about as much influence as your local city councilman. Certainly less than a United States senator, for all of their "new ideas." I mostly remember them selling a lot of bowling shirts out of Trash & Vaudeville and Canal Jean. But aren't those new ideas the thing, fortified by the same old guitar-bass-drums, that legitimized punk? And what about that other punk encampment, the United Anarchists, whose wistful idea of anarchy is something out of Burroughs or a Mad Max movie; arid landscapes, elaborate tough guys, and all. Didn't their professed view of life, of the ideal world, preclude the possibility of art? Dispense with it, in a world devoted to struggle, as unnecessary? Yet they sung of their dreams of mountains of excrement, of skewered children and gigantic insects, as artist-prophets, these nice middle-class boys and girls. I'm referring to American punks now. One had to be middle-class to come into contact with it here, to be aware of import record shops and college radio stations, just like Jay, Nat, Dave, and Richard.

A long way back to them, I'll admit. But a look at the attempted marriage of politics and art is always instructive, inasmuch as the robust dumbness of the one is inevitably incompatible with the sublime uneventfulness of the other. The artifacts of the politician are nearly always quaint, even as we labor, decades later, under the ramifications of his acts. The act of creation affects no one, touches no one. Its product sits, void of utility. "All is pointless," it seems to say, contentedly. Try mowing down the barricades with that one. They'll tell you about Enterprise Zones and Reasonable Force and after a couple of months of rehab they'll have you flipping burgers at McDonald's. That's why I've made Hi-Fi a half-assed moon 'n' june band—something we can all agree on for once; that they are not worth saving, that their ineptitude somehow makes the mishaps which befall them this evening fitting as opposed to tragic. Think about it: Mozart, getting his first gig in months, arrives at the recital hall and discovers that there's no piano! So he's out there in the snow-swept streets of Vienna, looking for a goddamn piece of shit piano so he can play the gig, eat, and then go back to, say, *The Marriage of Figaro*. Are you crying yet? This is Mozart, dust now in a pauper's grave, as we have been told again and again, as if what happened to his dead body matters. But Hi-Fi, God, "the idiots had to get their own PA system, haw!" If they were real people their feelings might be hurt.

But they are not, not their individual selves nor the name under which they are collectively known, which, like all other aspects of the band, they are dissatisfied with. "Hi-Fi" was the lackluster result of twenty minutes' discussion, and supplanted an equally insipid name like _____ or _____ (I don't care). Surprisingly, a poor name doesn't really seem to impede the progress of a band any more than a good one accelerates it. One of those rock and roll anomalies. So, Hi-Fi, then. The name only became the source of true dismay on two occasions:

1) Upon his return from England, Peter Dimitri, who will appear nowhere else in this story and who, for our purposes, "had it in" for the band, disseminated a lie of his own invention, to wit, that he had seen a band named Hi-Fi perform on the television show *Top of the Pops*, and that they were sure to be a Big Thing when Capitol Records released their first American album. As the successful result of this, various unreliable but implicitly believed sources began reporting Hi-Fi-sightings from as far away as the I-Beam in San Francisco. Jay's worst fears were confirmed, somehow, when he discovered, in the indy 45 bins at Bleecker Bob's, a single released by a band called the Love Rush on Hi-Fidelicatessen Records.

2) The appearance of the following item in the *Soho News*, week of August 6, 1980:

> On The Boards / j cheuse
> Appearing the 10th at **HEAT** (6 Hubert St.), the Hi-Fi's, whose members are so young that they have to be accompanied by parent or guardian to their own shows. Novel, sort of like the Archies meet the Ramones.

All the members of the band had already reached their majority in the dear dead days of the eighteen-year-old drinking age, so perhaps Mr./Ms. Cheuse was simply trying to generate a little excitement, get a few people down to the club that night. God knows, Hi-Fi needed it. Unfortunately, what few people were attracted to the club were repulsed by Hi-Fi's rendition of "Chinese Nigger," a tasteless song which failed to address the vital issues of piled excrement, skewered kids, and gigantic insects. At any rate, Nat and Dave were upset by the positioning of an article, "the," before the name, its resultant pluralization, and, to add insult

to injury, the addition of an apostrophe. Jay took it more philo-
sophically—a write-up is a write-up—but agreed that there was a
problem with the name. Here is a list of suggested new names submitted by various members of the band for consideration, along
with the reason each was rejected:

NAME	REJECTED BY	WHY?
The Idols of the Marketplace[2]	Jay	Too long
Stately Wayne Manor[3]	Nat	Fear of litigation
Beat Red	Dave	Too stupid
The Meaningless Intensifiers	Dave	Too *fuckin* stupid
The The[4]	Dave	Taken (and stupid)
The End	Jay	Probably taken
The Living End	Dave	Sounds like a nightclub[5]
Free Beer	Jay	Club owners won't go for it
The Id	Jay	Sounds like "The Yid."
The Ruling Class	Dave	"That sucks."
The Lost Child Band	Nat, Jay, Richard	Quorum breaks into a rendition of "Poor Little Buttercup."
600 School	Richard	Claims he attended one.
The Modifiers	Jay	Too trendy.
Big Room	Richard	Not trendy enough.
The Image	Dave	Too much like PiL
The Escorts	Jay	"We have to wear cummerbunds?"
Big Fucking Hammers from Hell	Jay	"Opening for Free Beer?"
The Mice	Nat	"Sissy night with the Lost Child Band and the Living End!"
Bandage	Dave	"Scabby."

[2]Nat offered to modify the name to "The *New* Idols of the Marketplace." This
was rejected as being too obscure.
[3]The original suggestion was "Stately Wayne Manor and the Batmen." A
dispute broke out over who would have to be Wayne.
[4]"And the Stutter Kings!"
[5]"A *fag* nightclub!" added Dave.

It occurs to me that now is an opportune time to explain that Dave is the member of the band in whom I have the least faith. As the preceding list shows, Dave is a pain in the ass, a troublemaker. He is the only band member with whom I have not consulted regarding this book. In fact, I would prefer that he not be in the book at all, but I needed a lead guitarist and there he was, Fender Telecaster in hand. He doesn't bother me much when I'm in San Francisco; he claims that the hills "weird him out," as they do everyone, which is why San Franciscans spend their time bleating talismanically about how wonderful they are for living in **Clean, Beautiful, Fog-Swept** San Francisco. One can never simply live in San Francisco (although they also bore you to tears with conversations about living simply before they roar off in the car they hocked the house for), it is a conscious decision for which one is forever entitled to be self-congratulatory. Forever, that is, until one moves to Oregon or Washington State to be rid of the filthy Bay Area. A curse on all their cottages! Actually, I feel better now, certainly a lot better about Dave, seeing as he and I see eye to eye on something for once, but there's something . . . ah, yes, the Fender Telecaster. The day we met was here in Brooklyn—it seems that aluminum siding and brickface "weird him out" as well, alas—and as he strummed a few chords with those iron fingers of his he divulged that he had gotten rid of the Jaguar and bought the Tele because he had an inkling that it was the "right" guitar to play right now. Strats were played out, he said; Springsteen played a Telecaster, and he just *knew.* Chunka-chunka-chunk,[6] those iron fingers. He really couldn't have cared less about how the thing sounded, any more than he cared about those lines, Girl all you need/to stop feeling blue-oo-oo/is come back to me/and feel my love so true. What was funny was that he had some strange idea that it was 1981; he had no idea that his existence didn't come about until years later. Telecasters are played! I wanted to scream, but hang on to the thing! Fender's turned Jap! How could he possibly know, though, I thought. How could he possibly know anything? And so he was conceived: a mindless creature, whom I have decided to make mad by endowing him with an overwhelming desire for comprehension. What a drag it must be, to be so dumb and to want to know more! Ha! Not that I'm particularly enlightened. Any writer who

---

[6]This is Lester Bangs's expression for the sound of a generic rhythm guitar, preferably played by one who is barely competent.

says he knows anything other than the helpless compulsion to obligate himself to the blackness of the world suspended within him is a liar. Perhaps it's *better* to be like Dave, to seek the heat and energy emitted by the things all around him. To glean the superficialities of things inherently superficial. Glint, glint. That's Dave! Chunka-chunka-chunk, is it really so difficult for him to fulfill his dreams? Are they such a tall order? These are the things that he wants:

1) To perform rock and roll music at the level of sophistication and accomplishment necessary to achieve success.

2) To achieve success.

3) To be able to afford whatever he desires.

4) To get fucked and sucked by many beautiful Girls, without strings.

I wouldn't mind those things, the last three items, at least. The fact is that I will be lucky to get this book published. Perhaps if I put down that Dave is snorting **COCAINE** in the men's room of a popular **NIGHTCLUB** which he will soon leave with a young stranger for some **HOMOSEXUAL INTERCOURSE**, and that a little later he will witness a **HORRIBLE ACT OF SENSELESS VIOLENCE** which will cause him to explore the **DEEP PSY-CHOLOGICAL ROOTS** underlying his **MEANINGLESS, DIS-SOLUTE LIFESTYLE**, understand the **GREAT TRUTHS**, and settle down to **STRAIGHTENING HIMSELF OUT** and **FI-NALLY WRITING THAT NOVEL**, all with the help of **THAT NICE GIRL HE HADN'T BEEN ABLE TO BRING HIMSELF TO COMMIT TO**, it'll sell a few copies and establish for me a reputation as a sensitive humanist who's been around the block a few, believe it. Call it *Big, Bright Zero*.

Jay would really be better off without Dave; Dave is actually destructive to Jay's execution of his thesis, the perfect rock and roll band. Unfortunately, I have decided that Jay's thesis is destined never to be realized, that Jay will always be playing weekday night gigs at CBs, or wherever. Perhaps I'll give him a break in the sequel. If Jay viewed the realization of rock and roll's "moment" as the unlikely juxtaposition of the slow, accretive process of trial and error against pure chance, working toward one end and allowing fate to handle the other, Dave's search was always for the simple expedient. He imagined rock and roll success to be a matter of choreography, and he was absolutely right. Dave was perceptive

enough to realize that fame's recipients are often remarkably je-
june, but because he had no sense of artistry the lack of clear
distinction between a "deserving" recipient and an "undeserving"
one infuriated him. In fact, he was as maddeningly frustrated by
this idea as Jay was by his own inarticulate vision, kept hundreds of
record albums as well as dozens of books dealing with rock and roll
artists and movements. Idiots like Dave always assemble gigantic
collections—there's that greedy acquisitiveness, of course, but
there's also a strange idea that by listening over and over to chord
progressions and reading apocryphal stories and staring at carefully posed photographs, one can get them to yield their secret
truths. To complement him in this whimsical respect, I've slapped
together Girl Bovary, to the tune of "One Hundred Pounds of
Clay." She's Emma's *other* daughter, and she doesn't have much to
say for herself. Actually, none of the women here do. It must be
one of those "guy" books. Perhaps P. J. O'Rourke will like it.

Let us take a look at the divergent approaches to songwriting taken
by Jay and Dave. First we should note that Dave worked at his
leisure, taking days and even weeks to complete a song. We have
seen the result. I think that it is fair, or at least useful, to assume
that the quality of the music to "All About Heartache" is commen-
surate with that of its lyrics. Dave also harbored some sense that his
songwriting sprung from the circumstances of his own life; that his
experience was all "grist for the mill." But, devoid of artistry and
incapable of synthesis, he could only manage to unite his experience (perceived as mostly bad) and his theme (Girl) with whatever
emotion the combination of the two brought to memory (mostly
anger). Nothing wrong with that, of course, except that these limitations were compounded by Dave's talentlessness and stupidity so
that the identical song might arise from Girl's arriving late for a
movie date; Girl's dumping Dave for some other Guy; or Girl's
shooting Dave and then leaving him for dead. It is incredible to me
that Dave could sit at home for weeks slapping together these
songs, steeped all the while in mystical marijuana (of course he's
a pothead), dreaming of his image adorning the backs of denim
jackets in Queens. Jay, on the other hand, worked quickly and with
facility, fully aware of his lack of talent and aided by one of those
bits and pieces that continued to flash at him (I planted it); the idea
that rock and roll was really a sort of clandestine form of comedy,
and a means of self-entertainment as well. After all, what did all

those guys in *Rolling Stone* and *Trouser Press* have to look so grim about? They were young, they were rich, and they had been placed on top of the world for playing A-D-E, A-D-E at extreme volumes. Jay looked at the pictures and saw a lot of guys who should be dancing and drinking and fucking it all away while they still had it. What was all this weight-of-the-world stuff when what you did was take planes, stay in hotels, and go into the studio once a year? Because you had to eat hamburgers, again? He loved hamburgers! As I've said before, a primping, posing, nostril-flaring, cheek-sucking guy like Dave was not exactly helpful to Jay. While Dave insisted on taking his time in "crafting" his "music," he had also insisted on a "no covers" policy for the band, oblivious as usual to the idea that the simple expedient sometimes consisted of playing "Twist and Shout" before a bunch of drunken businessmen at the annual Christmas party. "Sell out!" he would bellow, at the slightest sug- gestion of incorporating such a song into the crunchily stale set, and then run home to begin composing "Now I'm Laughin' at You, Girl" or "Shoe's on the Other Foot, Girl." All of Dave's songs cul- minated in a sort of revenge fantasy. Since "Turning the Tables (on You, Girl)" might take six weeks to evolve from Dave's experi- encing the "grist" of the cap left off the toothpaste tube, Jay was often compelled to write songs in an effort to imbue the act with some freshness. His songwriting was informed by his desire to turn rock and roll back on itself, not by spicing the lyrics with topical musings, but by lifting the lyrics directly out of their hundreds of antecedents and distorting them, as in a funhouse mirror, ever mindful of the leering innuendos and ridiculous, strained rhymes.

"Diner Goddess"
by Jay Lustig

Venus!
Venus!
You're my heart,
You're my soul,
You're my . . .
Venus!

When I saw you at the diner
I knew that you looked so fine
I had to have you girl
Pourin' soda at the fountain
and the change you were a-countin'
made me hungry!

So I ordered a Deluxe and
then I pulled out all my bucks—
I wanna tip—you—right!
Though the fries were like cement
I'm gonna give 20 percent
all through the night!

Venus!
Venus!
You're my heart,
You're my soul,
You're my . . .
Venus!

I hate to see you get the dregs for makin'
things work out like eggs and bacon
come with me!
You pop the toaster of my heart,
I'll put your water on to start,
just wait and see!

So won't you please turn in your spatula,
pencil, pad and paper hat you gotta
see this through!
You're my breakfast, lunch, and supper, we're
gonna seal our love in Tupperware
just us two!

Venus!
Venus!
You're my heart,
You're my soul,
You're my . . .
Venus!

If the audience went along with it, fine; if not, he could think about it later. Jay was aware of the audience without being preoccupied with it, as Dave was. But what an odd thing to make of the subject matter, especially compared to what Dave would have done with it. I say that because the song came about as the result of one of Dave's stories: while strumming, again and again, the chords to "Lola," he discussed his unrequited affections for a young blonde waitress he had met.[7] The story was boring, of course, most stories like that are, and from Dave, arrgh. After he had fleshed out the

---

[7]Curiously, this is the second time that Dave has talked and played guitar simultaneously—perhaps it's a tic. I'm merely surprised that he's capable of it.

essential details he began to concentrate on the minutiae of what had made this waitress so particularly attractive: the way in which she stood flush against the table so that the triangular outline of her crotch was plainly visible through her apron, her constant toying with the disobedient lock of hair that repeatedly flopped into her eyes, etc. You and I would be on our knees at that point, begging for mercy. Dave is so dense that he is incapable even of properly deploying the natural gifts of the fetishist. But Jay is a practical man, as we've seen, the kind of guy who shepherds a project through from cradle to grave. He stitches together his lyrics, slightly alters the chord structure of "Lola," and—*voila!*—a song is born. Jay figures they'll have it down by their (fifth) audition night at CBGB next week. Well, Dave was incensed. The song had been stolen from him. Stolen! If I were more merciful, I would have Dave pack up his guitar (Gibson Jumbo acoustic, black lacquer finish, gold-plated hardware, mother-of-pearl inlays) and take off at that point. Perhaps the mysterious figure in those photographs plays guitar as well? What I'll do instead is place in evidence a photograph of the band rehearsing this very song, "Diner Goddess." One of those types of photos that fans love: the band, stripped of its glitz, getting down to brass tacks. Why is it that depriving the celebrated subject of its image somehow reinforces that image? One can't push it too far, though—a photo of Kiss, in its heyday, working makeup-less in the studio was a definite no-no. A friend of mine has a theory that the fading of a certain television personality's star was precipitated by the resurfacing of some topless photographs that she had made years before for the calendars distributed by a farm supply outfit to its clientele. Her charm, on television, had revolved around the titillating concealment of those very breasts beneath an assortment of flimsy, revealing garments. Then the tit was out of the bag, as it were: there she was straddling a tractor, or whatever, clad only in high heels, G-string, and straw hat, milkweed protruding from her smiling mouth. No one needed her anymore. Besides, as my friend says, her tits were funny-looking. So, to the studio. What is odd about this picture is that it is a double-exposure, its images captured each time from the same vantage point in the room. The background of the picture is formed by two walls of the studio, one of which, apparently shared by a neighboring loft, is covered with egg cartons, cork, and other sound-insulating materials. The other faces the street, for in it is set a large rectangular window, so streaked with grime and dust that the rooftops and buildings beyond it are seen hazily and the reflection of the flash does not appear on its surface. The members of the band are at middle distance, grouped in a circle, facing each other. Richard, behind his drums, is at left. Clockwise from him are Dave, facing the camera; Jay, directly opposite Richard; and Nat, his back to the camera and facing Dave. In the right foreground is Nat's bass amp and next to it one of the small speaker columns that are connected to Jay's PA system. Across the section of the floor that comprises the middle and left foreground of the photo are strewn cigarette butts, a book of matches, two guitar strings, a guitar pick, and various cords traveling from instrument and microphone to amplifier. The inanimate items captured in the photograph remain constant, but the figures of the musicians are caught in two separate attitudes: one exposure depicts Richard striking the crash cymbal and floor tom, Nat hunching as he plays high up on the neck of the bass, and Jay singing, arching his back and tilting his head to meet the microphone he holds above it. The other exposure shows Nat gesturing as he speaks, head turned toward Richard, who looks back at him, hands in his lap, while Jay looks on, microphone held down at his side. Only Dave remains the same throughout the two images: arms akimbo, he stands looking toward the window, a slight scowl on his face.

We can infer from the fact that Hi-Fi went on to audition at CBGB a sixth, seventh, and eighth time before finally giving up that they did not perform too well that Monday night. One of Jay's flaws was that he was incapable of differentiating between a poor gig and a humiliating one, which is why we find ourselves this evening in a converted tavern in midtown Manhattan, so remote from the sort of venue Hi-Fi aspired to that it might as well be in Urbana. Actually, in Urbana the band might conceivably get a shot at a fraternity or ASU function, but that would be technically impossible, since I have decided that Jay is politically opposed to the Big Ten, Nat is terrified of driving, flying, and traveling by rail, Dave finds that agriculture has a tendency to weird him out, and Richard has it on good authority that the entire campus is sitting on top of a gigantic dump of highly toxic waste. How on earth did I put these people in a place like Cheaters? It seems too unlikely, too odd. But then again, Jay is the one who has called me to announce Hi-Fi's impending performances at such places as the University of the Streets, a latter-day commune with surprisingly stringent rules

concerning complimentary admission, and the convention hall of
the Youth International Party. I met Jerry Rubin there and he tried
to sell me, in quick succession, municipal bonds, time-share condominiums, a thirty-day vitamin and mineral "system," magazine
subscriptions, and an ounce of what he described as "Canadian
Brown." Actually, those were the only types of gigs I was interested in showing up for; call it morbid curiosity. CBs, Max's
Kansas City, and the rest were all known quantities, but these other
clubs could contain any number of ugly surprises. It seemed (and
still does) that a prerequisite for opening a nightclub in New York
City was the willingness to treat both patron and performer with
equal contempt. All of that is mellowing into the Good Old Days
now, though. Who remembers good old Max's, where the Nazi-
biker bouncers would herd you behind the velour ropes, kick you if
you blocked the aisle, and throw those who objected to being
treated like cattle headlong down the conveniently steep stairs? Ha,
ha. May the place burn in fucking hell. I remember Nat telling me
once that he'd played there to a relatively large weeknight audience
of about twenty people and wasn't paid because the manager didn't
"feel like it." Those good old days.

Cheaters wasn't quite in that league that remained solvent because someone big had gotten their start there, or because *New
York Rocker* reported, via hip code words, that it offered the best
DJs, prettiest girls, and cheapest drinks, or because it was a ghetto
for Fiorucci Punks and other Bridge and Tunnel types. It was just
another down-and-out bar that tried to revitalize itself by opening
its doors to third-rate acts like Hi-Fi. Sounds stupid, but it was
really America In Action!, right there at the dawn of the eighties:
"Cheaters President and CEO Mona Barron announced today that
the New York-based entertainment outlet would shortly undergo
a major restructuring which would involve, among other changes,
a facelift for the flagship midtown club and what Ms. Barron
described as 'a redirection of our marketing resources toward the
younger, more sophisticated consumer.'" What did they have to
lose—a cheap plywood stage, a couple of microphone stands, a
tiny ad in the *Voice* each week, a two-dollar cover after 9:00 P.M.
and *bam!* Instant Nightclub! Why not? Why should Hi-Fi appear
against a backdrop any more painstakingly conceived than its own
music? Have them there, then, making their entrances from behind
a pair of cheap folding screens depicting imitation Japanese prints,
bouncing up and down on that stage with its dubious capability of

supporting them, lit by a trio of inexpensive arc lights mounted on a track. It's where they belong. You can shake your fist at the skyline all you want, but the club scene in New York is really quite democratic, given what this term has come to mean: those bands that are any good and which hold out the promise of attracting crowds will eventually be given Friday and Saturday nights, and those that aren't are quickly detected and doomed to Cheaters and places like it. This is not to say that being showcased regularly at "name" clubs on weekends is an automatic guarantee of success— far from it. But those who find themselves, after a year or so, pushing their equipment through a deserted barroom at three o'clock on a Thursday morning are likely to remain there. Jay was already skeptical regarding the form of the music itself, but remained naïve about the machinations of the music industry, whose gears meshed smoothly even at the level on which he was operating. He had some idea that getting screwed was really Getting Screwed; that it happened to the big boys to the tune of millions of dollars. I am not going to be the one to tell him that he was Getting Screwed whenever some schmuck told him to be onstage as soon as the blue light came on, or else; nor will I tell him that he was Getting Screwed on those occasions when he was informed that it would cost $25.00 to have a sound man monitor the band's performance; or that he was Getting Screwed each time some nonentity, feeling that he was dealing with a slightly lesser entity, demanded something of him that was calculated specifically to humiliate him.

I must stop here. The Evil Nightclub Owner is such a venerable cliché that even as I write these words the image of George Raft, elegantly attired in evening wear and sitting flanked by two monstrous goons, laughs mirthlessly through a blue cloud (the image is colorized) of cigarette smoke as he reaches into his ornately carved desk and then carelessly tosses a packet of hundred-dollar bills at me. "Keep your nose out of where it don't belong, shamus," he says. Through the thickly paneled walls of his inner sanctum the hysterical laughter of the debauched carriage trade can just barely be made out. File it away. What I'm talking about is the utter periphery of an industry and milieu that devours its children and then offers the vomit for sale. Here is Jay walking into the midst of all this: first it's got an arm. Now it's got a leg. Ptui! It doesn't want him! Would it help a little if I describe him to you? Looks—I don't care. "Darkly Semitic." That's a sop to the bigots out there. Flannel shirts, corduroy pants, Stan Smith sneakers, quilted down jackets.

Now do you get the picture? This is Downtown New York City, 1981, where in order to appear chic and sophisticated you either dress like a thug or wear used clothing that once looked conservative on a CPA in 1965. This is one of the reasons why Dave and Richard, and to a lesser extent, Nat, would go into hyperspace each time Jay showed up for a gig looking as though he had dressed to run out for the *Times* and some bagels. Dave nosed around clumsily, like a blind newborn animal, tentatively teasing his hair with Dippity-Doo or purchasing a motorcycle jacket to wear. He really wanted to be Peter Frampton or Robin Zander; he really *was* aiming for Queens. Didn't want to weird anybody out too much. Richard, on the other hand, bought into the downtown thing whole hog. Whatever his sensitive antennae picked out as the "best" way to look in order to guarantee admission to the Mudd Club or Danceteria, he looked that way. He figured that he was better off imitating today the girls he was going to try to get over on tonight than settling in for some protracted uphill battle for a tomorrow in which *they* tried to look like *him*. So, Jay walks into the midst of all this, and among the things he encounters as he goes on his merry way is this:

LIVE MUSICIANS WANTED!!!!!!!!!!!!!!!!!!!!!!
for Midtown's most fashionable new nitespot. Rock'n'Roll, Blues, Jazz Welcome. Call Mona @ 581-0507

One presumes that dead musicians need not apply. Such solecisms do not bother Jay, however. I'll beg the reader's indulgence at this point and ask that you imagine for yourself the conversation between Jay and Mona. Certain cinematic images come to mind which may aid you in this respect—a vertical line splitting the screen into two equal rectangular sections, one of which is occupied by Jay and the other by Mona. Jay and Mona each make a big show of rummaging through papers when the question of a specific date arises, although neither of them has anything better to do. Concludes with a ringing ninth chord. Trang-g! Etc. Now, while you gorge yourself on these clichés, which can pretty much play themselves out in your head without any assistance, consider this: I constructed that advertisement so that red flags would begin waving madly in the minds of even the dimmest of readers. Something about the thing is certainly off. I'll offer a parallel that often occurs in the fashion industry: ads will appear, announcing that "new faces" are wanted for TV, magazine, and catalogue modeling.

Amateurs of all shapes, sizes, and deformities flock to the joint, and are told that they can't get any work without a proper portfolio, which can be prepared for them by the agency for the nominal fee of, say, $150.00. The real models are out there knocking them dead with their fuck-me smiles for a grand a day, and poor Andrea Marciano, the prettiest girl at Midwood High, is out a hundred and fifty bucks. I'll leave it at that, but let's have Jay hear it from someone truly leery of everything. Seriously, Nat draws the blinds and hides under the bed when he sees the Girl Scouts coming with their boxes of Cremey Yum Yums for sale. He's likely to mumble something about the Hitler Youth. Jay knows this, of course, I'll have to get you from here to there. So. By now the conversation between Jay and Mona is ended. Jay picks up the phone again and dials Dave, who does not answer because he is listening to *Houses of the Holy* through the headphones at top volume. Richard is unavailable, sitting now on a stoop on St. Marks Place with a young woman to whom he is enumerating the various types of attack helicopters employed by the U.S. armed forces during the Vietnam war. This leaves him with Nat. The phone rings. One, two, a total of five times. Finally, "Hello?" Ah, the burden that his inflection places on that word, as if the evil inhabiting the world seems to crystallize around the sinister device he reluctantly holds. Jay proceeds, after delivering his reciprocal salutation, to announce the news of the gig, using phrases like Ground Floor, Real Possibility of a Weekend, Good Door Policy, and the like. It is indicative of Hi-Fi's relationship with itself that Jay was frequently faced with the task of pitching the band both to outsiders and to its own members, with about the same amount of success on both ends. Nat is suspicious, as usual. The fact that his misgivings about the value of this gig or that one could conceivably have some basis in reality is beside the point. They don't. Nat is, to put it indelicately, a ball-buster. When Jay once told the band that it had been booked to perform before several thousand people at a free weekend concert in Central Park—their biggest-ever gig, at that point—Nat asked what the weather was expected to be on that particular day, six weeks hence. He would not, he said, entertain the thought of performing in inclement weather. He had little faith in the efficacy of the grounding devices built into the amplifiers and other equipment. He had heard stories. As it happened, the day turned out to be sunny, clear, and warm. There were indeed thousands of people in the audience, and Hi-Fi had had the remarkable luck of being scheduled to perform at 2:00 P.M., long before the crowd could be expected to start to thin. Between songs toward the end of the performance, Nat picked up a large pitcher of water that had been placed onstage for the band and poured it over himself, soaking his head, shoulders, arms and torso. When his fingers came into contact with the strings of his bass he received an electric shock, nonlethal but severe enough to knock him off his feet. If you ask him about it today, he will shake his head and comment about how suddenly that "sunshower" had appeared from "out of nowhere." In fact, this event receives mention in Nat's fifteen-page memo:

> 5/5/79 - Rock Against Racism Concert
> Central Park, NYC
> Received 1st and 2nd degree burns on both hands and contusion on left buttock requiring outpatient treatment at Roosevelt Hospital ER due to sudden cloudburst and unsafe working conditions. Incident necessitated replacement of Fender Precision Bass guitar (value—$350) due to short-circuiting of electronic components and warping of instrument's neck.

A lot of chutzpah. As I have said, there are literally thousands of witnesses who probably remember the unusual spectacle of Nat Phenomenon dousing himself and the live electrical appliance to which he was attached with a half-gallon of water. So we can expect that Nat's objection to the gig at Cheaters will have nothing to do with the pay, the conditions, or the venue—each of which, we have seen, is thoroughly inadequate in itself. Jay, although always cautious when discussing things with Nat, allowed a seemingly harmless comment to slip regarding Cheaters' status as a "bar and grill," although so far as I know the only food preparation going on there consisted of the bartender's obsessive pouring of pretzels into the bowls on the bar. "Steaks . . . ?" asks Nat. Yes, says the unwary Jay. "Chops . . . ?" Again, the affirmative reply. "Seafood . . .?" Yes, yes. "Shellfish . . . ?" Jay's answer is somewhat more hesitant here, he's finally gotten the message that Nat is leading him into one of the twisted labyrinths of his mind. He's been making it all up as he goes along anyway, something I can appreciate, and has no idea what to say—the lady or the tiger? "Yes. . . ." Aha! It seems that Nat has a moral objection to the consumption of shellfish, nothing that has to do with the arcane dietary laws of his forefathers—both he and Jay are thoroughly secular Jews. It stems from a childhood visit to a seafood restaurant, he says, where he had been permitted to select his own lobster from among those in the large tank near the kitchen. He claims to have had some idea that it was going to become his pet. Imagine his surprise when "Clawey" showed up dead on his plate; little crustacean eyes, though melted, wide with fright. Since then, well. The story is bullshit, of course; I suspect that Nat's parents would not have permitted a child under ten his own lobster, more likely would have steered the kid toward the fried clams or other "fun" food. I speak from bitter experience here. Besides which, the story comes from the mouth of someone who has absolutely no problem with dispensing controlled bursts of nerve gas to any insect he happens to encounter at home, watching its agonized seizures with a kind of detached fascination. Wouldn't dream of using a shoe or a newspaper—eww!—and speedily dispatching the little bastard. Jay says he's pretty sure that the place doesn't serve lobster. And it didn't, so Nat had nothing to complain about on that front, no way to refer to it as "Club Auschwitz" or any of the other insulting parallels that so-called animal rights activists come up with. Interestingly enough, Hitler was also very fond of lobsters and bade his scientists to find a way to painlessly prepare them for human consumption. One can only assume that the corps rose to the occasion with its customary experimental zeal. There has to be a certain amount of dissociation involved in the effort to reclaim the rights of all the other creations that Homo sapiens has spent millions of years evolving beyond. The contradictions inherent in the process might otherwise prove too much to bear—how else to rationalize the thousands of miles of jet travel; the gallons of fuel for the old Volvo or Datsun?[8]

The retrospective view of Nat's life is of a sort of parade of grievances, a type of anti-nostalgia that in some strange way must provide him with a sense of comfort. As the past recedes, taking with it its myriad ills, real and imagined, it must be a relief to think that they will not, in all likelihood, occur again, and that whatever good has happened can be summoned up. From such beliefs arise the idea of lucky and unlucky articles of clothing, utter terror of the law of averages, and other aspects of obsessive-compulsive behavior. Knowing all of this makes it very tempting to take liberties with Nat's character; to turn him into a slasher or a

---

[8]Although I've found, in the case of automobiles in particular, that a piece of technology can be lifted above its innate evil through the placement of the word "battered" before it.

transvestite or some other harborer of a lurid secret life. I prefer
that he become, later in life, one of society's professional neu-
rotics, an attorney. Most people, in their loathing of these men
and women, have the mistaken impression that their language is
designed to obscure and conceal. It is precisely the opposite case—
their language is intended to make everything blindingly clear. If
everything in the universe is incalculable and comprised of an
infinite series of stations, motions, occupations, voids, actions, reactions, causes, and effects, the attorney's task is to catalogue as
many of these as possible and then to apply them to a given
situation that looks, to the rest of us, as simple as the movement
from A to B. People who dislike attorneys simply distrust language. They like advertising, and they want their attorneys to be
like Gregory Peck or Henry Fonda, holding out their big hands and
talking about the Great Truths. I have a secret for you: the Great
Truths are really only all the things you can name in a list. In fact, I
submit that "apple" is truer than "justice." An apple is a round,
firm, edible fruit, with a protective skin that reddens at maturity
and a pale, yellowish flesh that tastes sweetly tart. You tell me
what justice is. Replies may be directed to my refrigerator box on
Market Street.

I really wanted to show Nat what I've written so far. I hear he's
gotten his shit together now, that he lives in a beautiful house in
Santa Monica, devotes himself to his wife and small son, and
works late into the night composing things like, ". . . defined as a
slow-moving motorized vehicle intended for use in agricultural
applications as a means of towing, hauling, or otherwise employ-
ing agricultural equipment and supplies and not for use as transportation on public roads or highways. . . ." That such people should
be considered normal by society and rewarded for catering to their
obsessions, while I am considered, in a word, a "weirdo," is in-
comprehensible to me, but there you go. On second thought, after
thinking about Nat, Nat Spielvogel né Phenomenon né Spielvogel and his lawn talk and golf talk and cellular phone talk, his
professed knowledge of mysterious places like Mazatlán and
Maui, I've decided that he can go fuck the pocket part in the back
of West's *Civil Procedure* and am sticking to my original plan
of total deceit. I've sent him a few hastily drafted pages purporting
to consist of the statements of people bearing suspect monikers
like Vanna Sang-Froid and B. J. Hornbeck, regarding his musical
and sexual prowess. Everything is expressed in superlatives. Any

moment now I expect the phone to ring, to hear the purring voice as he reclines in his ergonomic executive chair, those reminiscences about the "old gang." Vanna Sang-Froid?

As I have visited visions upon Jay, without cohesiveness; as I have given Dave the urge to comprehend, without intelligence, I have given Nat the impulse to hold his world together, to explain it categorically, without the benefit of any logic underlying his methodology. Oh, the poor man. He discovered early on that life provides few answers, especially to those big questions that occur to people mystically inclined: Where did I come from? Why am I here? When am I going? To have your entire life framed by those three monolithic unknowables, questions you would demand an immediate answer to within the context of something as simple as, say, a boring dinner party. Hence, he places himself at the core of the universe, or, more precisely, *as* the core of the universe. California's the perfect place for that, the people there neither talk nor listen. That he should determine that God does exist, because he saw the image of Christ in a cloud while pondering that very question. That he should freeze for long moments on the threshold, unsure as to whether he should walk with his hands inside of his pockets, to protect them from horrible accidents, or out, so that he can restrain himself in the event of a nasty fall. That he should, inspired by an argument with his wife, sublimate his rage via a vicious letter to the editor, and then, inspired by his letter, imagine his wife to be having an affair with the author of the article he was excoriating. This actually happened. Each component of his act fed silently upon the others. To the world, he looked like a man seated quietly before a laptop computer, that day's *L.A. Times* folded open on the table beside the sleek machine. Calmly he typed the words while, in his mind, his wife performed fellatio upon "Scoop"—her distended cheeks and lips, the very *sounds* of her perverted faithlessness. Meanwhile, the letter began to metamorphose: questioned the innocuous . . .; objected to the inert . . .; opposed to the insipid . . .; disturbed by the foolish . . .; annoyed by the ignorant . . .; angered by the mean-spirited . . .; enraged by the malicious . . .; nearly driven to violence by the neo-Nazi . . . finally he was done. Grinning, he showed the three single-spaced pages to his wife, who blandly remarked that it seemed a little overdone to her. His heart sank. She *was* fucking him, the cunt!

But that Nat, the obsessive, egocentric Nat of today, is really beyond our concerns. We're interested in the Nat who stood on that

tiny stage, "providing the upper half of Hi-Fi's rich vocal harmonies," as Jay would put it. How he became the sort of person
that he is now is a mystery. One supposes that Nat's progression
from overt psychosis to covert neurosis is a constructive change. I
realize that I'm using these clinical terms loosely, but how else
does one compare the Nat who picked fights with bouncers, tried
to set friends on fire, and gave every woman he became involved
with at least one shot in the chops with the other Nat, who, in the
words of a common friend, "crouches in terror"? So, circa 1981,
Nat is literally a bundle of nerves. He is both the most interesting,
and the weakest, character in this book, embodying all of the worst
traits of the others and undergoing a permanent identity crisis. The
idea of Dave McCall being a more holistically sound person than
Nat is hard to swallow and difficult for me to admit, but Nat is
helpless, helpless.

While Jay saw the phrase "to rock and roll" as defining the
achievement of a state of religious enlightenment, and Dave saw it
as the mirror-perfect reflection of that segment of society that
graced the covers of slicks like *Tiger Beat* and *16*, Nat's subliminal
take on it was the classic, seminal meaning of the expression: to
fuck. Rock and roll was the latest in a series of partially explored
and subsequently abandoned routes to the happiness he associated
with sexual satiety. The fact that he loathed and feared women is
not surprising, and proved an obvious obstacle to his attainment of
Nirvana. He managed to resolve the problem when his somewhat
scattered pathology cohered and hardened after he managed to
shed the baggage that came along with the experimentation of his
nascent sexuality. He devoted himself to the act itself, and his new
"method," absent the choreographed pageantry and the implicit
consent of his partner that were such a part of his earlier practices,
was something he alone could enjoy: the secret and exhilarating
fury given form by the sexual act, his delight in the concept that at
the moment of penetration his lover was simultaneously diminished, lessened in dignity and humanity. Maureen is really the
perfect beneficiary of all this rage, because she's actually a whore.
She once surprised Nat by taking him to a concert on his birthday.
The admission was comped, and as an added thrill the two of them
were allowed backstage to meet and chat with the headliners.
Maureen had previously secured this enchanting evening by sucking off, in succession, one of the club's front door men and one of
the band's roadies. Happy Birthday to You! Unable to reconcile

himself to her infidelities, and lacking the courage to defy her and commit some for himself, Nat ravaged her regularly, and in every conceivable way, all the while imagining himself to be one of her lovers, registering each sound that she made and each way that she looked as he felt that each must have perceived her. It is a short step from that to simply imagining both the lovers and the infidelities themselves. His wife's fictional liaison with Scoop of the *Times* suddenly becomes less unlikely. Nat confessed all of this to Maureen once, tenderly. Her reaction of utter revulsion startled him.

"I Wish You Were Someone Else"
by Nat Phenomenon

I wish you were someone else,
I wish you were someone else:
then I wouldn't have to be in love with you

I wish you were far from here,
not coming so close and holding me near:
then I wouldn't have to be in love with you

You get on my back,
'cause I'm always wrong—
but I can't see what I do

Oh, but if you leave me—
Oh, you know it grieves me—
Oh, I can't make my mind up with you

When we're lying on the bed
I feel the fireworks in my head
You do things to me, yeah,
that I've only heard about
But I wish that I were dead

I wish you were someone else,
I wish you were someone else:
then I wouldn't have to be in love with you

I wish you were far from here,
not coming so close and holding me near:
then I wouldn't have to be in love with you

You turn out the light,
everything's all right—
but I can't see what I do

Oh, but if you leave me—
Oh, you know it grieves me—
Oh, I can't make my mind up with you

Nat was no songwriter—no musician at all, really. With his considerable intelligence he managed to teach himself to fake his instrument with a remarkable degree of proficiency, but had no real understanding of it, no flexibility. But there is, to me, something oddly touching about this song, considering everything we've observed about Nat so far. Maureen, of course, thought that the song was about her, and flew into a rage. They had a fine argument that night, which culminated with the two of them giving each other black eyes, and then Nat went home to masturbate angrily, ejaculating into the huge porcelain bathtub in his kitchen and then methodically scouring it. But actually, the song was written by Nat to *himself*, out of the urge to break free not only of his illness, the limitations that it imposed upon his life, the image that it carried with it, but of the very lump of flesh that *was* him. Do you really think that your crazy friends are so non compos mentis that they are not as aware of their problems as someone with cancer, or a headache? Nat lived each day with knowledge of his helplessness; in a state of chronic low-level depression. He saw plain the hideous face most of us are fortunate enough to move through life unaware of: the world as an endless parade of garbage, dappled here and there with fleeting glints of beauty, of truth. Gone, as it moves back under the shadow. I wish he were someone else too.

Our last image of Nat, though, should be both typical and sedate, emblematic of surrender and sublimation. We can't really count him as newly among the corrupted, since the ambitions and dreams he abandoned for the mainstream were thoroughly corrupt from the outset. Had Nat actually become a rock and roll star, you can bet that there would have been plenty of "scandal": corpses in the pool house, arrests for indecent exposure, violent scenes involving waitresses. Now the most antisocial behavior that Nat engages in is when he fucks his secretary on the conference-room table, absently watching the traffic outside as it moves slowly down Santa Monica Boulevard. Indeed, I think that Nat, older and slightly more calcified, would provide the novelist with an interesting subject. The novelist would be John Updike, though. Why not? De-sex him, or at least establish sex as a sort of narrow, uniform activity that in itself inspires guilt and chagrin; grant him a gnawing sense of dissatisfaction with his absurdly successful life; a beautiful, aging, and alcoholic spouse; a vaguely delinquent child; a crisis situation that both intensifies and transcends the banality of his everyday existence, and you have all the requisite ingredients of a novel that will make members of the middle-class audience at which it is unflinchingly aimed shudder at the dark undercurrent that runs through their lives without ever making them fear for the loss of the mahogany sideboard or the shiny Volvo outside. I see Nat, this perfect product of the eighties, pissing and shitting compulsively, drinking gallons of water and taking vitamins by the handful, trying to eliminate the "poisons" from his body. "Working out," Christ, every drop of sweat a symbol of his effort to expiate what he recognizes as the corruption of his miserable life. That is to say that the economics of guilt are complex enough to have permitted the unspoken establishment of a kind of underground currency with which one exchanges virtuous acts for tainted pleasures. He reads this sanitized novel and through some feat of self-deception recognizes Updike as his chronicler. Don't ask me. Corruption really is a difficult thing to touch upon in a society where the act of turning on an electric light or brewing a pot of coffee is, in a sense, corrupt. Even as we sit around the table, sipping the Rich Colombian Brew and discussing the plight of exploited tenant farmers, the fact remains that Juan Valdez has retired for the night to his corrugated tin shack in the shadow of the mountain. I think that the idea that most people have of corruption runs along the same lines as Dave's: a rock and roll band dilutes its **"ALL ORIGINAL** reportoire" by incorporating into it a *cover song*—SELL OUT! "You're gonna take a dive in the fifth, kid. There's a nice taste in it for you." One day you're your own man or woman, and the next you're peering out of someone else's coat pocket. Nonsense. Our world is so thoroughly sophisticated, its realities filtered down to us in such dilute form, that at most they fill us with a vague sense of discomfiture, which is easily quieted. It is precisely our ability to simultaneously admit to the ugliness around us—Juan Valdez with an alligator clip attached to his scrotum—and ignore it that insures the perpetuity of abuse. There is nothing that is sacred, and there is nothing that cannot be overlooked. This is all very trite, I realize, but I needed it in order to get around to Richard's infiltration of my book. The photographs were really the clue that led me to discover his incredible subterfuge. After having noticed the presence of that stranger along with Jay, Nat, and Dave on the railroad tracks, I went back to check some preliminary notes I'd taken prior to embarking on the actual writing of the book. Each

of the characters was sketched out in one of the numbered sub-
sections into which the five or six handwritten pages had been
divided, and although they differed slightly from the way they've
turned out, they were more or less the same, with the exception of
Richard. Instead, I'd made an entry describing "Michael Bachmann, drummer," who was "a relative newcomer to the band, not
a member of Jay, Nat, and Dave's social circle, and outside the
perimeter of the St. Marks 'scene.'" It continues, describing the
dramatic climax wrought from this confrontation between "representatives of two different worlds," that is, the world of white,
middle-class Manhattanites who listened to punk rock and the
world of white, middle-class Manhattanites who listened to heavy
metal, but I forgive myself for the parochialism of my youth. At
any rate, that does not sound like Richard to me, nor should it to
you, considering that you've been duly acquainted with Richard's
prodigious grasp of transitory panache and observed him lounging
on a stoop on Depression Strip itself. But there's no way to compare the two of them physically, because knowing of the reading
public's predisposition to skip over such boring fare I generally
eschew comprehensive physical descriptions of my characters
except as a narrative device, i.e., "he hit his head on the top of
the doorframe *because he was so tall*" [italics mine]. Since it was
impossible to determine whether all that I had intended was a
simple name-change, and since I could not recall either having
made the decision to effect this change or the act of having effected
it, if indeed I did, I returned to the photographs to ponder Bachmann's short, wiry appearance in place of the familiar, tall,
endomorphic form that is signified each time I write the words,
"Richard Poindexter." I discovered then that somehow Richard's
image had replaced that of Bachmann on each of these photos. It
was a sloppy, crude job; anyone could tell at a glance that Richard
had been pasted in. The first photograph I examined was taken
before a chain link fence, topped with rusty barbed wire which has
been covered by a heavy canvas tarpaulin, folded double. On each
side of the fence, marking the left- and right-hand margins of the
picture, there is a massive steel stanchion supporting the railway
overhead. The bottoms of these stanchions are embedded in conical bases of concrete on which are painted broad diagonal stripes of
alternating light and dark color. Beyond the fence is a metal stairway climbing to a platform adjacent to the tracks above. On one of
the steps are two cardboard containers of coffee, from which steam

rises. The band, too, is on the far side of the fence, looking at the camera through the mesh formed by the interwoven links. At left is Dave, gripping the links of the fence with both hands and holding his body at an angle of approximately forty-five degrees to the ground. His leather motorcycle jacket, which is open, hangs from his body in a straight vertical line. His head follows his body's inclination and is tilted back, his eyes appearing as slits. To his left is Nat, standing with his hands behind him, planted in the small of his back, his chest thrust out. His stance is slightly pigeon-toed, and from the expression on his face it looks as if he is stretching after an act of physical exertion, possibly the scaling of the fence. Past Nat and slightly behind him, roughly in the center of the photograph, is Jay, who holds a rectangular guitar case in an upright, vertical position. The case is covered with a scuffed tweed fabric and has been plastered with decals bearing the names and logos of manufacturers of special effects boxes and other accessories and equipment. Jay's eyes are downcast, as though he is examining the case, or perhaps the trash that is strewn about the base of the fence on both sides: paper bags, cigarette packs, cans, bottles, newspapers, plastic garbage bags, a length of cardboard tubing, and other items too minute to identify. Richard appears before the fence, near the fencepost that runs parallel to the stanchion at the right-hand side of the photograph. His photograph has been taken in such extreme light that it is probable that, had he been there and had it been possible to capture him exclusively in this light, those on the other side of the fence would have been unable to distinguish his expression, his features, the very color of his clothing. The singular illumination of his figure is not the only indication that his presence in the photograph is counterfeit: there are certain discrepancies of perspective, of attitude, of positioning, that do not jibe with the rest of what is otherwise a fairly harmonious composition. He is turned slightly to his right, smiling as he talks to someone past the left-hand margin of the photograph (again, if we are to accept him in this context), hands thrust deep into the pockets of his tweed overcoat. He seems to be levitating above the debris at his feet. Behind his head, through the fence, the upraised arms of an unseen person are visible, the hands at the ends of them gripping the fence.

It's time to confront Richard and have it out with him. This will prove to be fruitless, of course. It's not that Richard lies. It's just that the pure information that flows into him finds its outlet only when tactically applied to a given situation, and then only in the form of equivocation, evasion, and allusion, the sum of which is enough to make you apologize for having bothered him in the first place. Later you realize that you are as empty as after having eaten McDonald's food. I don't in the least regret the loss of Bachmann. He would have been a bore; the kind of guy who uses words like *excellent* and *awesome* to describe the most pedestrian marijuana or blow job, who will tell you in great detail about the type of hero sandwich he likes to eat prior to inflicting internal injuries on homosexuals and blacks. What *is* interesting about Bachmann is that he and people like him are of the same class as Jay, Nat, and Dave. Same background, upbringing, and education. It's just that Bachmann and his ilk take their cue from the delinquents of Bay Ridge, while Jay, Nat, and Dave take theirs from the delinquents of the East End. It is likely that, in high school, both Bachmann and, say, Nat were interested in maintaining their memberships in Arista; in gaining entrance to the colleges of their choice. This, in a nutshell, is the "confrontation between representatives of two different worlds": Nat and Michael sitting around and swapping four-color brochures from Stanford and Brown. Hardly worth building a novel around, although it can be and has been done. Usually, though, the writer endeavors to lay a stretch of railroad track from one end of the book to the other, stipulating one side as "wrong" and the other as "right" and then condemning the hypocrisy of the distinction. Exit Bachmann, last seen in the vicinity of West 8th and MacDougal Streets.

My fear is that this tendency of Richard's toward disinformation will taint my book. I must lay out some ground rules, put my foot down with him. So here we are, then, in the dimly lit living room of a spacious Upper West Side apartment. A sort of casual metonymy will permit us to glean all of the necessary elements of character, so long as we understand that all of the following have been laid out for that specific purpose; in fact, we're lucky to be catching Richard in what might be called his environmental dishabille, but even so, he's moving, circling, impressing himself—what the hell. If he'd been expecting company, well, things would be looking a lot different. You know those houses where you come in, digitally remastered T-Bone Walker is blaring out of the stereo, a copy of the *Voice* lies on the couch beneath *The Collected Poems of Wallace Stevens* and *Conjunctions*. The schedule for the Cinema

Village hangs on the fridge, and below it are two postcards, placed side by side as if for comparative effect, one depicting the Honeymoon Suite at the South of the Border Motel in South Carolina and the other a dark, somber Rothko. A stack of unread copies of the *New York Times Magazine*. WNYC program schedule. A 1939 Remington Noiseless portable sits, gleaming and unused, next to the old Bakelite Western Electric rotary dial phone. You can just pile it on, you know what I mean, you feel faintly stupid in the presence of all this impedimenta, these Splinters of the Great Metropolis, the perfect balancing of kitsch and kulchur. Outside, the Puerto Rican superintendent picks his way gingerly through the broken Nieuw Amsterdam or Steinlager bottles, tossed out the window by the enlightened folks who were in attendance at a party here the night before. Dumb spick. Anyway, Richard is swiftly moving toward this, he's merely a series of exhibits. But we're going to catch him unawares: we glide past an elegant sideboard on which a note has been placed. Near to it on the burnished mahogany surface is fifty dollars, two twenties and a ten. A dogeared copy of the latest edition of *Jane's Fighting Ships* rests on the dining table adjacent to the sideboard, along with a book whose title is made up of those words whose charm lies in the imprecision of their coinage: *Geopolitical Infrastructure of Protoindustrial Empowerment* or *Protoindustrial Infrastructuralism and the Geopolitics of Empowerment*. Does it matter? The book's there, it's a wedge of brightly colored space bearing the same relationship to the external world as an Armani suit or a BMW. My father used to have a friend who dutifully carried a dogeared copy of *Finnegans Wake* onto the subway with him every day. Richard is seated in an easy chair, balancing on his lap a telephone and a copy of the *Physician's Desk Reference*, talking to an operator manning the twenty-four-hour Anheuser-Busch switchboard. He has to know whether or not bottled Budweiser is pasteurized since he has just ingested an MAO-inhibiting drug. Spotting us, he waves us further into the room and motions for us to sit down. I shall infer that our visit is taking place sometime near the date on which the events of the book as described in the first section take place, because twenty-four-hour consumer hotlines were not as common in those days as they are now, that being before the consumer was "empowered." A quart of beer that cost ninety cents then costs two dollars now, but that's just sour grapes. The point is that Richard would undoubtedly be loath to utilize any means that are common knowledge, given that the hoarding of uncommon, to all appearances exclusive, information is Richard's particular métier. That is my stern commentary on our determinedly ignorant civilization: that Richard, for his possession of data easily obtained through levels of research familiar even to Physical Education majors, should be deemed by his peers to be a formidable and oracular presence. Yet not all of this is bullshit and mirrors—Richard did, after all, get into the book. Perhaps that bodes well for its commercial potential: leave it to Richard to jump on the bandwagon before it departs. No doubt that at the moment that the book's success reaches its apogee, Richard will desert, releasing Bachmann from wherever he has kept him in captivity and vigorously denouncing the book as a commercial sham, or, more likely, treating it with the same sort of contempt that he lavishes upon last year's clothes. Is it possible that Richard scouted out my book on his own? Not likely—his powers have little to do with imagination or ingenuity. He obviously availed himself of some obscure secondary source. Let's take a closer look at that note on the sideboard, now that Richard's had to run out for canned beer pursuant to the teachings of Budweiser Central. At first glance I thought it was a note from his father, who has departed for the weekend, but a closer look reveals something else.

FICTION JOBS MONTHLY

April
*Complete Listings Each Month of Positions Available
in Current Works-in-Progress*

ADD TO THE CORPUS OF LITERATURE

Works in English

Ball, Ernie *Lather, Rinse, Repeat*
This collection of interrelated stories poignantly captures the joys and sorrows of everyday life at a Wyoming trailer park. If you like a relaxed environment and friendly, decent people, this is the job for you. Completed first draft. *Needed: Wilma, beauty shop proprietress (WF, 45-50); Don, park manager (WM, 60-65).* Available Immediately.

DiMarzio, Coyle *Summer Songs*
In this bittersweet coming-of-age novel, Tod, a teenager from Ossining, NY, comes to terms with the conflicting emotions wrought by his

summer job as an attendant at the local mental institution; first love, with Freyja, a newcomer from the city; and the receding joys of child-hood and "the gang." Roughly one-half complete. *Needed: Various inmates (M, ages vary). Polished interpersonal skills and a "hands-on" attitude are a MUST! Starts June.*

Dunlop, Jim *The Dennis Alternative*
Gourmet and CIA operative Dean Cooney follows a labyrinthine trail of international intrigue which leads him to James Dennis, a world-re-nowned child psychologist, and his sinister plot for world domination. Outline complete. *Open call for aggressive self-starters. Pharmacoepic experience a plus.*

Fender, Leo *Sick of Dying*
In the not-so-distant future, the evil Trigton Corporation mass-pro-duces genetically identical beings to cater to the needs of the upper classes. A miscalculation results in the "Flint" series, a race of immortal savants whose introduction ushers in a period of bloody strife. Waiver required. *Needed: "Jeremy Rivetts" Series, I-IV. Must stand under 5'7", have red hair, freckles, eyeglasses.*

Gibson, S.G. *The Wobbly Tumbril*
SACRE BLEU! If you can keep your head while the pressure's on, then this picaresque historical comedy, relating the adventures of Michel and his simple-minded brother, Nicolas, as they travel throughout post-revolutionary France during the Terror, is for you. Research fieldwork currently winding up. Biling., Fr/Eng. *Needed: Peasantry, Minor Aris-tocracy (Open Call). July Prod. Date.*
INCROYABLE!

Hofner, Viola *Cherchez la Femme, or, The Strange Attractor*
This anecdotal romp presents the mosaic of the downtown New York scene during the 1980s in all its glory and squalor, as seen through the dilated eyes of a jaded observer. First draft complete. Closed shop. Exlnt. benefits include very generous vacation pkg. *Needed: assorted white goddesses (w/**own** pedestals). Submit **professional quality** demo & photos.*

Ludwig, Skinner *The Toby*
What supernatural force links the fate of young professor William Montgomery and his family to that of a clan descended from slaves? The answer is to be found in this terrifying novel, set against the moody backdrop of New Orleans. **THIS COULD BE YOUR CHANCE TO "SHINE"!!** Second draft half complete. Competitive salary and full benefits pkg. including life, med., 3D, ℞ *Needed: John Hoppy, skeptical Departmental Chair (WM, 50); Dr. Henri Scateau, expert in the occult (WM, 65); Cleonetta LaForge, family matriarch (BF, 97); Boo Radley, mute handyman (WM, 32). Avail immed.*

Marshall, "Stack" *Cross Talk*
WHERE WERE YOU "THE DAY THE MUSIC DIED"? Denied their beloved music therapy by a cruel twist of fate, nine residents at a halfway house gather to offer their conflicting versions of the chain of events leading to their deprivation. Beginning with laughter and ending at the brink of an apocalyptic horror no society could bear to confront, *Cross Talk* packs a shattering wallop. No experience necessary. Lunch, carfare, and medication provided (as necessary). *Needed: Big Paul, insensitive orderly (WM, 27).*

Pearl, Tom *The Demanding Breast*
NEW FACES * NEW FACES * NEW FACES * NEW FACES
Actress by avocation, waitress by trade, and detective by accident, Libby Giblitz attempts to penetrate the mystery of the "Virgin Manuscript," which has disappeared during a transatlantic flight. Is it merely a clever fake, or is it a true and complete accounting of the relics of the Passion, the sister manuscript of *Eruct, Umbilicus*? Libby's spunky travels throughout downtown New York and the capitals of Europe will keep you on the edge of your seat. Perfect for upbeat, creative types. *Needed: Ben Nelson, Skip Valdez, Libby's former lovers (WM, 25). Starts May.*

Rickenbacker, Dolf *Too Broad For Leaping*
SICK OF COMMUTE / SMOG / TRAVEL. . . THE CITY? A set of unlikely circumstances sends Bronwyn Ragg, a savvy, urbane marketing executive, "back to the soil" in rural Vermont. Initially reluctant, she learns first to respect, and then to love, the rocky terrain. First draft complete. *Needed: Kate, wisecracking best friend (WF, 25-30); Ezra, crusty Yankee (WM, 75). Start at any time. Principals only—no developers.*

Roland, F. Xavier *First Made Mad*
A riveting, insider's account of life "behind closed doors" at a gigantic film studio. Jerry Spalding, a young screenwriter, weighs his sense of artistic commitment against his desire for success as his deeply felt project is turned by studio executives into a commercial sham. Outline form, being ghosted. HAVE YOU GOT "★" QUALITY? *Needed: Andrea Marciano, starry-eyed young hopeful (WF, 19).*

Shure, Mike *Up from Neva*
An intense, New York-born, Jewish intellectual travels to the USSR, with results that are both entertaining and enlightening. His experiences with everything from memalists to muzhiks, from perestroika to pierogi, both shatter his illusions and enlighten him. Ideal candidates will be athletic and skilled in the art of self-defense. Letter of intent signed.

The listings for my book and Ms. Hofner's are circled, and in the margins are some notes taken in that form of shorthand—f u cn rd ths—so absolutely representative of current thought. Strike all the vowels from this burdensome language; the eye will infer the presence of what the hand does not miss having written; productivity will increase and all will be well in the land. That is, until the day that the eye does *not* infer the soothing, rounded texture and sound of those vowels, never having seen them. This will lead, of course, to the sort of chaotic imprecision that most of us flee to the printed page to avoid. Imagine going to the deli and ordering a sandwich. You choice is to have it on "wht brd" or on "wht brd." You want it, of course, on wheat bread, not white, but in this case the code is indecipherable even within its context, compromising the interpretive foundation upon which the principle of f u cn rd ths rests. Either that or the manufacturers of ry brd will experience a staggering windfall. In a classified advertisement words are condensed for purposes of economy, and it's a fairly interesting task to take two or three English sentences and squash them; blast their nuclei, the vowels, out of the words in which they are embedded while still communicating the essence of the message. Not exactly an intimidating job, but an exercise of judgment and craft nonetheless—who hasn't placed a classified and then rushed to check it when published? Richard's turned the process on its head, though. He had to stop several times while making these notes to consider the truncated spelling of various words. Took him twice as long as it would have if he'd just written them out. All for the purpose of sustaining the illusion of Movement!, of Speed!

Richard's sleight-of-hand is centered on his carefully prepared appearance of what I can only describe as insouciant urgency. What I have hitherto done is to present a gallery of characters, the components of this band, Hi-Fi, whom we have observed and become familiar with, whose actions and motivations possibly even intrigue us. They are discrete elements of the oblivion that exists beyond this flat, sharp-edged world, and although they are affected to an extent by the events through which they move, their behavior is characteristic. With Jay, Nat, and Dave I worked out their schematics and then shoved them into the laboratory so that we could watch them perform with fidelity to their design. In Richard's case, we are left only with that series of exhibits. In other words, Richard cannot be written *of*, he can only be written. The hoarding of those little nuggets of information, the continued preoccupation with those facts and figures, gleaned from *Jane's* and other publications like it, with which he sought to dazzle the members of his junior high school class, has now achieved a sort of transcendental grace. What he "knows" is what he "is." There is something sinister about the man whose *shoes*, whose *eyeglasses*, tell you the whole story. I think of Dave, whom I had at first mistaken to be a kindred spirit of Richard's. What a rank amateur he is by comparison; capable only of conveying himself and his desires. One can look at Dave, or Jay, or Nat, and easily dismiss any one of them without hesitation or fear of subsequent regret. A very finite world, ever contracting, is what they seem to represent. The very act of forming Hi-Fi, of running it at a loss, defines their limitations. There are gigantic blocks of activity surrounding them with which they shall never acquaint themselves. But Richard's image leaves you tingling with desire and ambition. Remember, this is Richard's "aboutness," not "tall, endomorphic" Richard. Get up right now and run to the nearest copy of *Cosmopolitan* or *Vanity Fair*, examine an ad for a brand of booze or perfume or a line of designer clothing. What is beckoning to you? It ain't the Seagram's, is it? Not on your life, not since Midwood High. Of course, at times all of us signify one thing or another; or several things; or one thing at one time and another thing at another time; or mutually exclusive things simultaneously which contextually can be interpreted as a manifestation of irony—the various permutations, while not endless, are surely extensive. For most of us the painstakingly structured cocoon in which we wrap ourselves cracks and breaks under the stress of the most minimal contacts with the outside world. You're better off dead, really: nothing can disturb your myth once you are at rest;[9] your anecdotes and posed photographs take on the sturdiness of legend. This state of imperviousness is perhaps what Richard is attempting to achieve in life. I know one thing only about him: he moves through each moment as if he is caught in the bright illumination of the flashbulb. To be with him is to be with the unspoken promises of the advertisement. Somewhere within him is the hint of a better, brighter life, which will reveal itself if you'll just take his hand. This is all very terrifying to me since it is a trick which I have never mastered. I can never "hint" at anything because what is unwritten is simply the whiteness of the page and

[9]Albert Goldman may disagree with this.

is not to be inferred: f u cn rd ths is *not* If You Can Read This.

If I haven't already made it clear, Richard isn't simply a particularly facile adept of conspicuous consumption. The vulgarity to be found on Rodeo Drive is really only once removed from the old cartoon image of the heiress dragging her mink coat across the floor. It fills you with a sense of hunger, all right, but one that is misdirected. It is not a question of a wish for self-transformation, nor even a desire for a shifting of personal circumstances to wealth from relative poverty, but a queer feeling of shame in the face of others' ostentatiousness. Richard is a much more intelligent kind of catalyst. If Richard's "aboutness" on a given evening is "Beverly Hills" or "East Hampton," it is simultaneously "Avenue D" and "Secret After-Hours Club." There is a sense with him that your own mutability depends upon his relinquishment of one of those little nuggets. So much depends/upon/a black suit/jacket/ glazed with chalk/dust/beside the white/pool cue. "Gotta go, gotta meet some people," says Richard, after having banked the eight ball into the corner pocket, thrusting the warped cue back into the umbrella stand near the bar and slapping the dust off his jacket. "Down around Rivington Street," he says over his shoulder in response to your shouted question. Then he is gone, leaving you breathless. Block after block of crumbling tenements, but now somehow imbued with a dazzling aura of glamour. Actually, what Richard does is usually crushingly bland. I happen to know that tonight—the night of the canned Bud, MAO-inhibitor, and quick game of stripes-and-solids—Richard is going to a "tag party," where each invitee is handed a can of spray paint upon entry and encouraged to contribute a graffito to the walls. The occasion: the signing of a local band to a small but nationally distributed label. Although all present will be white, there will be a collective attempt to emulate, as closely as possible, what are perceived to be the behavioral characteristics of young urban blacks. Yo, Richie be def! This is really a monstrous, clunky bore, tinged with racism, but at the same time it is at the cutting edge of fashion. That you might arrive at either of these conclusions is the reason why Richard alludes to the party but leaves you alone to play another game on the coin-operated, three-quarter-size pool table.

So, the obvious question arises: What is Richard, King Signifier, doing with an outfit like Hi-Fi? A straight answer, as usual, is easily avoided. Even as we scoff at the philistine farmer, with his pickup truck and NRA membership, we eagerly consume the bounty of his land; even as we snicker at the man who hangs ugly paintings on his walls and keeps in his oak veneer particle board bookcase the monthly accretions of his membership in the World's Great Literature Club, we covet the high-tech stereo equipment whose manufacture he oversees in his capacity as plant manager. I see no reason why the phenomenon shouldn't work in reverse. Richard has his doubts, though. Hence, this contribution to Hi-Fi's set, a sinuous, articulate tendril undulating from the stage at Cheaters.

"Style Bite"
by Richard Poindexter

You know I've seen a lot of things
that I think you'll never see—
and I've been a lot of things
that I think you'll never be.

And, baby, let me say about this:
you should really have no doubt—
whenever a place has an inside
I'll be the one lookin' out.

And if you play, maybe I'll comp you;
get you in; say you're with me—
it doesn't matter who I know.

And just like A to B what follows
is a given; nothin's free—
just bear in mind the quid pro quo.

Talk to God on Sundays,
talk to me on Friday nights.
My speech has no inflection,
but every word I say is right.
Your company's requested
at a pre-determined site.
The host and me, we're really tight.

So if you want to see the place
that everyone and no one knows—
achieve a transcendental grace[10]
With which the territory goes

Play your cards right, I'll keep mine close
to my vest, I've got some plans.
I only hope that you know all
the steps when we begin to dance—

---

[10]the bastard!

> Talk to God on Sundays,
> talk to me on Friday nights.
> My speech has no inflection,
> but every word I say is right.
> Your company's requested
> at a pre-determined site.
> The host and me, we're really tight.

The song sounds remarkably like "Starry Eyes." I mentioned this coincidence to Richard and, coolly appraising my shirt, he told me that I didn't know what I was talking about. He was interested in the Manchester sound. The Manchester Sound. And, he hastened to add, he didn't mean Joy Division or the Buzzcocks. Then he was gone.

I have two picture postcards which I have placed side by side on the refrigerator for comparative effect. On one is a photograph of the Beatles, taken around 1963, depicting them clad in old fashioned two-piece bathing suits, standing in a row while lifting their straw boaters and stepping forward with their left feet with something less than chorus-line precision. On the other is a photograph of the New Kids on the Block, each of whom looks pensively and unhappily at the camera. I'll leave out any discussion as to the relative merits of the two groups. I will say that the Beatles shoulder the blame for having unleashed the famed British Invasion, making them responsible, in a sense, for some of the most terrifyingly rotten bands ever to occupy the Top Forty. I know that to some the British Invasion now represents the high-water mark of popular culture. The Beatles, the Stones, the Who, the Kinks, et al. But can we really lament the recent decline of popular culture when more than twenty-five years ago "I'm Telling You Now" by Freddie and the Dreamers hit the number one spot in the Top Ten? "A triumph of rock as cretinous swill," as Lester Bangs would have it. What is striking about these two pictures is the ineptitude of the hype machines that brought them into being. Here we have the Beatles, harbingers of the sixties, posed as if they were members of a music-hall troupe which conceivably could have entertained their grandparents. The New Kids photo is really quite generic, its curiosities more subtle. Those moody expressions are descended from sources at least as archaic as those underlying the Beatles' ridiculous pose, although it takes a moment's reflection to realize this. Fortunately for us all, a moment's reflection is an unnecessary

effort in these fulfilling times. But I can see an apprehensive publicity man, in a moment of insight not fueled by market surveys and
test results, grasping this and rushing to pull these photos from
distribution. But to replace them with what? Something "new"? I
doubt it. If one were to graph popular culture, one would find that it
runs an unwavering course throughout time, indicating no declines
or rises. That it might appear more sophisticated or intellectually
challenging at some points than at others is merely typical. Any
good con lets the mark think he's ahead. Popular culture is interesting in that it nearly always reveals the zeitgeist without in any true
way reflecting the society that sustains it. It is strange that Greil
Marcus has trouble coming to terms with this when Flaubert understood it implicitly decades before mass communications. I dis-
tinctly heard a "no fair" out there. Well, what can I say? Flaubert
walked the earth; he breathed air, farted, and probably pissed in the
sink now and then. I claim the right to compare any other human
being to him. Mr. Marcus would do well to reread him. All those
reams of paper devoted to understanding the Sex Pistols. Some
people got rich taking potshots at "Society," is all. John Lydon and
Malcolm McLaren understand. Hunter Thompson understands.
Oliver Stone understands. But what happens when you crawl right
up Society's asshole and then convey the stink of its dank innards?
You will be ignored, for one thing. You will be condemned, if
you're lucky. You will be pegged as a bourgeois. I'm laughing now
as I think of all the fool "artists" I know, living conspicuously grim
bohemian lives while aiming at the Big Time. People who think of
art as a vehicle for mass change and think that mass change will be
any more reasoned than anything else done en masse. Radical
reactionaries who renovate their lexicon to accommodate the sensi-
bilities of the AFDC recipient, the physically challenged, the
underserved community resident, the African American. You're
telling me a poor crippled black woman on welfare gives a shit
what you deign to *call* her? Right, she'll argue with you about it as
soon as she's done bundling up her newspapers and separating her
trash for the recyclers.

This brings us back to Hi-Fi, via the scenic route, as usual. Some of
you have doubtless commented on the fact that I have selected easy
targets myself, in the form of four boys barely out of high school.
But I insist that by omitting so much about them, presenting only
their essence while pointing them in the direction of the future,

we can, with geometrical logic, draw certain conclusions. That is, youthfulness is neither an excuse for nor the cause of their salient traits. A venal and stupid boy, like Dave, will mature to be a venal and stupid man. Simple as a turd. People like Richard do not really exist to begin with, they bend and twist, groaning like metal subjected to harsh and unbidden climatic change, but moving, always moving, so that even the traces of what they had been oscillate in the distance. Nat was a politician even at the height of his mania; now the tautology of motive underlying his life manifests itself as parcels of time and event separated from one another by the verbal screens he deftly throws up in order to dismiss them. Jay, well, Jay. He'll make money, or art. Hunger is the undoing of many a man. He may become a rock and roll star, which some will see as ultimate vindication, or he may disappear into some quiet suburb, which some will see as ultimate failure. He won't be fooling himself, however, which effectively disconnects him from his three associates, and from a lot of other people as well. This book is for him. These people are not "symbols," but they are representative—I know them; they live. As I have implied, they might as well be four freshman congressmen, or four young farmers, or four surgical residents. Rock and roll was an option, and something I once knew a little about, so I seized it. People shatter from the inside of thwarted dreams every day, and live there, fragmented within such casings, until they die. Otherwise, they simply die: the meaning of life. They're not really representative of popular culture, you say. Well, who knows. I wouldn't be surprised if, with proper management and promotion, they found themselves with a million or so paying customers, people who actually looked forward to their record releases and concert appearances. It is no accident that I have locked them in time at this juncture, the very day of Ronald Reagan's assumption of the presidency—I wonder what would occur if I were to hand them a note while they're onstage, tell them that they are all staring into the maw of an era which will make even their grandiose dreams appear modest. That by its end it will have left nothing uncorrupted, undiluted, unsold. That even the age which succeeds it will carry the sickness; that having tapped into the vast reservoir of middle-class guilt it will utilize that guilt in ways that appear cynical even in light of Reagan's eighties. It really was an odd time to come of age in the United States. It was as if the map of the nation had turned into the picture of Dorian Gray.

Bearing all this in mind, I return us to the photograph that opened this section. Turn back to it, if you like. It is human nature to attempt to evoke a sense of nostalgia when describing a photograph like this. Lost Sweetness. Surrendered Innocence. But none of its parts, examined discretely, will admit any nostalgia. It is indisputable that many of the things I held dear ten years ago when I focused that camera have since been blasted into oblivion, or altered beyond recognition; that the elevated railroad track on which the members of the band are posed has been razed; that the buildings behind their figures have been converted into luxury condominiums; that a chic restaurant has replaced the bodega where we bought coffee and cigarettes before scaling the chain link fence separating us from the forbidden tracks. And yet how willing we are to approach the things we love with ignorance; to forget that those warehouses and factories were once the site of unceasing exploitation, that every activity on those railroad tracks was once overseen by men of greed and corruption, that, after they had been unloaded from boxcars at sidings very near to where Hi-Fi stands, a once-common sight on the avenue below was that of thousands of lambs, preceded by a Judas goat, being led to their slaughter.

DUB 3
(Vocals)

The vocals, because they are the essence of the popular song and tend to define it melodically, should always be left until last; the frosting, as it were, on the musical layer cake. This rule applies doubly if the vocals employ harmonic or contrapuntal effects.

—Gifford, supra, at 154

We've been talking about Stochasm, Snowman, Stately Wayne Manor, and some other bands. What about Hi-Fi? When was the first time that you saw them?

It must've been right after Mona and I opened the club, or I should say Mona opened the club and I did whatever she allowed I was capable of doing, which meant mostly tending bar. Not that I minded so much, you know, let her handle all the bullshit with the contractors, I don't read mechanics magazines or any of that, you'd see her with the blueprints—blueprints, right, for a stage made out of two-by-fours, no wonder I lost my appetite when the bill finally came—but anyway, yeah, I like to wake up fresh and rested in the mornings so it was her baby and welcome to it. So Mona puts this ad in the *Voice*, "musicians wanted," and the response was zip, which kind of relieved me, really, I thought maybe I could talk Mona out of her idea of becoming a big time nightclub queen, we used to sleep over the place and I'm pretty easily awakened by noise, for one thing, and Mona had made me hang on to my day job at the library so I wasn't getting a whole lot of sleep as it was. Should've just stayed there, at the library, nice and quiet and a check every two weeks, instead I'm standing behind the bar, reading in the *Post* about how some guy two blocks away on Eighth got his head blown off for being a little too slow to suit a stickup man, the door constantly opening and closing, you know, you could never keep your hands and feet warm enough there. Yeah, my daily life was just *full* of things that kept me interested, fuckin place, pardon my french, was so slow that most of the time I had to invent work for myself, you know, polish the bar, empty the ashtrays, keep the bowls full of pretzels, all the boring bartender bullshit, and I'm thinking, "I'm as capable as I ever was—why is there a lump in my throat all the time?" But you couldn't bring anything like that up with Mona, she'd tell me I was thwarting her dreams. Her word, thwarting, not mine, thwarting her dreams if I asked if I could maybe take a night off, if I asked if maybe we could close at 2:30 instead of 4:00 A.M. after a night with maybe six customers spread out. Anyway, the ad, she puts this ad in and after about four weeks of running it she gets a call. Who did she get a call from? you ask, well me too, it's the sweet mystery of life, there she is with her Mona Lisa smile and her pad face down against her chest, I thought maybe Buddy Holly came back from the dead to play at Cheaters! You can see the tension I was under at that point, I used to have constipation, but I had the runs every damn day at that point. I used to actually think about murdering her, can you believe it, murdering her for what she'd done to our nice quiet life—it was like a joke, you know, let's own our own business, great, let's have live music to entertain the lushes, terrific, let's turn this place into a real nightclub, fantastic, and then it's the big pain in the ass. I am *not* the kind of guy walks around bitching about the raw deal he gets from life, but even my friends, the two or three Mona approved of, they were running from me like the plague, and I'm thinking to myself, "My father was a good man, he worked his whole life in the fuckin slaughterhouse just so his son could get a job in a library, not have to worry about a goddamn cow falling on him, and this fuckin bitch wants me to be George Raft with the spats and the cigarette cases and the table lighters and on West 40th Street, yet." I learned lessons from life, I knew who to get next to and how to get by, but this was unreal, you know what I mean? And even as she's turning me into part of her little fantasy, I'm still not good enough. I'd try to come over to her in the bed and she's like, "My sex life is perfectly satisfactory." At times I very much wanted to leave home, I'd start laughing or crying for no reason, and then I'd just throw up. "No one understands me, Don— I've always had talent, I've always had dreams, now you're not going to thwart my dreams, are you?" Sure, sure, I have dreams myself—I always wanted to be Frank Sinatra, personally, but I keep my mouth shut of course.

What happened the night that Hi-Fi performed at Cheaters?
They were really a bunch of brats. I don't begrudge anybody anything, but I'll tell you, I wish anybody had gotten famous over them. They come in, they're pissing and moaning right off the bat, "Whaddaya mean there's no PA?" "Whaddaya mean we can't bring food in here?" "Whaddaya mean we only get sixteen bucks?" And the one not in the band anymore? With the funny name? Fuckin guy was *possessed*, I swear he was, he kicked over all the drums, he goes out and smashes his little tart of a girlfriend right

in the chops, and then, after we let him back in for God knows what reason, I catch him snorting coke in the *ladies'* room! I got acid stomach anyway, do I need this? I'm like, "You think this is fuckin CBGBs? You think you're at one of your punk rock faggot friends' houses?" He was out on his ear after that, just for the principle of the thing. I *hated* it when those punk bands played, I'd stand there not believing my eyes, those poor little rich kids up there in leather that'd keep me eating for three months, screaming to that moron noise, you think *I* don't feel like swearing at the top of my lungs sometimes? Those rock groups were like having a nightmare every night. I'm standing behind the bar, trying my best to concentrate on the stupid job, Mona's walking around in some getup that'd embarrass one of the whores on the corner, getting drunker and drunker. I've had some strange experiences, I been around, I'm trying to hold onto my temper while getting put down by a bunch of snot-nose kids who are so goddamn stupid that they're ordering gin and tonics in the dead of winter. What kind of guy am I? I have a cough all the time, but never worry about my health, you get me? I don't dwell on the fact that I'd be much more successful today if people hadn't had it in for me. I'm not a pervert and the only time I ever stole was from the greengrocer when I was a kid. So why is it that I feel like smashing things all the time? Why is it that I'm never able to just sit and daydream? Like you're supposed to after a life of hard work? Not that I'm the kind of guy who takes days and weeks and months to get things going. My family loves what I have chosen to do with my life, always supported me, so I have a positive outlook. My sleep is fitful and disturbed as it is without me trying to figure out life. Don't you understand that my head hurts all over?

Are you telling the truth?
     I don't always tell the truth, but my judgment is better than it ever was.

Did anything significant happen after Hi-Fi began to play?
     Mona began to dance, really crazily, I mean, she came out of the office, kind of weaving around, drunk as hell, and I thought she was just going to sit down at the bar and have herself another drink, but she walks out to the middle of the floor and just starts throwing herself around, I thought to myself, "She's having a fit, this is it, I'm free!" But then she quit, she's dripping sweat, she comes over,

"Don, my whole body is hot, why is my whole body hot?" What do you say to that? I poured her a beer. She started to do that often, I really think she went nuts around then. First the dancing—after a while she didn't need music anymore—and then the comment about her hot body. Then she started complaining that she was hearing things, oh boy, did she flip! She'd also say these things, like, "I am above the law," and "There are foreign objects in the Pepsi," and then she'd accuse me of writing letters about her to Page Six in the *Post*. I'm in pretty good physical health, so what if my soul leaves my body now and then? Those were the nows and thens. After the performance, quote unquote, was over, I remember I decided to refuse to speak, for some reason. I wiped the bar, checked the bottles, but wouldn't talk to anyone. The little brats filed out, the place was real quiet—nobody was talking. Mona came out, she put her head down on the bar, she was crying, and I put my hand on her hair, told her I'd make everything all right for her. She bit me. I'm thinking, "I'm well-liked—I'm *very* well-liked by the people who know me. I take my angina pills and don't bother people. So what if I dismembered small animals at school? I had to, it was biology. My father, in the slaughterhouse, wanted me to bring home a Regents diploma. I am a good bartender and don't dwell on the book of Revelations, which I see coming true around me every place I look. I take shit from morons, I read Evan and Novaks, yet my life must be bad if my wife bites me and all of my body tingles and burns." The creeps in the band came up, I paid them off, and Mona stumbled back to the stage, right in front of everybody, gets up there and starts moaning like some kind of animal. What can you do?

Where Are They Now?

Hi-Fi, with its new drummer, Michael Bachmann, is world famous. Richard Poindexter studies accountancy at San Jose State University. I am an inventory control supervisor with the text-book adoptions division of a major publisher. Mona died after neglecting to treat what was posthumously diagnosed as alcoholic hepatitis. Paul Marzio lives in Williamsburg, Brooklyn, where he is at work on a novel. Maureen Ferret has become a prostitute and works in the vicinity of Laguna and Fell streets in San Francisco. Miles Miller is salad chef at a fashionable New York bistro, the Nova EboraCafe. Jed disappeared in 1983 after leaving his Chelsea apartment to buy a roll of film. Girl Bovary has a one-half ownership interest in a Phoenix, Arizona, boutique. Mimi Miller lives with her brother Miles and is presently unemployed. Susan Dennis committed suicide on Christmas Day, 1985. Sean Dennis was institutionalized for seven years and now lives with his father in Greenwich Village, spending his days tending to his bulletin board. Cheaters was destroyed in a fire of suspicious origin in January 1982. I can't hold any of this shit in.

We've been talking about the Tumblers, the Contradictions, the Meaningless Intensifiers, and some other bands. What about Hi-Fi? When was the first time that you saw them?

I'm sorry, I knew that you wanted to talk about them. I have this bad habit of keeping on a subject until others lose patience with me—I hope you haven't. The first I ever heard of Hi-Fi was when Jay Lustig called me in response to an ad I'd placed in the paper, the *Voice*, I think. You see, Don and I had just purchased the bar and it wasn't doing very well—it had been one of those chains, you know, a Blarney Stone or something, and I really didn't want *that* kind of clientele. We fixed it up and raised the prices, and that took care of that, but it didn't bring us a new clientele to replace the old. So I hit upon the idea of turning the place into a rock club. Obviously it's turned out to be a good idea. I needed to do something, Don was slipping into mental illness at that point and, not understanding the severity of his problem, I thought that this project would be therapeutic—I'm a sucker for men like him, unfortunately. I loved my father very much and he was a hopeless drunk. They're all father-substitutes—a common enough syndrome, I suppose. Anyway, by this time Don was referring to himself as "The Librarian" and taking care of his "archives," as he put it, which were really just this vast network of cork bulletin boards on which he hung everything—and I mean *everything*. He hadn't yet started complaining about his phantoms—he started to see people and animals that simply weren't there, that's when I realized that I had to have him committed. But even so, I was already sufficiently dissatisfied with our lives together, wishing constantly that we could be as happy as others seemed to be. I desperately wanted some kind of life in that club, some outside element. So Jay called and we talked for a while—not just about the gig, which we took care of right away, but about this and that. He was charming, he was ambitious, he was witty—everything that poor, sick Don wasn't. I remember that while I was talking to him

I felt as if it were a scene in a romantic movie—you know, a turning point for the beleaguered heroine. So I guess I fell a little in love with him—with all of them. God, they were such fresh, such funny kids. I was always surprised that they never hit it really big—but I guess it was just a matter of timing. Jay, of course; dopey Dave, who could sometimes be a pain in the neck; Nat, sober, serious, Nat; and Poindexter, who I used to call Professor Corey—he had an answer for everything. I remember the first thing that Jay asked me in person was whether I was a lesbian. In retrospect, it was really a rude, intrusive question—but I managed to answer, as calmly as possible, that no, I'd never been particularly attracted by members of my own sex. Then he asked me if I liked to play drop-the-handkerchief, which struck them all as tremendously funny for some reason, and I got over my shock and started laughing with them. I've never been one to exaggerate my misfortunes, but I just opened up to those kids, and the terrible feeling I'd been having in the pit of my stomach just disappeared, like that. I was able to look in the mirror, all smiles, and say, "I'm an important and valuable person!" It sounds silly, I know. I guess I'd been right, in one sense, about the therapeutic value of converting the bar into a club. For the first time in years I was happy to be a woman—I stopped feeling angry, stopped feeling blue, stopped losing myself in romance novels. I even remember the one I was in the middle of and then threw away—*Too Broad for Leaping*, it was called. They started coming around a lot after that. Nat would read me poetry that he'd written—beautiful stuff. Jay confessed to me that his feelings were easily hurt. Dave and I walked through the children's zoo and teased the animals there together. Richard confided that his secret wish was to become a forest ranger. Meanwhile, Don and I had started fighting, bitterly. I am fairly easy to beat in an argument—but I couldn't give in on the day that I went upstairs to find that he'd mutilated the publicity photos that the band had given me! He'd sliced them into pieces and then put them on the bulletin board, mixing them up with other pictures, of deformed people and lambs and farm equipment—and then he came in and started yelling at me that any man who is able and willing to work has a good chance of succeeding. His face was twisted with rage! I found it hard not to give up hope, but I just couldn't give in. I asked him point-blank what it was about the personal articles of others that so strongly attracted him that he felt compelled to handle or steal them. He told me that he had plenty of self-confidence and that he wanted to sell the bar and become a discount florist. It was at moments like this that I thought life simply wasn't worthwhile.

What happened the night that Hi-Fi performed at Cheaters?
Which one? They had a residency. I suppose you're talking about the "Inauguration Bash"—that's the one everybody remembers, the one that everybody's interested in. I remember trying that day to call them, let them know that the PA had been broken by some trashy band the night before, some really pretentious band called the Strange Attractors. I couldn't get in touch with Jay, Dave never heard his phone because he liked to play his records with the headphones on, Richard was out, someplace, and Nat simply wouldn't answer the phone, ever. So they showed up, and they got angry when I told them the bad news. It was the first time that there had ever been a rift between us—I felt like I was melting. I'd bought a beautiful new dress, just for them. But again, I couldn't give up. I argued and argued to get them to see the truth. Jay stood there, nodding, I don't think I ever loved him more, while Nat and Dave set a few small fires in the back. Richard was busy with his drums. Don leaped out from behind the bar, embraced Jay, and told him never to put off until tomorrow what he ought to do today. He added that he didn't mind being made fun of and suggested that he and Jay ought to open a nursery together. The man always lied if he thought he could profit from it. I couldn't stand it any more, so I went into the office and began to cry. A little later I heard Jay calling Paul Marzio from the pay phone in the alcove. Then he and Nat left. It was quiet then until Maureen Ferret, Nat's girl, called to say that she'd be late and to please tell Nat—she was going to church with her grandmother. I never liked Maureen, and my resentment of her was probably exacerbated by this comment—I hadn't even spoken to, let alone worshiped with, any member of my family since I'd married Don. I got an urge to do something harmful, something shocking. I decided to tell Nat that Maureen was with Miles Miller, allowing him to photograph her in the nude. That led to trouble later.

You're talking about Nat getting thrown out?
Nat was never thrown out—he was like a little brother to me, I wouldn't do such a thing. Paul Marzio was thrown out. I should backtrack a little and explain that Paul had been the original bassist

for Hi-Fi, but he decided to quit—bigger and better things, you know the old story. He joined some other band, they were really bad, the Brave Lobsters. Paul was usually OK, very sweet, a little shy, but he fell in with this evil psychopath named Mike Shure, called himself Mike Tumor, he claimed he was Jesus Christ reborn, or something. Anyway, Tumor and these other two members of Paul's band, Michael Bachmann and Jeremy Rivetts, showed up at the club a little before the set began and Paul went with the three of them to the ladies' room to do some cocaine. I'm no prude, I understand that such things will occur at parties or other affairs where there is lots of loud fun, but Maureen had gone out and somehow hit her head against a dumpster—that's probably where you got the idea that it was Nat who was thrown out because Jed, at the door, thought that Nat had somehow inflicted this injury on her. I explained that Nat believed that women should have as much sexual freedom as men, and even Don said "One's hardest battles are with one's self!" Anyway, we had to get her cleaned up, she was bleeding, and Paul and these three creeps were in the bathroom. I couldn't ask Don to take care of it, for reasons that should be pretty clear by now, so I knocked on the bathroom door and called out as cheerfully as possible, "You boys are presenting me with a problem that is so full of possibilities that I can't make my mind up about it!" I was trying to make light of it. I heard Tumor make some sort of remark about the fat lady singing, thanks a lot, and my muscles began to twitch and jump. Nat was next to me, he had his arms around Maureen, who was crying, and he said, "I don't care about what happens to me"—and he hit the door with his shoulder, broke it in. Tumor and the others scattered, and Nat went right for Marzio, "I'm not feeling well and I'm angry!" Marzio lost it, started crying, begging for forgiveness, and suddenly I felt as if I'd done something wrong or evil, an unusual feeling for me— I'm usually pretty happy. Maureen started complaining that her head and nose were swelling, expanding, that I should take care of her right away; she was so insistent that I felt like doing the exact opposite of what she requested, so I took her into the office and sat her down, left her there, she was screaming, "Why is everybody trying to destroy me!" It was the first time I'd ever really done anything dangerous just for the thrill of it, she was turning purple from crying or from the bruises or something, and I just shut the door on her. Nat was alone in the bathroom, he was just standing there, swallowing convulsively. Everyone just seemed to lose control, to go a little mad, at that point. Jay and Miles Miller seemed to take over then; Miles had his camera out, started taking pictures of the bathroom, the door broken off its hinges, the blood on the floor. Don was screaming at them to stand up for what they thought was right, Jay was directing Miles, who was telling me that he was interested in becoming a police photographer, and the regular popping of the flashbulb and Jay's calm, authoritative voice offset Maureen's ranting from the office— something about her head being restrained, something about wanting to get to Heaven and get it over with. It was like a race or a game—Miles was clicking his shutter as fast as he could, Jay had him by the shoulders and was spinning him around, Nat had begun to clean up the bathroom by himself. I didn't know the rules, but it all seemed to make sense, in a way.

Are you telling the truth?
Most people are honest chiefly through fear of getting caught.

Did anything significant happen after Hi-Fi began to play?
Not that I can think of, no. I seem to remember Jay up onstage making some kind of joke about how they'd all been sent to the principal's office—but I wasn't feeling too well by then, my speech was slurred and my voice was hoarse, so I went up to Don and told him that I was hot, please give me a Pepsi. My hands were shaking and I spilled some of the beverage when I lifted the glass to take a drink—Don had insisted on buying these tall, skinny glasses, liquid spilled from them quite easily—and he complained that I ate and drank like a pig. I ignored that, tried to enjoy the show, but then Maureen started up again—I'd all but forgotten about her. "I am a smart and capable person! I take classes at Hunter! Why are you plotting against me? Stop following me!" Miles came up and said he'd take her out, buy her an orange drink or something. In response to my questioning look, he told me that he'd never take unfair advantage of Maureen's situation. It was kind of a bad scene—after the audience had left I took Jay aside and told him that they'd made over two hundred dollars but that I'd have to deduct almost the entire amount to take care of the broken door and the cracked mirror in the bathroom. He said that he understood, but I could tell he was angry, and he threw the money at Nat—said since it was all his fault, he could keep it. Nat stood up without a word, started to go outside, and then I remembered

to tell him that Maureen had gone off with Miles. That was the trouble I mentioned earlier—he was now convinced that the two of them were having an affair, thanks to me. He went out and I saw him throwing up in the gutter.

Where Are They Now?

Jay Lustig is a stockbroker with a discount brokerage house on Wall Street. Dave McCall studies ritual self-mutilation in the United States, and has contracted with a publisher to bring out a book on the subject. Nat Phenomenon is a senior associate with the Los Angeles office of a law firm specializing in insurance defense. Richard Poindexter graduated from a certificate program at the Albert Merrill School and insists that he will soon be attending Oxford University. Hi-Fi broke up in June 1983, after releasing an album through the small but nationally distributed label with which it had signed. Don McOral committed suicide on Christmas Day, 1985. I own several successful nightclubs and discotheques in New York City. Paul Marzio has been in a coma since slipping and hitting his head in a motel shower in Urbana, Illinois. Maureen Ferret lives in San Diego, where she is at work on a novel. Miles Miller is a commercial photographer, portraits a specialty, and has just moved into a two-bedroom condominium at 1049 Park Avenue. Jed is now a media consultant to Mayor Dinkins. Girl Bovary resides with her mother on St. Marks Place and reputedly "takes classes." Mimi Miller is an internationally known film actress, who most recently appeared in the hit action comedy, *The Virgin Manuscript*. Susan Dennis is founder of a radical feminist group, the OA&F. Sean Dennis obtained a graduate degree in psychology and is now a licensed therapist. Cheaters outgrew its original location and is currently situated on West 26th Street. I love these kinds of dramatics.

We've been talking about Paste-Up, the Tobys, the Mice, and some other bands. What about Hi-Fi? When was the first time that you saw them?

It's funny you should ask that, because the day I met them was the day most of my troubles began, terrible troubles, and I know where to assign responsibility. It must have been in 1979, when I was still going out with Dave. I hadn't really met any of his friends yet, I don't remember which of us had made the unspoken decision not to become involved with the other's "scene," as they say. I remember we used to laugh about how our relationship was almost as if representatives of two different worlds had gotten together. Anyway, one day Dave told me that he'd met this guy named Paul Marzio. Dave responded to an ad Paul had placed, in the *Voice*, I think, and dropped by his house with his guitar, a Fender Telecaster, not that that's important or impressive, and they sat around and jammed. Paul asked him if he'd like to join a band he was forming with another friend of his, Jay Lustig. Dave really wasn't very good at that point, and he thought that playing with other people might help him to improve. So he joined, it was Dave, Jay, Paul, and Mike Bachmann, although Paul was using a stage name, Nat Phenomenon, pretty silly, right?, but we were all still teenagers, thought we were getting past the parochialism of our good burgher parents and nursing at a fresh new breast downtown, on St. Marks. Lots of luck. My parents used to go away quite often to Europe, not that that's important or impressive, and we were living at the time in a very spacious apartment on the Upper West Side, so one day when they were away Dave called to ask me if perhaps they could all drop by, watch cable. We were the first people I knew with cable, not that that's important or impressive, but still, people *were* impressed. So I said sure, and over they came. Jay made the strongest impression on me, at first—he was obviously the leader. Dave was, of course, a known quantity. Michael was a little nervous and hyperactive, but he had a certain charm and we got along fine. But it was Paul I fell for, really, I'm damned if I know why, the sick fuck just swept me off my feet and it was *because* of his sickness. He and I stood in the kitchen talking for hours, he told me how he couldn't stand the sight of blood, yet would often examine his phlegm for traces of it, how he was sometimes beset by inexplicable depressions, how he was terrified of communicable diseases. I remember thinking, "This is it, my life has begun at last, I'm never going to enter another science fair with some lame project having to do with monitoring the growth of common houseplants; pretty soon I'll probably be indulging in unusual sex practices!" My thoughts were racing so fast I was glad I didn't have to articulate them! My homelife was pleasant and satisfactory, I'd been receiving college brochures from Stanford and Brown, but I knew that within a couple of weeks I'd be sneaking into movie theaters, that everything would be out in the open and I'd never have to try to decipher people's hidden motivations again! Lots of luck. Anyway, the rest of them were in the living room when we rejoined them, concealing small items in the folds of their clothing and making fun of my parents' stereo. Criticism hurts me terribly and earlier we'd been talking about names for the band, at that point they had a rather pretentious one, the Id or something, so I just lashed out and told them that they ought to name their stupid band after my parents' stupid stereo.

"Hi-Fi"?

Well, yes, that's what I meant, although it was actually quite a good stereo, a Pioneer, I believe, not that that's important or impressive, it was just old-fashioned, and so it said "Hi-Fi" right on the front, they bought a new one soon afterwards. I'd been hoping that this would hurt them, somehow. Their poking fun at the stereo was a personal insult to me, so I wanted to injure them back. But they *loved* it, they thought it was the best thing since sliced bread, so I cheered up and offered to cook them a nice big meal. I set the table in the dining room, joyfully told them to come and get it! and Jay asked me if my conduct was controlled by the customs of those around me. I guess I answered yes, because he knocked all the plates and glasses and silverware off the table, the glasses and plates were shattered on the tile floor, then demanded paper plates and stormed off with them. I heard drunken laughter from the living room, I certainly felt useless. When I was a little girl I always gravitated toward milieus that tried to stick together through thick and thin, lots of luck, and here were these louts straddling my parents' Chippendales, not that that's important or impressive, arms folded across the seatbacks, screaming out "I Didn't Raise My Boy to Be a Soldier." *Apocalypse Now* was on HBO. Michael got up and leaned out the window which overlooked Broadway, trying to pick fistfights with "faggots," as he put it. Paul calmed me down a bit, told me that he was never happy unless he was roaming or wandering. Jay pointed out to him that he was afraid of driving, flying, or traveling by rail. It was frightening and exhilarating to be with them like that. I've often lost out on things because I couldn't make my mind up, so I decided then and there that I wanted to be part of their world, even though Dave had carved his initials in an antique mahogany sideboard my parents owned, not that that's important or impressive.

What happened the night that Hi-Fi performed at Cheaters?
We're certainly jumping ahead quite a bit—I really hate it when

someone cuts me off like that. I thought it was important to give you some background, I used to keep a detailed diary of this sort of thing, leather bound with kid ecru finish leaves, not that that's important or impressive. Anyway, Paul and I had been going out for about a year then, but it was a losing battle. He'd really begun to flip out, whenever something bothered him he'd begin to sing "The Game of Life" at the top of his lungs, wherever we were, insisting that I take up the backing vocals and scolding me when I sang off-key. I'd prepare a nice meal, string beans and roasted peanuts and Parmesan cheese, or spaghetti squash with dried Chinese mushrooms and white clam sauce, and he'd accuse me of putting ground glass in it. He'd awaken me when he couldn't sleep, which was often, to tell me of the thoughts and ideas which disturbed him. He'd take out my diary—that's why I finally stopped keeping it—put on a white housecoat of my mother's, Chanel, not that that's important or impressive, and tell me he was going to "read my chart." He started taking books out of the library on fits, seizures, and convulsions. I can go on and on but what I remember most clearly is the amount of weight I lost, the way that I couldn't really piece together a lot of what I'd been doing, it was like living a nightmare, although it was nice to be able to fit into the size five outfit I'd picked up, at Charivari, not that that's important or impressive. I'd cry, wondering what I'd done to deserve such punishment. Just when I'd hit bottom, I met Miles Miller. His sister Mimi and I were best friends, we were in high school together, and by sheer coincidence it turned out that Miles had gone to school with Jay, knew Hi-Fi, and so we had a lot in common, really hit it off. I'd already started playing around a little behind Paul's back—it's such ancient history now I'm not ashamed to admit it— but with Miles I could tell it was the real thing. Lots of luck. So we started to have an affair, he was tender and sweet, everything Paul wasn't. Making love to Paul was like making love to a machine, I swear. Anyway, we consummated the affair on Election Day, I remember that vividly, because Paul and I had a remarkable phone conversation in which he kept insisting that reading comprehension scores were going to decline as a direct result of Reagan's presidency, obsessed with it, I heard all these papers rustling in the background while he was talking to me, all these latinate demographer's expressions like "per capita" and "median" and that damned rustling paper, he was foaming at the mouth, really. I called Miles up and he came right over, I think I asked him to help me out with a camera I'd just bought, a Nikon, not that that's important or impressive, although the decision to purchase it was actually the most important one I'd ever made, but we both knew what was going to happen. I had never felt better than I did afterwards. Filled with all the self-righteous justification of fresh, new love. Lots of luck. So by the time that the gig at Cheaters rolled around, not only had Paul gone completely around the bend but Miles and I were pretty heavily involved, and apparently we'd gotten a little indiscreet because someone spotted us together that day at a four-star restaurant in the Village, Hoodwinks, not that that's important or impressive, and ran straight down to Prince Street to tell Paul. Paul called dozens of times at my house, Miles's house, left these crazy messages like, "The top of my head is tender, stop with the voodoo!" and "You think you're clever, you think you've put something over on me!" Whatever he was thinking, he just had to call and express it. The funny thing was that Paul had been suspicious even when I was still faithful to him; it had become an ordeal to come down to the gigs because he'd started writing these horrible songs about me, "Now I'm Laughing at You, Girl" and "Shoe's on the Other Foot, Girl." I'd stand there, a phony smile pasted on, while he stared at me with this incredible look of loathing and contempt on his face, singing these lyrics about some terrible slut who had absolutely *nothing* to do with me. The others, of course, picked up on it, started writing graffiti about me in every men's room on the Lower East Side. I'd get exhausted, my head hurt all the time, I had to get out of it somehow. Miles and I decided to tell Paul that night that we were in love and that we didn't want to carry on behind his back any longer. I'd bought dozens of self-help books, you know, *How to Get Out of a Losing Relationship,* that sort of thing, read them all, as if studying those words, all that advice, and all those contrived scenarios set down in the quiet of a book would actually help me deal with real life. Lots of luck. We arrived late, around ten or so, Paul was all over me right away, he dragged me into the back, started *sniffing* me all over, really scary, "You think you're such hot shit because you know hot shit people like Miles, huh?" I ran out, I wanted to be in sight of the others. Jay and Dave were at a table, and I sat down with them. Paul followed me out, stood on the stage and started waving a copy of *New York Rocker* at me, "I know what you wrote about me in here! *Well, I'm up on top, looking down at YOU!*" Jay asked him what he was talking about, and he just went on, about how he and his mother and father were being followed and photographed by secret intelligence agents, that he had nothing to hide, his mind worked as well as it ever had, he could handle money and alcohol, other people's opinions of him didn't bother him. Michael had been chatting with Miles at the bar, and I guess this pissed Paul off, because he took his bass and swung it like a baseball bat at Michael's drums. I was so embarrassed, I hate it when people pull stunts like that even if they're not motivated by blind rage, this beautiful drum kit, a Tama five-piece, not that that's important or impressive, just flying to pieces, and Michael very calmly grabbed Paul by his collar and waistband, just like in a cartoon, and tossed him out onto the street. Michael just wanted him out of his sight for a while, I guess—we all did really. But then he disappeared; it was well past the time that the band was supposed to do the sound check; the place had already begun to fill up with the ten or fifteen people who had come down to see them. Michael and Jay went out to look for him because they were getting concerned about appearing on schedule, and the people who owned the club were giving them a very hard time about it. Miles and I were sitting at a table up front, trying to act nonchalant, you know, chatting with people who came over to say hello, this horrible night getting mixed up in these moronic conversations, "No, Paul never has stage fright, yes, I like Hunter very much," bla bla bla. Michael rushed inside and told me to come right away, I got up to go out and Miles was right behind me. Paul had broken his hands on the windshield of a parked car, a Jaguar XJ6, not that that's important or impressive. His knuckles were bleeding and his fingers were all splayed as if they were deformed, and he had this twisted grimace on his face, either he was smiling or wincing from the pain. Jay and Michael said that they had better go back in, cancel the gig, and I told Miles that he better go on inside with them. I took over. Paul was in a pathetic state and I had done it to him; I suppose that was the rationale I had at the time. In the back of my mind I suppose I also knew that he couldn't really hit me with those hands. The only "reason" I could imagine Paul having would have been some sort of desire to free himself from something, his anger or his pain from being so ill or even something as ridiculously simple as his obligation to play in the band. It's hard to remember, I really wasn't being terribly analytical at that point, standing there in subzero cold with a man blabbering about fainting spells and dizziness and reptiles and the saintly goodness of his mother.

Are you telling the truth?

My memory seems to be all right.

Did anything significant happen after Hi-Fi began to play?

Just the fact that they played was pretty significant, I think. Some guy who nobody knew, but who knew how to play all Hi-Fi's songs, volunteered to fill in for Paul. It turned out to be Richard Poindexter and the rest, as they say, is history. I was introduced to him before they went onstage—Jay said something about needing to get my approval because of all the good help I'd given them, Dave and Michael began to laugh hysterically at that but it didn't matter at that point. I had Paul sit on the curb in an illegal parking zone, told him not to move, he expressed a certain amount of concern over his future sexual potency, but said it would be fine if I went and chatted with my new friend. He made it clear he was referring to Ronald Reagan, but I elected to ignore his implicit accusation. It's usually pretty hard for me to make small talk when I meet someone new, but with Richard it just *flowed*! I knew that I'd never be bored with a man like him, that there'd always be something exciting to keep me interested. I thought I was losing my mind, but I was falling in love again! I reluctantly excused myself, they were going on and I had to get back to Paul. When I came outside, Paul was being rolled by two ragged men who'd obviously come over from the Port Authority. I am against giving money to beggars under any circumstances—they spend it on alcohol and drugs and it encourages them to continue their cycle of self-destructive behavior—so I ran up loudly clapping my hands and stamping my feet. I helped Paul back inside, took him into the ladies' room and tried to get him cleaned up. He said that he heard voices assuring him that he'd be able to feel a sense of pride in himself again, didn't I? but I said that I didn't, adding that my hearing was as good as other people's. His hands had begun to shake and I was relieved when he told me that they were feeling clumsy and awkward; at least he was now tenuously connected to reality.

What happened after the performance was over?

We weren't there for that, I took Paul over to the emergency room at Roosevelt Hospital while the band was still playing. I remember stopping to buy some paperback at a newsstand, a sci-fi thriller, *Sick of Dying*. I can read for a very long time before my eyes get tired.

Where Are They Now?

Hi-Fi, with its new bassist, Richard Poindexter, is world famous. Don McOral moved to Wyoming, where he manages a trailer park. Mona Barron is a diet counselor for Jenny Craig Weight Loss Centers, Inc. Paul Marzio disappeared on August 29, 1982. I am an Account Coordinator for Dun & Bradstreet and frequently pretend to be an artist of some kind. Miles Miller sells hand-painted T-shirts on Astor Place. Jed completed a course of study at the Institute for Audio Research and now engineers and mixes sixteen-track recordings at his own studio near Grand Army Plaza in Brooklyn. Girl Bovary works as an Animal Health Technician at the Peninsula Humane Society in San Mateo, California. Mimi Miller's nude, partially decomposed body was found beside a hiking trail near Aspen, Colorado. Susan Dennis work as an operator/counselor at a twenty-four-hour suicide prevention hotline. Sean Dennis has had sixteen letters to the editor, all dealing with aspects of popular culture, published in various sections of the *New York Times*. Cheaters was purchased by new owners in 1984 and achieved a certain renown after its premises were used for location shooting of scenes from a melodramatic film about the emptiness of urban life, *Big, Bright Zero*. I feel weak all over.

We've been talking about Double Exposure, the Taxi Avengers, Bandage, and some other bands. What about Hi-Fi? When was the first time that you saw them?

I'm sorry, but I get some headache whenever I start to think about the good old days, quote unquote. Hi-Fi was supposed to be therapy for me; talk about the cure being worse than the disease. My mother had met Jay someplace, probably through her ad in the *Voice*, and got this bright idea that if I were maybe to become involved in the band it would get me back into circulation. She didn't think I got out enough; this was her way of describing my nervous breakdown, which I won't go into so much: everybody's got problems. The usual, some vague disturbance which you don't pay any attention to until the symptoms become too much to ignore. I would become embarrassed, for no reason, and break out into this annoying sweat. I'd stumble and bang into the walls sometimes when I tried to walk. I had recurrences of the hay fever and asthma that had gone away when I hit fourteen. Et cetera. My mother thought fresh air and sunshine would fix all this. Finally, though, I had an attack in which I remained completely lucid although I couldn't control my movements or my speech. Mom gave up on the healing power of nature then; shipped my ass to Bellevue. They pumped me full of Thorazine, sensible souls. I remember a movie was on the tube in the ward, *Birth of the Beatles*, just some stupid TV movie with actors playing all the parts, and apparently I was muttering something about them being the *real* Beatles, and then I started believing that these people were not only the real Beatles but that they were also my friends. Talking to them, offering them advice, "Get rid of that lousy bassist! That drummer doesn't fit in!" You know. So Mom interprets all this stuff I said while I was babbling like a bag lady to mean like I had a real, serious interest in this kind of thing. And so she prevailed upon Jay to let me in the band to play drums—there was an old Slingerland set at the club that I used to bang around on sometimes—strongly hinting of course that the door to Cheaters would always be wide open for them. Jay took the bait, too: it's always easy to find someone who wants to be Jimi Hendrix—in fact, Nat and Dave were both playing guitar in the band at that point, what a mess—but drummers are harder to come by; the equipment's more expensive, it's harder to fake it. And the idea of being able to play Mom's club must have sounded pretty good, too. I think Hi-Fi had done like six audition nights at CBGBs at that point. So Mom brings them around to meet and chat with me while I'm still lying in bed at home, afterwards she's like, "Well, now that you know them, how about it?" "Mona," I say, "I do not like everyone I know." Then she leaned on me: "You *never* like anybody. Don't you want to go new places and see new things? I'm doing this for *you*, so that you don't turn around in ten or fifteen years and say that you robbed yourself of the best years of your youth. Don't you ever daydream? About belonging?" Frankly, no, but my own inclinations would never ever dissuade my mother from taking things into her own hands when she felt the time was right to do so. She's the one who sat me down when I was two to explain to me all of the main facts of sex. Two! But I was actually pretty adamant about this. I did not want to "belong." I have never wanted to be a "team player." I did not want to be publicly anonymous, you know, stuck in a sum-of-the-parts kind of thing. Mom didn't get this at all. I could not explain it to her. I honestly believed that my thoughts and ideas would be stolen by these people. I probably haven't expressed myself clearly enough. I mean I thought my ideas would be subsumed by the group. I wish I weren't so shy, I wish I could belong, but I've always felt alone. It's not as if I believe I'm condemned to live a solitary life, or even like I'm bitter that I have—everybody's got problems. This must be a bore for you. You're a journalist, a rock critic, whatever you are. Spice it up a little, some lurid innuendo here, some baseless rumor there: Richard Poindexter is a kleptomaniac, Jay Lustig belongs to a cult. Throw that right in there, be my guest. Anyway, in order to make a peaceful life for myself, I go against my own better judgment and join the band. So I'm sitting uptown with Mom and she's giving me one of her pep talks: "Sometimes I can't believe the way you've turned out. Your mother has always enjoyed a good time, been known to flirt, to get around—*these aren't unpardonable sins!* To you, everything tastes the same: bland. You'd just as soon sleep all day as at night. I hate to treat you like a child, but at your age I'm worried. You're too old for your 'moods.' I understand, you think I'm just getting on your back because I have nothing better to do. It's not true—I'm your mother! I worry! Frequently! Come on, take a chance, step on a few cracks!" Then Ms. Self-Confidence freaks out: "Oh my god. The PA's broken. I'm breaking out. I need a drink. Run down to Prince Street and tell them."

Hi-Fi?

Yeah, it's the day of my first gig with the band. All the way down to Broadway-Lafayette I'm wondering how it must feel to be as happy as other people seem to be; to come from a home filled with love and companionship; trying not to feel anxious and worried. I wouldn't treat a dog the way she treated me. I kept telling myself, "*Everybody's* got problems!" Just another mumbling fool on the IND. I'm reading all the ads on the train, that's enough to make anybody realize that someone somewhere is worse off than them, but I kept alternating their blunt messages of hope and fulfillment with my own thoughts: "Like to Get Your Contractor's License?" "Love between a mother and son should be the strongest of all." "Like Science?" "Friends should share." "Like Hunting?" "She should worry about what I do, not what I don't do. She should worry about who I'm with, not who I'm not with." "No, yes, no, yes, no, yes." Black, white, black, white, black, and white, replacing each other as I looked from ad to ad. By the time I got off, I was a wreck. I walked over toward Prince Street, looking for a little camaraderie, a little gossip, anything to get my mind off my mother and her annoying habits. I felt like a sleepwalker. Someone was standing outside with the equipment, but I didn't recognize that it was Nat until I was right on top of him. Suddenly, I couldn't make up my mind whether I actually wanted to talk to him or not. I just wanted to go back home and crawl back into bed, stay there. It wasn't worth it, belonging, all that clubbishness: I knew everything would get torn apart or disintegrate sooner or later anyway. But he'd already seen me coming. "Hey Nat," I said, "bad news, the PA's busted." "I knew it," he says. I tried to make conversation: "How's it going? All ready for tonight?" "How's it look?" "How's Maureen?" "Fine I guess." "I hear Strange Lobster is giving Marzio the boot." "I don't know." "Hot today, huh?" "Yeah." "Well, Reagan's it now. We're in for it." "OK." "At least I don't have to ask you to put me on the guest list any more." "No." "See that new chick at Veselka's yet? Foxy!" "I eat at Leshko's." "Has Jay written the new bio up yet? With me in it?" "How should I know?" "Gonna wear something special tonight? Onstage, I mean?" "Some T-shirt things." I felt pretty pathetic. My heart was pounding and I was having trouble breathing. I mean, did he want to talk about sex? Or what? What was I doing wrong? "Well," I said, finally, "I guess I better go up and tell Jay about the PA." "Don't bother, I'll take care of it." He moved to block the door. I knew something was up, but I couldn't figure it out and I wasn't going to push it. I still felt very unsure of myself. "Well, I'll see you up there." I went over to West Broadway and stood there trying to figure out what to do, where to go. All those shops on the main drag were chanting a song of exclusivity at me; the old wop neighborhood of railroad flats further west was just as solid and homogeneous, them screaming out the window at each other; and back the way I came was Nat. Strike three. I knew he'd still be standing there in the same spot, I just wanted to get out of his line of sight. Finally, I just went uptown. A little later the other shoe dropped.

You're talking about getting thrown out?

Yeah. The phone rang and Mona answered it, and in a couple of seconds she came mincing into the room, this stupid grin on her face. I wanted to smash it in for her. I picked up the extension and it was Jay. We waited until my mother hung up the other line. He sounded really nervous, like he was reading from something he'd written down. "When I assume a responsibility I take it very seriously. I have a duty to this band, I have to follow it. . . ." I don't really remember what else he said. As soon as he said that I knew I was out. Something about Nat being interested in playing drums, the economy of the power trio sound. They'd just wanted to play the club, of course. I told him that I didn't want to stand in their way, Mr. Nice Guy. God forbid I should act mad in front of somebody. This time, though, I didn't feel mad for a while. I sat, and I thought, and what I thought about was my dependency, my mother's making all the decisions and choices for me; I brooded over all of this, and got more and more agitated and restless, started pacing and muttering, and finally I went downstairs to the empty club. It was warm and dark. In the back, the stage was lit and I saw the old Slingerland set up there. I grabbed a chair from one of the tables and went at it, just smashed it to pieces: I tore all the drum heads, I stomped on the cymbals until they were cracked and bent. I flipped out, I went into the bathroom and started screaming and kicking the door, pounding my fists against the mirror. I totally lost it. My mother came in, she grabbed me and she took me into the back room, sat me down. For once she was in total sympathy with me. She hugged me and kissed me while I cried and retched and she checked to see if I'd hurt myself. I was OK. She sang me a little song that sort of calmed me down:

> Disappointments are for the books;
> They're passing fast, just like your looks.
> Keep your dreams to yourself, it serves
> To focus you, and to calm your nerves.
> So, when the sky looks black with pain,
> Smile, it's just like a springtime rain.

Are you telling the truth?
My way of doing things is apt to be misunderstood by others.

What happened that night when Hi-Fi performed at Cheaters?
Oh, what a night. After I calmed down a bit, my mother was back on me again. "I just don't understand you, you're pathetic." So much for family solidarity. Well, everybody's got problems. She told me that she wanted me to stand up straight and tall and face them. In fact, she wanted me to tend bar that night with Don. All I wanted to do was sleep, but she took me upstairs and got me one of Don's white shirts and a greasy clip-on bow tie and then she gave me a crash course in bartending. She showed me how to mix

easy drinks, like stuff over ice and gin and tonics. She told me
to check the stock a lot to make sure we weren't getting low on
anything and told me to always keep the bar clean, "nobody likes
to drink at a bar that's wet or greasy or has dirty ashtrays on it."
After we were done, it was almost time for them to show up. She
said, "Kid, you're going to do great. I find a lot more fault with you
than I should sometimes." Then she went into the back room. I was
alone. When they came in, I was busy at the bar. I turned around,
pretending to look at the rows of bottles, but I was watching them
in the mirror. I knew I couldn't do that forever, so I faced them and
started wiping the bar. I couldn't say a word. I started thinking of
the bed again, safe and warm. They looked just as uncomfortable.
Finally, Jay came up to the bar. Before he had a chance to say anything, Mona came out. "Stage is back there, dressing area's behind
the folding screens. Sound check's an hour and a half before
showtime, and we want you onstage at eleven o'clock, no bullshit,
OK?" It was embarrassing, I could feel my neck starting to blush.
I've always been jealous of her directness, her ability to confront
situations like that. Later, we're standing there and I'm begging her
to let me handle it in my own way and Jay comes running from the
back, "Where's the drum set? Where the hell am I going to find
a drum set at the last minute?" "Phone's over there, Jay," I said,
finally, just to prove that I could say something. But when he came
out of the alcove, Mona couldn't resist asking: "Did you get
lucky?" He started cursing at her; she looked over at me. Typical.
The situation just resolved itself, finally. I said whatever was
expected of me, "watch your mouth or you're out of here," something like that. Jay and Nat got somebody to lend them a drum set
and they went off in a cab to get it. With them gone, I felt a little
better. Dave and Richard came up to the bar and they were both
apologetic—they said the whole thing had been Nat's idea, that
they hadn't agreed with it. When Don got there I went to the back
and sat with them for a while in the dressing area, it was a real eye-
opener. They said that the band had been on the verge of breaking
up for a while and that this would probably do it. Then Maureen,
Girl, and my sister showed up. They were shocked by the news.
"What a scumbag!" said Maureen. Mimi told me not to worry
about it, "they suck anyway." Girl gave me one of the T-shirts
she'd made, she said she'd had me in mind for it. It had this picture
of a serpent eating its own tail. By now I was feeling wildly
excited, on top of the world. Getting kicked out had been the best

thing that had ever happened to me! *Everybody* was coming up to me, "I hear you got fucked over by Nat and Jay." So when Nat and Jay got back with the drums, they were greeted by a very hostile atmosphere—especially Nat. I was back behind the bar, talking to Maureen, and Nat came up and asked Maureen to please come and sit with him, he wanted to talk. They sat at one of the tables across from the bar, and out of the corner of my eye I could see that they were fighting. At one point Nat looked at me and gestured, and Maureen said, "Fuck off! You're crazy!" She got up and left, and in a second Nat was after her. A couple of minutes later, Jed arrives and he says that somebody who looks like they're from the club is beating up on a girl outside. Just then all hell breaks loose, Maureen comes running in just a step ahead of Nat, she looked horrible, her lip was split and her hair was all in her face.

Who was in control?

Sounds strange, but I was. Jed was at the door screaming at Nat to get the fuck away if he didn't want to get hurt. I could tell that he was about to become unhinged too, so I asked Mimi to take Maureen into the bathroom to get cleaned up and then I went up to Jed and told him that I'd handle it. I went outside, it had become freezing cold. "Please go home," I said to Nat, "everything'll be much easier to handle tomorrow." He was looking pretty bad himself, he was crying, but he'd started to calm down. "Please let me in," he said, "please, I'll be good." I said that I didn't think it would be a good idea, that he'd better go now. I could see him starting to get angry again. It was weird. Really thoughtfully, he goes, "You're a good looking guy, you know that? You're a real good looking guy." "Please go home." I reached over to touch his shoulder, but he jumped back. "Keep your fucking hands off of me! And keep your fucking hands off my girlfriend!" "Go home, Nat." I went back inside. In the bathroom, Maureen was doing a little better. She kept saying that Nat was the Devil, and she was in Hell. I put my arms around her and told her that I'd take care of her. She kissed me, and I knew that for better or worse my entire life had just turned a corner. When I came out of the bathroom, Jay was waiting for me. "I'm really embarrassed to ask this, but we're going to need someone to play drums now." I said I'd fill in.

Did anything significant happen after you began to play?

When we went on, there was a big cheer when I was introduced.

I felt very energetic, very happy. I screwed up the intro of the first song, but other than that I was OK. Maureen was sitting at one of the front tables with Girl and Mimi, and she and I were looking at each other throughout the first song. Mimi got up at the beginning of the second song, but she came rushing back a couple of minutes later, spilling her drink as she ran down the aisle. I saw her whisper something to Maureen and then Maureen looking around nervously, grabbing for her purse. It was Nat, he'd gotten back into the club somehow. There was nothing I could do. He sat at the table opposite Maureen's and just stared at her. By the beginning of the third song she'd started staring back. When they smiled at each other, I knew that was it. At the beginning of the fourth song, he had joined her at her table. Soon after, they left.

What happened after the performance was over?

I don't really remember. I guess I was in a state of shock because everything was returning to normal. I felt like fucking Cinderella at midnight. Everybody's got problems. Everybody in the club left right away—big party at Nat's house. The band packed up quickly, so they could get to the party before it was too late, and Jay thanked me for filling in and said he hoped there were no hard feelings. Then he asked me who to see about getting paid. I guess I can't blame anybody for grabbing everything they can in this world. I just sat there silently for a few moments, spacing out. He punched me gently in the shoulder, waved his hand in front of my eyes. I told him to go talk to Don about the money.

Where Are They Now?

Jay Lustig is an A&R man for a small but nationally distributed label. Dave McCall is lead guitarist for a local heavy metal band, Kwire Böiz. Nat Phenomenon committed suicide after stabbing Maureen Ferret to death on Christmas Day, 1985. Richard Poindexter now performs as a hip hop artist under the name MC Dex. Hi-Fi broke up in August 1981 after its seventh unsuccessful audition at CBGB. Don McOral won the New Jersey State Lottery in 1987 and lives in retirement in Pine Bluff, Arkansas. Mona Barron Miller McOral moved to Ossining, New York, where she works as an administrative analyst at a mental institution. Paul Marzio manages a motel near Fairvale, California. Maureen Ferret was murdered by Nat Phenomenon on Christmas Day, 1985, but has become famous in death through her autobiographical novel,

Stuttering on the Truth. I live with my sister, and spend my days tending to my bulletin board. Jed is now a limousine driver/armed bodyguard in the Los Angeles area. Girl Bovary was born again and now lives in Toronto. Mimi Miller is a waitress at a Wall Street topless bar, Henrik's. Sean and Susan Dennis develop and conduct inspirational seminars for wealthy executives around the country, and their manifesto, *The Dennis Alternative,* is entering its third year on the best-seller lists. Cheaters was sold in 1984 and is now the site of a Chinese restaurant that does a brisk lunchtime business. No one cares much what happens to you.

We've been talking about Endnote, Benjy and the Idiots, and the Escorts. What about Hi-Fi? When was the first time that you saw them?

This is kinda funny. I went to high school with them. They hung with the fag crowd, the punk rock crowd, so I wasnt friends with them or nothin. I got along with Jay OK, he didnt dress like a queer like the rest of em. Take him aside, Im like, "Jay, youre cool. Why you hang out with those punk rock assholes?" So I was pretty open-minded about the whole thing, I think. The others were just a buncha little pussies. Me and my friends, we liked to play practical jokes on em all the time, like, we beat the shit outta Spielvogel at a party once. What a blast. I go, "Hey Nathanael, oh Nathanael." He hated bein called that. Hes dressed in total punk rock bullshit, shit hangin from his clothes an shit, stupid blind nigger sunglasses on. He says, "What?" and I say, "I wanna shake ya hand, man. Really, thats some outfit you got on. Maybe you could gimme some tips." So he holds his hand out, dumb fuck, and I grab it and my bud Mike smashes him over the head with a chair. "Oh, how punk you look now, Nathanael." We booked, laughin all the way to Positively 8th Street. But I didnt really know anything about the band until later. Tell you the truth, I was kinda shocked when I found out. We all thought a band was something you went to Ticketron to get seats at the Garden for. Im not gonna say this to Jay, of course. Hes going around, passin out fliers. "Come on, Jed. Come down. You gonna hang around 8th Street lowerin property values your whole life?" I gotta admit, I had respect for him. He had a lotta balls sayin this to me. Were laughin at him, though. "Youre in a band? You? Playin rock and roll? Get outta here." He goes, "Actually, were gonna play some Urban Blight covers." Mikey goes apeshit, "Really? Urban Blight? No fuckin shit!" What a momo; Jay was fuckin with his head an shit. I love Mike like a brother, but hes got the brains of Garfield the cat. Maybe not even. Ill never forget what Jay says next: "If Ronald Reagan gets elected president, then I can make it playing rock and roll. Itll mean there are moren enough idiots to go around." Fucked if he wasnt right.

Are you telling the truth?
I believe there is a God.

Did anything significant happen then?
From my personal point of view, no. We got outta school right after that and I had some trouble getting started. I applied to Hunter and I got in, you just hadda like breathe on the mirror, but I dropped out. I hated school, I was lousy at it. I was hustlin to make a little money; no big deal, I was still livin at home. I got a job as one of those jerks on the corner shovin things at passerbys, the place folded, then as a foot messenger. Mostly, I dealt weed. My parents were on my ass to get my shit together, theyre both big-time professors at NYU. "Here, look," Id say, "Im an artist. Im drawing a beautiful flower for you." We fought a lot. It didnt help any that I looked so lousy next to my fat-ass brother. Class pres, editor of the newspaper, going to Cardozo on a scholarship, all that shit. Fat faggot. It got to be this routine, like, at supper wed be sittin around and my brother would be like, "so the tort fees are found to have abrogated the Dudiov care and thus was libel. . . ." Im cringing, my old man goes, "So, Jed, is it true that city boys wear out the soles of their shoes before they wear out the tops?" Another big laugh at my expense. Sweatin out dinner every night, I was feeling lousy, very low—you cant trust your family, who can you trust? About once a week or so Id replay all the scenes like little movies in my head, getting very excited when Id come up with all the cool things to say I hadnt been able to think of when they were gangin up on me. So one day I see this ad in the *Voice* and I apply for a night job as a bouncer at this club, Cheaters. I figured it was a good idea because a, it would get me out of the house all night, b, now they couldnt bug me about getting up late, and c, something exciting like thatll usually pick me up when Im feeling bad. I mean, I couldnt believe I was gonna get paid to make people be afraid of me!

What happened the night that Hi-Fi performed at Cheaters?
That was a weird night. Id been workin at the club maybe two,

three months. Turns out it was a shit job, my bosses, this fat drunk bitch named Mona and her crazy husband Don, were a pair of cheap fucks. I got a cut of the door and they stiffed me on that, even. I kept it mostly because of what I told you about already, plus there were fringe benefits, like booze. But still. Anyway me and Mikey and a couple other dudes are sittin around talkin and we get this great idea to rip the place off. They had a PA and some other stuff, we figured itd be good for a couple hundred. The idea was Id take a piss before I left and leave the bathroom window open, it looked out onto this little airshaft Id checked out a couple times, no big deal to get in. I figured they asked for it, chintzy bastards. So that night, the night were gonna do it, Im kind of full of energy. The usual lousy bands playin—they only had lousy bands play there—they were called the Redheaded League, they all had red hair, get it, ha. Dons literally bangin his head against the bar. He hated it, I think thats what made him crazy. He was always comin up to me, "I love flowers and trees, Jed. I love the smell of fresh meadow grass and clean air. I cannot feel the entire right side of my body. I'm losing my sight. That woman has taken control of my mind and my body is following." Youd pat him on the shoulder, "Thats too bad, Don. We all got problems, Don," and hed wander off. Hopeless, he was like a little kid. Anyway, make a long story short, we do it, no problem, except we have a fuck of a time puttin the PA speakers in the trunk of Mikeys Camaro. Later, downtown, were outside Positively 8th Street with a slice and guess who walks by? Jay Lustig and Nat Spielvogel the Fag. Havent seen em since school. Jay hands me a flier. "You gonna come down? Were gonna make it now, I told you." I look down on the flier and you know what it says. Nathanael says, "Nice PA. Whered you get it?" Im tryin to keep calm. "Keep the fuck off it, Nathanael." Im hopin Mike doesnt open his big dumb mouth. I know that if Im smart I can finesse the whole thing, think something up. But the Fags looking and looking at that PA. He goes, "I've seen one just like that somewhere recently." Jay knows somethings up, but like I say, hes smart, hes like, "Theres millions of those around, come on, lets go." But Spielvogel just cant stop looking at it. Thats when I knew Id have to do somethin about it, keep his mouth shut for him.

You're talking about getting Nat thrown out?

Thrown out. Killed. Crippled. Like I say, I knew I hadda do something. I could see it now, at supper, my father going, "Well,

Jed, you've made quite a mess of things, as usual, but maybe your brother can defend you." If I was an only child I could handle jail. The next day I felt all weirded out an shit. I mean, Id done shit, but Id never done a *crime* crime before. I kept thinkin that people were watchin me, followin me. My throat was all dry and I kept drinking gallons a water an shit. Just my luck, my dads only got office hours that day and hes back in the house around two oclock. "Jed," he goes, "I've been wanting to talk to you." I dont need this. "Jed, I know you value your friendships, and I think that's admirable. But I think you're riding for a very long fall. I think your friends are using you." My ears, theyre ringing and buzzing. Did he know? How could he? I know this is supposed to be the big father thing, caring and sharing precious moments, but aside from my other problems all I can think about is the constant bitching, "Why can't you be more like Jeff? Why can't you write prize-winning papers while saving people from burning buildings?" I hated his guts. "Jed, what I'm getting at is, do you have any plans for your life at all? Do you have any idea of what you'd like to be?" "A sportswriter, I guess?" That shut him up for a second. "Well," he says, "then *be* one!" Then he goes off, "Your mother and I have been talking about this, about *you*—" I started laughin like it was a dirty joke. I booked, hadda get outta there, I just wanted to be left alone for a while. I went over to M&O and got myself an excellent sandwich, they take a loaf a French bread thats just a little bit stale, so its kinda crunchy, and cut it in half the long way and put on like a mountain a boiled ham. Then on toppa the ham they put on like another mountain, of Swiss cheese. Then they put lettuce on, iceberg lettuce, not the hard white part but the soft green part. Spread mayo and mustard on the top parta the bread and youre in business. Eat it with a quart a Bud and maybe a bag a Ridgies. So Im sittin there finishin my sandwich on a stoop next to Rocks in Your Head, Im about to head over to Positively 8th Street to hang for a while, and then I notice something very, very interesting happens. A little further down Prince someone comes out of one of the buildings carryin two guitars. He puts them down on the sidewalk and turns around and I see its McCall. Right behind him is Jay, hes schleppin an amp. They both go back inside and then Spielvogel and Poindexter come out rolling this big trap case with drums on top. The drums fall off when theyre bumpin it down the step, I can hear Poindexter from where Im sitting, "Youre a fuckin *scrub*, you know that?" Spielvogel goes back in, comes out a second later with another amp and another guitar. Poindexter finishes putting the drums back on top of the trap case and then he goes back in. Spielvogel waits a sec, looks in through the door, and then gives him the finger, goes and gives the drums on top this little, wimpy shove. What a *pussy.* So hes out there alone. Im thinking, "what an excellent opportunity to convey my sentiments to him," an shit. I go over. What do I have to be afraid of? The faggots scared of fucking *Richard Poindexter.* I didnt want to hurt him; I just wanted to make sure he understood things from my personal point of view. When he sees me, he looks like hes gonna puke. "Hello, Nathanael. I was thinkin it might be a good idea if you kind of forgot where you saw that PA." Now hes trying to tell me he doesnt know any-thing about any PA. "You disgust me," I say, "you insult my intelligence with your little smartass mouth. You should show a little respect, an shit." Im very tense, and were walking in this like little circle, facin each other, its a bore, Im like, "Is this a *fuckin* square dance? You tryina fuckin *hypnotize* me?" I reach out, yoke him, get him in a headlock. "Everybody dies, Nathanael." Just then, window opens, this faggot sticks his head out, like, "Leave him alone! You big bully!" Im like, "Speak when youre spoken to, faggot." I let go of Spielvogel and reach up to the windowsill and pull down this big faggy plant. It gets all smashed. "Remember what I told you, Nathanael." I left thinking that Id made quite an impression, had an influence on him. All my nervousness just went away like that, I knew I wouldnt get into trouble.

You were "in control."

I go over to Positively 8th Street and hang out for a while, then we go to Mad Hatters for some pitchers, Im feelin really stoked, what you said, like Id taken control of things. Better than sex. Im tellin Mikey, "All we gotta do is come up with some story about where we were last night, stick to it, and were set." Anyway, its gettin kinda late, so I score a little coke, do up a couple a lines in the bathroom, and grab the train uptown. Im feelin very intense, its one of those weird nights in New York when all the nuts come out. Theres some crazy guy on the train drummin on the seat in front of him; some nigger lady with an accent screamin at the top of her lungs; this guy whos just a head goes rollin by on a skate-board, shakin his cup in his teeth; and when I get off at the Port of Authority its even weirder than usual. One of those nights. So I dont even notice really when I pass this guy and some skank on

40th, hes whackin her and slappin her head and shes tryin to kick him and theyre both cursin and cryin.

Could you detect some sort of pattern or order?

I dont get you. I mean, it mighta had somethin to do with the Reagan thing, there were the usual bullshit marches an shit, probably some of it carried over. So I go inside Cheaters and theres Don, the usual lameass expression on his face, "I'm so glad you finally got here. There's been trouble, we were broken into last night. They came in as easily as if it were a doll's house, a doll's house. I can't take the strain, Jed, I need to be near growing things. Mona's no help, she's drunk, she's coming on to all the young boys." Then he goes, like hes not even her husband, "She's going to get into trouble one day." "Be a man, Don," I say. Do I give a shit about his personal problems? Do I want to talk about them? Then the door bangs open and its the skank I saw on the street gettin beat up, "Help me, help me, hes gonna kill me." Im totally comin down an shit, I cant deal with this, I go to do up some more coke and some assholes locked himself in the mens room, so I try the ladies room and its open, empty. Im pouring the coke out onto this little mirror I carry and I hear this commotion outside, lotsa shoutin and bangin around an shit. The door flies open and its the skank *again*, I spill all the fuckin coke, really pissin me off, and shes with a friend a hers whose tryin to pull a guy, the guy on the street, offa her, and then I see the guy is Spielvogel, just lunging and lunging at her and he puts his arms up, puts his hands behind his head like hes fuckin *relaxin*, but hes makin a double fist and I see someones hand reach out to grab his hair, his head, and he just slams it outta the way bringin the fist down on her, I remember she just goes, "Oh," and then blood starts pourin outta her nose an shit, and he tries to do it again and I grab him "You wanna fight someone, asshole?" and he yells out, "Youre a fuckin thief, you stole that fuckin PA," and I pulled him into the bathroom with me, it was weird, I just pulled him away from everybody outside like takin a piece out of a puzzle, and I slammed him against the stall "You fuckin pussy" and hes "You faggot" and I flip "*Im* a faggot, huh? Im a *faggot*? *Im* a faggot, huh? Im a *faggot*? *Im* a faggot, huh? Im a *faggot*? *Im* a faggot, huh? Im a *faggot*?" punchin him each time. I was totally outta control, I couldnt stop hittin him, the little cunt Im *defendin*, for chrissake, what an idiot, is jumpin on my back, "Get off him, get off him!" I have this whole audience of people just gawkin outside the bathroom, and I finally stop when I'm tired.

What happened after this "performance" was over?

Spielvogels not movin at all, theres blood like all over the place, my hands are all swollen and sore, someone goes, "He killed him!" and I turn around, look at them all still in the hall outside the bathroom, like Im gonna *explain* to them, but I choke, I cant say a word, then some people push into the bathroom and theyre all helpin him an shit, hes *fine*, I didnt hit im that hard, but of course hes playin it for all he can get, "Oh, it hurts so bad, oh, I cant see," fucker, my attitude, sonofabitch started beatin up on a chick, but still, you know, Im feelin all alone an shit, nobodys comin up to me, you know, like, "good job," or shit, and Im, like, "Whats the fuckin point?", whatever, their stupid game, like, their rules, cops come in, "Looks like youre gonna be takin a little trip," cop *bullshit*, who cares, fuck this shit, "I got friends," whatever, you know, Monas "get him out of here," to me, like, "I'm sure they'll love *you* on Rikers," my ass, *bitch*, Im "I ripped you off cunt I took your fuckin PA and I wish Id killedya," not sayin it, not *stupid*, but, you know, fuck *her*, asked for it, Im wantin the cops to take me outta there, all the people, buggin the hell outta me, Im thinkina takina machine gun, *BUDDA BUDDA BUDDA BUDDA!*, blood and holes and broken glass. Blaze a glory.

Where Are They Now?

Hi-Fi is world famous. Don McOral and Mona Barron perished in a fire of mysterious origin that consumed their apartment building in May 1986. Paul Marzio is a CPA working in the Chicago office of a Big Six accounting firm. Maureen Ferret is a television actress who has gained renown through her appearances in thirty-minute "infomercials" advertising such products and services as tax-free municipal bonds, time-share condominiums, and vitamin and mineral systems. Miles Miller works as an advertising copy-writer and claims to be working on an "insider" novel. I am incarcerated at Attica Correctional Facility for unrelated offenses. Girl Bovary has been trying to figure out how to attract and marry a rich man for seven years. Mimi Miller is a consultant to civil engineering and construction firms, specializing in doctoring environmental impact reports to be submitted to the Department of the Interior and other authorities. Susan Dennis edits *Sunshower*, a literary magazine out of Bend, Oregon. Sean Dennis lives in a refrigerator box on San Francisco's Market Street. Cheaters was closed by the New York City Police Department on January 22, 1981, after it was determined that the management repeatedly violated State liquor laws prohibiting sale of alcohol to persons under eighteen years of age. I get a raw deal out of life.

We've been talking about MMPI, the Golden Girls, the Lost Child Band, and some other bands. What about Hi-Fi? When was the first time that you saw them?

Hi-Fi first burst onto the national music scene in 1981 with the release of its witty debut album, *Go On, You Insolent Mouse*, which widely appealed to aficionados of both mainstream and alternative music. The disc yielded three original Top Forty hits, "Lyin' Only When It Matters," "More Sensitive Than Most," and "The Daily Grind (Gettin' Me Down, Girl)," and the band cracked the coveted number one slot with its ska-flavored cover of the Sex Pistols' "No Feelings." These successes took both Hi-Fi and the independent label with which it had signed by surprise, and within the year the band's contract had been purchased by Cronus—but only after the larger label agreed to give the boys complete artistic freedom.

A seasoned club band, Hi-Fi had spent two years honing its act to a sharp edge before enthusiastic audiences in the New York City area, somehow managing to combine a sense of intimacy between itself and its fans with an energetic, larger-than-life stage show that left audiences screaming for more. With each of the boys contributing original material to the band's growing repertoire, Hi-Fi synthesized elements of hard rock and New Wave, giving birth to the exciting "Deli Rock" sound and breaking completely from the punk rock tradition in which it was rooted.

Hi-Fi.

The founding member and guiding spirit of the band was, and remains, Dave McCall. The son of a second-generation abstract expressionist painter, the boy begged his father to purchase an electric guitar for him after watching the Rezillos perform on *Top of the Pops* during a visit to London. Painfully picking tunes out on the cheap Fender until late at night, Dave slowly mastered the instrument and soon began penning his own songs. Even early efforts, such as "Dreamin' of Sex, Girl," show signs of the blistering honesty and poignant self-reflection that would become hall-marks of the mature McCall style. Shy and easily embarrassed, Dave was coaxed before the footlights by an enthusiastic teacher, Robert Bobtak, who had heard the youngster softly chording his instrument and singing quietly to himself in a stall in the boys' room. Persuaded by the educator's sincere interest, Dave entered the school talent contest where he performed "I Write the Songs" before a packed auditorium. Although he placed second in the judging, Dave later reminisced, "It was amazing how popular I was in school after that."

Jay Lustig would seem an odd match for the shy, mannerly McCall. The son of a second-generation abstract expressionist painter, Lustig had by the age of sixteen earned a reputation as a troublemaker and truant. He had also, however, inherited his father's sophisticated reckoning of the marketplace and, spotting a potentially lucrative business in recording and producing the many bands that had sprung up in and around New York, he established Zounds studios with the proceeds from the sale of a Bob Thompson painting. Running the operation on a shoestring, he bided his time while repeating his oft-expressed conviction that "If I could find a city boy with the suburb sound and the suburb feel I could make a million dollars!" The stage was therefore set for the day that Dave wandered into the studio with his guitar, seeking to record a sound-on-sound demo of a song he had written for a girlfriend, "Russky Man." Seated behind the console, Jay was intrigued by both the song's dynamic beat and its solid commercial potential, and he persuaded Dave to soften its biting, acerbic lyric. The result of this propitious collaboration was "All About Heartache," the first Lustig/McCall composition. The partnership immediately bore fruit: there followed a withering indictment of the emptiness of urban life, "Peculiar and Strange (Walkin' through the City)," the satirically bland "Summer Song (Never Been in Love)," and the presciently terrifying "Scary Family," inspired by the arm's-length intimacy engendered by the proliferation of classified personal ads.

But even the most determined duo do not a band make, and Dave and Jay soon realized that they would have to recruit an ensemble specifically tailored to their distinctive sound. Writing off all in-struments other than guitar, bass, and drums as effete, the two embraced the "power trio" arrangement as the most practical means of harnessing their raw yet polished energy and began their search for backup musicians. The first hurdle was cleared early on, when Michael Bachmann, an Industrial Arts major at the High School of Music and Art and an acquaintance admired by Dave for his clothing and formidable intellect, was persuaded to purchase a bass guitar with a cash prize awarded to him for a wooden fruit bowl he had entered in the school's semi-annual exhibition. Although Michael's experience with the instrument was limited to childhood guitar lessons at nearby Greenwich House, he soon proved himself to be more than a mere thumper, whose dexterous fretwork provided a fluid yet rock-solid foundation to the band's inchoate sound, and whose vocal abilities graced the upper half of the band's rich harmonies.

The quest for the right drummer met with less initial success. The band's first choice, Colin Hanton, was a remarkably gifted musician whose promising career was sidetracked by a tragic case of manic depression, and his periodic hospitalizations proved to be incompatible with the band's ambitions. Their next recruit, Tom Moore, left for more pedestrian reasons: at age seventeen, his parents would not let him stay out for Hi-Fi's frequently late shows. Jimmy Nicol was more reliable, but after a short period it became evident that he simply was not as dedicated as the others to their goals. The timing of Nicol's departure was unfortunate, for shortly afterward local impresario Peter Dimitri, who admired the band's unique energy and presence, offered them a berth on the Tri-State tour he was promoting, which would kick off six weeks later with the "Inauguration Bash" at Cheaters, the new Mona Barron–Don McOral rock palace in Manhattan. Rather than give up on their dream, this new incentive spurred Dave, Jay, and Michael to intensify their quest for the right drummer.

Coincidentally, Richard Poindexter, a self-styled "bad boy" who had moved effortlessly from art rock to punk to ska, each time leaving broken hearts and indelible memories of virtuoso performances in his wake while establishing a reputation as a dangerously polemical percussionist and trendsetter, was at this time nearly fully recovered from an unfortunate drug mishap which had left him partially paralyzed. Although jealous competitors had written him off, Richard realized that his diminished motor capacity and unerring sense of backbeat could lend itself to the new, cruder "power pop" sound that was beginning to gain momentum in New York, and he began the arduous process of teaching himself the new rhythms on practice pads while still convalescent. News of Hi-Fi's search came to him through the insular rock world's ever-active grapevine, and after reviewing some demo tapes the band had recorded at Zounds he contacted Jay and expressed his interest in signing on. Several marathon rehearsal sessions later (wisely preserved on tape by Jay, and soon to be released as *Changing Voices: The Cold Taxi Sessions*), the new Hi-Fi was ready to make its debut at Cheaters.

What happened the night that Hi-Fi performed at Cheaters?
Emboldened by the new lineup and energized by having constantly tested the very limits of their creativity in the fiery crucible of those rehearsals, Dave, Jay, Michael, and Richard completely revamped the band's stale set, infusing it with a searing political edge. Now at the top of their form, Dave and Jay composed no less than seven new songs to debut at Cheaters: the anthemic "No One Seems to Understand Us," Dave's bitter and timely indictment of the dawning Reagan era, "I Smell a Rat (DC Current)," a harrowing song of psychological dissociation, "I Can't Keep My Mind from Wandering," a comic account of an encounter with bureaucracy, "Don't Get Impatient," a bitter paean to self-help platitudes, "I'm Not Anxious," the sharply satirical "I Got Mine (Don't Worry 'bout His)," and the bleak "I Wish I Were Dead."

Having obtained the coveted next-to-closing spot, the band appeared onstage at about 2:00 A.M. before over a thousand excited fans, many of whom had waited in line overnight to purchase tickets, enduring sleeplessness and a blinding snowstorm. Although earlier in the evening there had been problems with the sound system, these had by now been resolved and the band performed with deafening clarity, driving the crowd to all but forget earlier masterful performances by such bands as the Identical Strangers, Sandwiches, Again?, SpeedStick, and the Lab Rats.

Did anything significant happen while the band was playing?
For all of the elaborate preparations that had been made to ensure that the interior of Cheaters was the most lavish ever conceived of for a rock discotheque, scant attention had been paid to the structural integrity of the former warehouse in which it was situated; and many of the renovations were, in fact, illegal. It was later determined that these renovations had been expressly approved by one Armand Oso, a senior building inspector for the City of New York, who was subsequently dismissed from his position and indicted for bribery and extortion under color of authority. As

a result of Oso's malfeasance, the roof of the building collapsed, in the absence of certain load-bearing walls, when runoff from melting snow accumulated on the rooftop because drainage pipes had been removed from the building's facade for cosmetic reasons. The disaster occurred roughly halfway through Hi-Fi's fire-breathing set, and the torrent of water that cascaded from the ceiling shorted out the instruments and equipment while simultaneously dealing each of the band members a serious electrical shock. The show was immediately stopped and the curtain brought down before the anxious, aroused crowd was fully aware of what had happened. The result was sheer pandemonium, the model for all "Deli Rock Riots" that were to follow. Without stopping to think, the maddened throng rushed the stage, where the club's security forces, led by Jed Solowicz, an ex-Hell's Angel, were overwhelmed, ultimately being driven back into the ladies' lounge, where some of them were beaten to the ground. Meanwhile, from across the street, hundreds of the disappointed fans who had been turned away from the sellout performance now streamed through Cheaters' unattended front doors, adding to the chaos.

Who was in control?
Bedlam reigned.

What happened after the evening was over?
The members of the band later recalled the days and weeks that followed as an "unreal" blur, as they suddenly found themselves at the center of a growing storm, with Jay's off-the-cuff remark to a reporter that the band was "more popular than Reagan, now" only adding to the controversy. Hysterically denounced by the mainstream press but increasingly popular among many young people, Dave and Jay finally were obligated to call a press conference, at which Jay, with his winning blend of mockery and innocence, pledged "to try not to destroy anything." Somewhat sated, the media eased off on its attack, and Agitpop Records, a small but nationally distributed label which had halted negotiations with the band at the height of the furor, signed Hi-Fi to a two-record deal. Dave and Michael were able to quit their jobs as bulb-counters for a company that maintained theater marquees, and Jay closed Zounds as a commercial studio, devoting its facilities entirely to the band. Soon the controversy had been completely forgotten, and with no enemies in sight, Dave, Jay, Michael and

Richard guardedly released *GOYIM*. The rest, as they say, is history.

What sort of pattern or order could be detected in the band's subsequent career?

After the success of *GOYIM*, and the move to Cronus, the band released *Crossing the Sea* (1982), which reached number one and spawned the monster hit, "Peculiar and Strange (Walkin' through the City)"; *World of Light* (1983), which topped the charts for six weeks on the strength of the number one "Ghost Talk (Hearing Things)"; *Cora in Hell* (1984), a change-of-pace album greeted enthusiastically by critics and fans alike, which embraced a mellow sound exemplified by such megahits as "Hate to Leave Home, Girl"; *Ice Palace* (1985), the multiplatinum return to the band's earlier hard-edged sound, which featured the record-breaking chart-topper "Innocent and Extremely Dangerous"; *Synthetic Wax* (1986), an early experiment in sampling the work of others, which despite critical acclaim, sold poorly, although one song, "People Are Talking," entered the Top Ten; *Mean Bloody Things* (1987), a curious critical and commercial failure consisting of twelve variations on the same song, "Stab"; the resurgent *Oracle* (1988), which again established Hi-Fi as a force to be reckoned with, yielding the number one "I Only Hurt the Ones I Love"; *Blues Landscape* (1989), a relaxed, affectionate look at rock and roll's roots, which featured "Can't Concentrate with You Around"; and the band's magnum opus, the magnificent triple-album *Triad* (1990), which was divided into three distinct parts: "The Uncanny," "Props," and "Livelong Day." *Triad* was heralded as the dawning of a new "golden age" in rock and roll, although the competition has yet to rise to Hi-Fi's level of accomplishment, and the album gave birth to no less than *nine* Top Ten hits: "Give It Up," "The Words in My Head," "Dumb Thoughts (Welcome to McBrain)," "Scared Every Day (The *New York Post* Song)," "Take It Easy—Give It Hard," "That Hurts Too," "I Like to Watch," "Don't Listen to Them," and "Lemme Out!"

In addition to these accomplishments, Hi-Fi starred in two feature films, Sy Hathaway's award-winning documentary *Lonely in a Crowd*, which examines the rigors of touring, and Jim McKinley's offbeat *Firewalkers*, in which each of the boys plays one facet of a multiple personality. Dave, Jay, Michael, and Richard have each tried their hand at solo recording with varying degrees of success, notably with Dave's *A Fool of Myself* (1988), Richard's *No Worries Religion* (1987), Jay's *Don't Rush Me—I'm Almost Out* (1989), and Michael's *Conceited Fella* (1988). However, rather than squander their energies on their separate hobbies and interests, the members of the band usually unite around a common purpose and, like brothers, close ranks against outsiders.

Hi-Fi is now enshrined in our culture, having raised rock and roll to the level of high art. They are so firmly embedded in the landscape that there is a sense with them, as with religion, that they have always been what they are to us today, and that they always will be. There are, of course, the smirking Cassandras who would have it that Hi-Fi will one day seem quaintly archaic, outmoded, obsolete. Fortunately, millions ignore these dishonest cultural policemen, recognizing that Hi-Fi truly stands apart from the crowd. Hi-Fi—now and forever.

What about Nat's getting thrown out?

Although it is against our policy to comment publicly about ongoing litigation, it is our position that Mr. Spielvogel's allegations are baseless and without merit.

Are you telling the truth?
Interview's over.

Where Are They Now?

Hi-Fi is preparing to release its new album, tentatively entitled *Lambs to the Slaughter*. Nathanael Spielvogel is a security guard in Hawaii, a beloved counselor at Christian summer camps, and a sometime autograph seeker. Don McOral was arrested for cocaine smuggling and subsequently entered the Federal Witness Protection Program. Mona Barron's autobiography, *Nightclub Goddess*, is currently number five on the *New York Times* Best-Seller List. Paul Marzio has changed his name to Paul Marshall and is a member of a paramilitary sect in western Idaho. Maureen Ferret is involved with the Color Xerography Collective. Miles Miller is a spokesman for World of Our Friends (WOOF), an animal rights organization. Jed Solowicz died from head injuries sustained when he was thrown down a flight of stairs during a bar fight in November 1988. I am married to Dave McCall and am press agent and occasional backing vocalist for Hi-Fi. Mimi Miller is a graduate student studying commodity aesthetics at Reed College. Sean

Dennis is now "God of Currency," a metamorphosis which he claims to have undergone after his abduction by extraterrestrials. Susan Dennis is a librarian in Bedford Falls, New York. Cheaters renamed itself Floodgates, the Barn, and Ludäche Coalworks before finally closing its doors. The old building that housed it now contains luxury condominiums. Got a smoke?

We've been talking about Depression Strip, Ten-Year Plan, the End, and some other bands. What about Hi-Fi? When was the first time that you saw them?

It gets me very angry and depressed the way so many people have been coming round lately, trying to paste their own prejudices and preconceptions over all this ancient history. You'd be surprised how many silly, ignorant things I've heard and read recently about this, about something I certainly know all about, and I decided to go public because I think it's my responsibility to set the record straight. I'm not a hothead, but I cannot afford to worry about other people's hurt feelings in this respect. I'm very disappointed by the way people have been distorting all of this, so even though I'm a very private person and am reluctant to discuss myself and my private life, I'm once and for all going to try to bring all this out into the open. That was a very special and unique time and place—lightning doesn't strike twice, as they say. Obviously it's in the best interests of the people in control for them to sow a lot of confusion, keep everybody guessing.

Who is "in control"?

If you don't know, I needn't explain it to you. It should be quite obvious, with all of their little smoke-and-mirrors tricks, the way they try to keep everybody in the dark about things. The fine hand of Supreme Authority is everywhere apparent. I'm right and I'll be proven right. Now, where were we?

Hi-Fi . . . ?

Right. Miles and I had got to know Girl at the University of the Streets. We had introduced her to the work of Debord and the concepts of *détournement*, which we were then applying to our work with the Art Redistribution Project. Girl seemed to be a nice enough person, a little bit shaky. All of her plans were vaguely artistic in some way, but very safe. She was interested in photography, for example, but she felt that it would be perfectly acceptable to work commercially. We tried to persuade her that she was making a mistake, but this only caused her to give up on the idea. I remember her as being very man-dependent, in a bourgeois sort of way. The sex was permissible as long as it was preceded by a night of dancing, a taxi ride home. You know what I'm saying. She was very shocked when she found out about Miles and me. Incest was remarkably disturbing to her, just as she found it equally disturbing that Miles had quit Harvard after a year, that I'd lived with a Sandinista officer. But that was simply the way she'd been brought up to think. It was all deeply subversive to her and, I think, a bit exciting as well. Actually, I think that this glint of pliancy in her nature was the only reason that we tolerated her. In any case, Miles and I had just authored an essay, "Rock and Roll: Oppression and Its Asexual Progeneration." It was a candid, insightful piece, not a little cynical, which examined rock and roll's perpetuation of its own mythical stature as the embodiment of rebellion, even as it became a multibillion dollar industry. Needless to say, the members of the so-called leftist press wouldn't touch it, since they ignorantly insisted that this musical form of prostitution would one day flower for them. It created quite a storm just by circulating in manuscript. At any rate, we were just about to shelve it, rather than go on beating a dead horse, when Girl walked in with all of her romantic palaver about a "punk" band that she knew; their songs of revolt and all that. She even thought that it was somehow fashionable that the bassist, with whom she was involved in a sex affair, would regularly beat her and force her to engage in sado-masochistic acts. Of course, when it came down to it, she admitted that her friends' goal was to sign a contract with a multinational communications conglomerate, to amass capital and to indulge in commodity fetishism of the most spectacular kind. When she asked our advice, as "real revolutionaries," as to the best way that her friends could achieve their degraded goals within the framework of their meretricious brand of radicalism, some of our number were in favour of expelling her, even of doing away with her. But Miles seized upon the idea of co-opting her in her ignorance, turning her means to our own ends. "Unless we are all prepared to accept the twin concepts of uncertainty and fear that govern the lives of the bourgeoisie, to believe in a future over which we have no control, to believe that we have been placed in situations guided by others, then we cannot pass up this opportunity!" It was inspiring. For the first time in a while I felt as if I cared about something. Despite what Miles had said, we had all felt as if we'd been drifting of late. The climate had changed from one of bemused tolerance of our existence and purpose to one of outright hostility. Difficulties and obstacles were piling up. The baying apologists of the left were shamefully preoccupied with appeasing the forces of repression and tyranny, and the fascist Reagan was about to take office. Miles moved each of us to childlike wonder, and to righteous anger. We all knew that we could still do things of great benefit to the world, and that it wouldn't be a matter of walking on water. Although, for the sake of formality, we agreed to sleep on the matter, I think we'd all decided individually that Miles had spoken the truth. The next few days we were all very busy as we met to forge a consensus about what we were going to do. Miles and I had some trouble swallowing the absurd, careerist "ideas" of some of our then-associates, who seemed to embrace the goal of parlaying our manipulation of the band into a source of cash. These so-called experts were swiftly excluded, and as the matrix reductively evolved to contain me, Miles, Mona Barron, Don McOral, Jed Solowicz, and the unwitting Girl, a sense of serenity descended upon me. I freely shared in the exchange of ideas, shedding my customary reticence. We had all taken on a tremendous amount of work, but it was worth it to beat the manufacturers of spectacular diversion at their own game! We chose Inauguration Day as the date on which we would make our debut. A Prohibition-era night-club was our theme—decadent fun, even as the world is hammered into its complacent grave. We then cast ourselves in different rôles. I was to be the cigarette girl, Miles the officious portrait photographer, Don the evil owner, Mona the ebullient chanteuse, and Jed the hulking, truncheon-carrying bouncer. Girl and her friends would play rôles as well, of course, but we chose not to share these with them. Then we began to decorate our nightclub. Each of the tables was set under a canopy designed to resemble a shanty. The wall behind the stage was painted in a startling trompe l'œil fashion to depict marble, chrome, brand-name motifs, electronic gimmicks, all radiating outward from the mouthpiece of a gigantic radio-era microphone. Newspapers were pasted onto the walls, and slogans painted over them: FEEL SHAME IN THE FACE OF OTHERS' OSTENTATION, YOU ARE THE PRODUCT SOLD BY POPULAR CULTURE, A "GREAT MAN" 'S OBITUARY IS JUST ANOTHER PRESS RELEASE, THAT WHICH WE CALL CULTURE BY ANY OTHER NAME

WOULD SMELL AS PUTRID, and many, many others. Objects we'd gathered were hung on the walls as well, a pair of skis were crossed with a gleaming scythe, an old air-hockey game protruded from a gigantic coffee can in which we'd also placed a large hose, painted to look like a drinking straw. All that our little creation needed was a name. We finally decided on "Cheaters," which we slathered across the window of the storefront in lurid, fluorescent paint, forming the letters with care and precision but allowing the paint to run in rivulets down the length of the window and to gather in a pool on the floor.

Was there any pattern or order to all of this?

It was necessary for us to create a specific atmosphere. The "nightclub" was purposefully decorated in an odd, incongruent manner; elements of false need and squalid exigency placed jarringly side by side. Our plan was to redo the auditorium of the University as a sort of cell in which the effluvium of the dominant capital-culture would be trapped; and thus stand revealed in all of its rancid glory. Finally, when we had finished, we instructed Girl to bring her band to see us. We were nearly shattered when we realised the extent to which they carried the sickness as well. They existed within a hierarchical order, subscribing fully to the onerous concept of specialisation. They spoke of things in terms of sin and redemption, disappointment and satisfaction, leaders and followers. We asked them to play for us, couching it within the terms of the only degraded language they could respond to, I believe we said that we wanted to see them "at work." Their songs consisted of a stereotypical litany of misogyny, impatience, and teenage angst. We were quite dismayed; it seemed as if there were no way we could use this pedestrian chaff. But we realised that their rejection of the vanguard was their strength. Like Girl, they were pliant and eager, and Miles had an epiphany—we had merely to present them as they were. Surely their lifeless, amplified clichés would be interpreted as a sublime manifestation of irony. We "agreed" to let them perform on Inauguration Night.

What happened the night that Hi-Fi performed at "Cheaters"?

Miles and I were rather nervous and upset. Earlier in the day we had found, to our embarrassment, that Girl, who had now become like one of the family, had informed the media of our performance. I had thought that she had come to understand our methods, but it seemed that she still clung to her conventional notion of publicity as a means of dissemination. I tried to explain to her that this was not a "fishing expedition" in any sense; that it was an organic undertaking oriented toward a complete break from the core of "event," as we had been trained to understand the concept. I took her out for a hamburger to do this, I thought that it might settle my stomach. The idea of the plasticene spokes-whores of the media raking my ears with their crooning, revisionist interpretations made me nauseous. At the coffee shop, Girl presented me with the T-shirts she had fashioned for the band, per Miles's specifications. They depicted Saturn, emblematic of those who would devour their young; a lighted tower, signifying the inaccessible spires in which decisions governing our existence are made; a bat, symbolic of all bloodsucking parasites; and a jagged arrow pointed toward the groin, the true locus of tawdry sentiment. She had done them perfectly, and I forgave her her cheap tabloid dreams. If she had sought succour in the scaly tentacles of Liz Smith and Suzy, within the fashionable pages of the exponents of "redemptive" literature, like the atrocious Hofner, she would soon no longer need to. How could she know? I realised this when we took a walk after the meal, and she insisted on traveling down streets that she had been on hundreds of times before, claiming that it made her feel secure to walk within the confines of the psychogeographical box that had been plotted out for her decades before her birth. This too would break apart, its shards the redirected energies of those trapped within it. The day seemed full of possibilities. When we got back to the University, Miles had had another insightful idea. He had removed the public address system from the stage—the band's prosaic grievances would be stifled beneath the droning, futile technology to which they were enslaved. Unfortunately, he had not counted upon the sheer atavistic willfulness of the band's leader. In fact, it looked for a moment as if it might come to violence. We're fully prepared to treat people roughly, if necessary.

You're talking about the band getting thrown out?

We considered it. Jed, in fact, was aching to put into praxis the "abstract authoritarianism," as he put it, that he represented. However, since the band's performance served as the cornerstone of our presentation, we simply pretended to be amused by their repulsive sense of entitlement. I led them to the locked room in which Miles had hidden the equipment and in the end they were reduced to unleashing a torrent of scatological insults, with which they presumed to shock and intimidate us. Their failure to do so was absolute, but it was nevertheless an unpleasant experience. Still, it added to the aura of tension and in order to preserve it we began to provoke them in any way that we could: toying with the equipment in which they took such proprietary satisfaction; tousling their hair; I sat in one's lap and whispered suggestive words into his ear while staring at another, and then suddenly slapped his face; Miles repeatedly popped his flashbulb in their eyes. When I presented them with the T-shirts Girl had made, one of them stayed behind and attempted to entertain me with a vulgar anecdote. It had something to do with "tits." Failing to impress me with this, he stripped to the waist, ostensibly to try on the T-shirt. I couldn't help but start laughing. He implored me to take him seriously, told me that he read the newspapers and enjoyed attending lectures on serious subjects. I silently marveled at this. All of that corrupted knowledge, all of those false needs articulated with such muscular righteousness in song, pivoting around an immense blockaded wellspring of sexual energy. I augmented my genuine mirth with feigned laughter, and he predictably reverted to form, calling me a "cunt-licking dyke," which is so completely off the mark that I went into hysterics: I am attracted by members of the opposite sex. I left him to his confusion. Soon, they were seething with rage. After we had all dressed—I wore a skimpy, backless outfit and carried a huge tray filled with plastic skulls, Miles had on a used sharkskin suit, fedora, empty eyeglass frames, and he carried an ancient Speed Graphic reflex camera we'd found somewhere, Mona wore a gold lamé dress with matching pumps and purse, and Don and Jed dressed in formal attire, white jackets and all the rest, although only Don wore spats—we came out and discovered that the band was making a show in itself of busily assembling its equipment onstage. This was worrisome; Miles and I realised that their pretentious veneer of professionalism was readily apparent. Fortunately, only a few people had arrived, mostly associates of the band who were anxious for a "free show" and rapt before this display of manly business. Still, it was necessary to take corrective action before others began to gather, particularly the unwelcome members of the press who would take heart at the sight of something so reassuring and familiar as the band's dignified, choreographed preparations, their laconic and deliberate communications with one another. We began to bring them beer, in order to break down their repressive poise into pure elements of impulse and reactivity. By the time that they took the stage, they could barely walk. Even before they came on they had become the center of attention, although not in the way they had intended. It was like having a pack of wild animals on the outskirts of a primitive settlement. Miles was going from table to table, snapping photographs of the people beneath the shabby canopies. In many of them the members of the band and their entourage can be seen in the background striking each other, throwing things, stuffing food into their mouths, and setting napkins on fire. When Mona opened the show, they created a disturbance which all but drowned out her recitation of the "Bubba Song," a kind of sound poem. Its augmentation by the ambient noise did the song justice, filling the edentulous newsmen with the dread and loathing that they might otherwise have shunted aside in favour of ignorant ridicule of Mona's performance. Now there was no turning back, for any of us. We wanted blood to run from the walls!

Are you kidding?
I have strong political opinions.

Did anything significant happen after Hi-Fi began to play?
They staggered onstage, mumbled a few incoherent remarks to the audience, and then began tuning up their instruments. Sensing that they were still clinging to vestiges of expertise, Mona and Don began wildly applauding, while Miles and I tossed handfuls of the plastic skulls I still carried onto the stage. This added to their already considerable disorientation, and they all began to play, although not at the same time, and two of them began braying into the microphones. The effect was to send chills down my spine. The members of the audience who were part of the band's entourage were booing and following our example by throwing glasses, bottles, coasters, ashtrays, bits of the shanties, and other debris at the band and then at the other tables. Those who had come at our invitation joined in the destruction as well, adding to the types of items being thrown paperback books, sexual paraphernalia, playing cards, shoes, religious icons, and newspapers. The pusillanimous colporteurs of information hadn't counted on this, and they attempted to leave, but Jed blocked their exit—the truncheon was quite real—and they were obligated to remain cowering in

their shanties, looking about furtively as if some imaginary saviour were coming to rescue them.

What happened after the performance was over?

The band had stopped playing in the middle of that first song and begun to argue amongst themselves on the stage, all the while being pelted with the flying debris. The drummer and bassist were most vehemently at odds with one another, and the other two stayed off to the side, hands on their hips, watching. The drummer cemented what he evidently felt was his epigrammatic preeminence by telling the bassist that he'd prefer to work with "girls"; at which point the bassist struck the drums with his instrument, dropping it and racing from the stage when the other rose, in appropriately threatening posture: another ritual male superiority spectacle. After that, the spell was broken, I'm afraid. There was something almost tranquilising about watching these two loutish boys rolling about on the floor. We attempted to salvage the evening, to reclaim the stage and the attention of the audience, but it was a lost cause. The gladiatorial combat riveted even our friends, and the genuine uneasiness of the press was replaced by a sense of haughty disgust. Sure enough, the stories that appeared later were arrogantly dismissive: "OUTLAW" ROCKERS ON OUTS, CHEATERS CHEATS AUDIENCE, NOSES ONLY THINGS BROKEN IN "BARRIER-SHATTERING" EVENT. Girl had obviously been accurate, if simplistic, in her press releases. And that was about the end of it; of the movement, of everything. There was chaos and then there was recuperation, but for one instant there had been a glimpse of something new and naked. In ten years I haven't seen anything like it, but I can wait. In the meantime, this story must be preserved truthfully.

Where Are They Now?

Jay Lustig is an independent television producer and the creative force behind such programs as *Daddy Mac*, which chronicles the adventures of a kindly, wise fast-food franchise owner in the inner city. Dave McCall is an asbestos-removal worker. Nat Phenomenon is a first-term member of the California State Assembly. Richard Poindexter died of complications arising from AIDS in 1990. Hi-Fi broke up when clubs refused to book them after they had earned a reputation as the "Guest List Kings." Don McOral was killed in a freak automobile accident in Yellow Springs, Ohio, in September 1984. Mona Barron grants interviews for a fee. Paul Marzio works as an office temporary in San Francisco. Maureen Ferret drives a BMW and owns a home. Miles Miller is an account representative for NYNEX. Jed Solowicz manages a Seattle-based limited partnership that purchases and restores Victorian homes for resale. Girl Bovary teaches computer-aided drafting at a technical college in New York City. I help ordinary women achieve their maximum potential for fitness, beauty, and health. Susan Dennis believes that God communicates directly with her via the television game show *Cheaters' Club*, which coincidentally is produced by Jay Lustig. Sean Dennis collects and sells political memorabilia. Cheaters was dismantled the day after the performance, and the University of the Streets closed in 1983 after being evicted from its storefront location, which is now the site of Los Tramposos, a fashionable Salvadoran bistro. Tall women tell tall tales.

We've been talking about Iron Fingers, Shaggy Dog, the Image, and some other bands. What about Hi-Fi? When was the first time that you saw them?

The egg didn't break when I flipped it or after when I lifted it from the skillet to slide onto the bacon, on the bread. Hands shaking from coffee after coffee at Homer's all night long and into the daylight; a fucking miracle. "It's school again tomorrow, Jay," I kept saying it but I didn't really care: I liked sitting alone with him on the same side of the booth, his arm around me while he ate a Cheeseburger Deluxe and then breakfast. Something about coffee shops; big horseshoe counter, kitchen hidden behind a huge aluminum cabinet filled with dishes and glasses, ready orders waiting on top. Jay showed me how the waitresses walk slowly, sensibly, joining cup and saucer only an instant before placing it in front of you. Wonderful, he said, to eat food you neither wanted nor were able to duplicate at home. Runny eggs, dotted with yellow grease, three friable strips of bacon joined at the edges, shapeless hunks of potato shot through with soggy onion and minute particles of green pepper, all served on a cracked ovoid platter with an undertoasted English on the side. Ice cold pats of golden butter. He started to tell me about the band then but stopped to laugh at the way I ate. I slid my bagel over to him, stuck with coffee. It turned a pleasant golden color with cream. He started telling me about the band again back at my house while I made him a sandwich. Fame. Fortune. Fucking. Food. It was what he wanted. I could help him a little. He stopped again to warn me not to break the yolk. A stupid way to have it, I thought, the golden fluid exploding into his mouth. "Please tell me about the band," I said to his ass while he looked through the refrigerator. I wanted him to fuck me. He ate the sandwich hungrily, wiping his hands on his pants legs. I tried to get him to tell me more about the band, watching his jaws working, but it didn't matter, I only wanted to excite him, be interesting for him, to envelop everything he touched and was aware of, by listening to or feeding or opening myself to him. I took him into my bedroom. The golden sunlight tracked the wall. I watched it while he moved over me. In the afternoon when we got up and walked through the street together I felt vibrant and warm even in the stinging cold, the new love was organic and had grown out of my own abiding hunger, just as all things rose wild from within the grain of his. Paralyzed emotions roused to excited fluttering as he talked to me, walking the quiet blocks toward the river, golden sun burning red over New Jersey, telling me of the covenant that existed between coffee shop patron and coffee shop, a breach of which he took very seriously indeed. Dunkin' Donuts on Kings Highway had perpetrated such a violation, serving in place of the large stale hunks of French bread he had expected with his soup two cellophane packets of saltines. He bought a hot dog from a vendor on the pier and ate it as the sun went down, its last rays catching in his hair and affecting it with a golden nimbus. He had saved his crackers, he said, until he had eaten half the soup, then had crumbled them methodically into the bowl, wiping the crumbs from his hands into the bowl, and churned the soup with his spoon until it achieved a pulpy consistency. The sun disappeared, and I felt we were caught in an attenuated penumbral zone between the golden meaninglessness of the city and the darkness beyond it. It was temporary of course. The band. I loved him, but the band. When I met them I realized the extent to which I was gambling with Jay. Their secret language divided us, always. I struggled to understand the way in which he would melt golden cheeses into his corned beef hash, he was happy with their candy bars. I conceded the point to them, brought candy bars to their rehearsals for him. He would eat them, silent but for his chewing. The jaws working. When we were alone it was bliss, for me. We would walk from Prince Street to Canal, I was completely lacking in my habitual paranoia or even prudent self-consciousness as I threw my arms around him, stuffing my hands into the pockets of his jacket, his jeans, feeling with delight the empty wrappers there, moving my fingers into any interstices and freeing the crumbly edible things wedged in them, disengaging myself only to allow him to handle the battered telephones, car stereos, and circuit boards piled in the sidewalk bins. Sometimes we would turn down Mott and on one of its jagged shifts we would descend a flight of stairs, the shadows traveling up our bodies as we moved, to find ourselves in the vestibule of a restaurant, golden carcasses hung in the windows flanking us, and he would peer at the menu while pulling his cash from the chaos of wrappers, slips of paper, and keys in his pocket. I would usually pay. I would pay for anything, for him. Inside, I would pass my untouched food to him. He would explain the various sauces, their traditional uses and his particular preferences. I would amuse him by picking at things with my chopsticks, while he worked expertly with knife and fork. "The band is doing good," he would say. "The band sucked today," he would say. I endured the band for him, because I could endure nothing without him. I suddenly began to enjoy attending parties. The electricity of the crowd was stimulating and in some way at a remove from the serenity and calm I felt, leaving him near the chips, circulating. All of my worries would disappear. The stasis and decay I saw written plain on the everyday faces of my friends, his friends, wiped clean and drawn again in bright party colors. I couldn't make fun of them, though. Looking at Jay, elbow deep in the punch bowl, I ached for them and their lack of what I had. Nat and Girl standing talking, her coolly lovely in a golden summer dress, bathed in the kitchen fluorescence, smiling at him over the lipstick-stained rim of her Styrofoam cup, him somber in his greys and browns; both fumbling for the region where flirtation yields to physical contact, lost in thwarted desire; even as Dave and Maureen danced close with one another, caught in the amber of their own decimated past, rhythmically moving over to me—I look quickly at Jay: head back, inverted quart of beer between his lips—"Do you think Nat and Girl want to break up with us?" "Should we mind?" Giggling, evidently satisfied with the conversation because the particular contingency it addressed seemed remote. Richard with Paul Marzio, they smiled into Miles's camera, Paul jokingly flexing his biceps while Richard moved out of the way of his elbow. "I was in . . . a gang," Richard said, for no reason. I have this picture. My brother has it, who sat on a couch, sedate enough as Mimi talked to him, then suddenly shivering, twitching, trying to retract his head between his shoulders. Thorazine. Lost in the golden moments. Later, in my room, I realized that I might as well be living in a cabin in the woods or mountains with Jay, for all I needed the others. The room was mysterious and churchlike as he slept, lamplight streaming from under the crooked shade and spreading across the bluepainted walls, which ended a few inches short of the ceiling, the paint cracking where it had run. His clothes were draped over a chair without him in them, I looked at them, they were his. Maybe I was stupid to think that it could last. Forces were at work, even then. Even though I wasn't privy to all the gossip, I knew that my preemptive candy bars had rankled. Jay had made an attempt to explain the "code" to me, but was unable to evoke it with the same clarity that he brought to bear on culinary matters. To this day I understand only that I broke the code. I have purchased hundreds of records, dozens of books dealing with rock and roll, studied them in an effort to get them to yield their golden secrets. Which are generally consistent: the band is a closed system. The band is married. The balancing of divergent personalities creates a holistic unit, which is exclusive, even as these personalities are shared with the world. Perhaps Jay hadn't wanted me to understand, had actually wanted me *not* to understand, a reflection of my own hopes: that he had loved me too, and needed for *me* to destroy the affair. Jay never choked on what he *needed* to say. His tongue would be clotted with his evasive admonition about the "code," and then he would tell me the truth about pizza: that pizza is not a baroque construct, and is best enjoyed as a simple concoction of bread, tomatoes, and cheese. That Americans in their ignorance—he would gesture toward New Jersey, golden sun burning red—use it as a foundation on which to place *other* things, which they have enjoyed in *other*, perhaps more appropriate, contexts. Sausage, pepperoni, and mushrooms he would allow, although not at once, and he approved of anchovies, although he disliked them himself. But some pizza was harsh and artificial, even the sounds of its various names were alien: *ham* pizza, *barbecue chicken* pizza, *pineapple* pizza. I realize the true extent of loss in my life, as I pour crumbled Oreos over my vanilla yogurt. I stopped going to the rehearsals, just waited at home for him to drop by afterwards. I would sit at the far end of the table, watching him eat, his sleeves rolled up, his eyes on his plate. I could sense some imperceptible alteration taking form, far beneath the exterior he presented. Although the deliberate way in which he consumed the food appeared unchanged, self-absorption was now its raison d'etre. A woman can tell. He offered token comments about the band, unpasteurized beer, other things that might be taken as having some connection with his life, by someone else maybe; not by me. I was in love but in a hurt and angry way, and I began to retaliate, perhaps unconsciously, paring down the elaborate dinners I'd been making until eventually I was serving him soup, or sandwiches. One bleak winter night early in the new year I walked home from Sloan's with dinner—his dinner—in a paper bag. It had begun to snow, huge wet flakes that lingered just on the far side of rain, soaking everything. Golden blotches of lamplight spread across the slick black streets. The Keds I'd put on for the three-block walk up Waverly Place were wet through, and the grocery bag was disintegrating in my hands. When I reached to unlatch the gate in the wrought iron fence separating my building from the sidewalk, the bag tore open as I shifted it in my arms and the groceries spilled onto the ground. Two cans of tuna fish, a loaf of bread, some celery, a box of raisins, a little jar of Hellmann's. I had gathered up the other items before I noticed that the jar had shattered, fragments of the broken glass inlaid in an amoebic blob of mayonnaise. I was standing there, frozen with confusion, the rest of the food piled in my arms, trying to figure out how, or whether, to clean the mess, when I heard Jay: "Sandwiches? *Again?*" I looked up at him, through the screen of falling snow, studying me from the other side of the gate, his arms akimbo, and I noticed what appeared to be a look of disgust cross his face—a slight curl of the lip, the subtlest suggestion of a rolled eyeball—as he watched me. Whatever it was that I believed I had discerned, it passed swiftly and his eyes shifted, inevitably, to the splintered jar and the mayonnaise, running now in viscous, oily rivulets. We watched it silently together for a few moments, and I was still watching it move and form when he said that he was going to Homer's. After he had gone, I went inside the house—*fuck* the mayonnaise—where I discovered with an odd sensation of pleasure that I was chilled to the bone. In my room I changed into dry clothes, tossing my wet things into the bathtub, and then I came out and poured myself a surprisingly large glass of gin. I was not a drinker. Our father, Sean's and mine, was very strict about drugs and alcohol, but he approved of both if their use was, however vaguely, medicinal in nature. As I drank it a facsimile of loving warmth enveloped me, the germ of a bad habit. Actually, I became incredibly drunk. I thought to sit and brood over the future of the

thing, me and Jay, but the sense of calm, behind my eyes, no sense
of time, drifting from one gauzy fantasy to another: concrete eval-
uation was impossible. I set aside my problems, but I couldn't
leave them alone, either, hammered them into pleasing shapes.
Finally, I urinated, a slow spreading in my crotch and thighs. There
was no shame—I bent this infantile cataract to my will as well,
shaping it into agreeable contours: Jay on the threshold of my
room, lit from behind so that his expression and features were
obscured from me, crossing to the bed and lifting me, tenderly,
carrying me to the bathroom and removing the soiled clothes,
wringing them out over the tub so that the golden fluid drizzled
into it, cleaning me gently and then taking me back to bed, joining
me there. I fell asleep, blissful, in my mess; awoke, wretched. I
undressed and showered, wanting to linger in the tub but conscious
of time, hours had passed since Jay had left, he had had hundreds of
thoughts over which I had no control, some of which, probably,
had to do with me. I called his house, there was no answer. By now
he would be with the others, telling them everything, they would
of course advise him to drop me, friendly and concerned advice,
right. When I left the house, I found that it was astonishingly warm
outside. The mayonnaise had congealed in brownish whorls radiating from the pieces of glass, and tiny black flies rose from it as I
passed. Everything was sharp-edged and distinct in the winter sun,
people walked more slowly, their coats open, moving in and out of
cool shadow and the unexpected pockets of golden light reflected
off the melting snow all around, a gentle day, the children in the
schoolyard on Greenwich Avenue played hopscotch and other
warm-weather games, their heavy coats stuffed into the chain link
fence, ignoring the snow lying in bright patches on the asphalt.
There are days, in New York, when everything seems possible, in
whose configurations you can see the lines and angles of a coveted
fate. In simultaneously exploring both them and the depth of your
golden vision you seek a rigorous mathematical precision; try to
get the very names of the things you pass, the adjectives that
qualify them, into your apprehension of them. These you sort and
attempt to reconcile with the millions of other things you've seen
and experienced. Purely associative; happiness has no logic. The
peculiar clarity of the day propelled me forward, to Prince Street,
where I burned like a moth. When I arrived, bearing edible gifts,
Jay was outside standing guard over the equipment. I loved him
so. But his change of heart was immutable, he accepted the food

silently. It was a sandwich, and my little joke fell flat as I watched him devour it. What did I expect? I can only ask that question in retrospect. That he should hold up the half-ovoid of bread, meat, and cheese; admire it, offer a few reassuring and apologetic words, toss it aside to embrace me? The jaws working as he crammed it into his mouth, moving in rhythm to the little steps he took. Fucker. The weather, too, was gone: the temperature was dropping and a stiff wind had come up, taking the snow from the freezing piles at the edges of the sidewalk and blowing it, in swirling gusts, so that it struck me like sleet. I felt drugged. He didn't want me any more, didn't need me. How trite. Not that he said any of this. He said "You're on the guest list" with about the same inflection he would have used if he'd been reading off the license numbers of the cars parked nearby on the street. All around the city reconstructed itself as a crystal of ice, deafening arctic weather emerging from the day's lambent deception. Jay waited, sticking his forefinger inside of his mouth, cleaning the fragments of food from between his teeth and gums. "Well?" he said. "Well, what?" "Aren't you going to apologize for being such a bitch?" Suddenly I saw him as a gigantic, frivolous insect—which I loved. Sucking the greyish mush off his fingers, licking the golden mustard from their tips, fixing his dark eyes on me while he rubbed his forelegs together. A freakish and enduring image. To this day I feel a sense of proprietorship when I see others walking the streets with their strange pets, pigs and snakes, remember Jay manifesting himself as a fly or cockroach, there on Prince Street, for all to see, if only they looked closely enough. But soon enough it had passed, his human form returned, hairy hand rubbing at some grease spot on his down jacket, angry at me now as he began to litanize his complaints: sex with me disgusted him, I was a stupid repressed Catholic school-girl, I was playing with fire, I was useless at parties, around his friends, he went on and on. He belched and I realized how badly I had to pee, so I left him then, telling him that I'd see him uptown later, feeling strangely emotionless, almost analytical in my disturbance. Things break down and end and their energies are scattered and I figured I'd go uptown to see him tonight *just to make sure* so that I wouldn't have the regret of uncertainty piled atop my other regrets. Which I was sure would pass quickly, right, nibbling on the edges of truth when cornered. When I arrived back home Sean was there, in fine fettle. It was a pleasure to see him; if cold logic and calculation were defined by Jay, my sandwich in his stomach and cruel words on his lips, I wanted no part of them, would *rather* be around poor Sean. "I am the agent of the Logical God," he announced, hovering outside the bathroom. "Plop, plop, fizz fizz. *If* you were in trouble with several friends who were *equally* to blame, would you rather take the *entire* blame than to give the others away? *And*, if you made a *conscious* decision to do this, based on some concept of morality, would such a decision *diminish* the act, virtuousness-wise? The type of trouble itself is unimportant, here." I told him yes to one and no to the other, mindful of my fizzing. I loved Sean. He made others, including our father, nervous, but he and I enjoyed a strong bond. When we were children he helped me to overcome my shyness, had talked me through many nights in dark, frightening rooms. So we talked now, quietly, first from opposite sides of the bathroom door—he called it "the scene of the crime"—and then together, in the dining room. He was angry for me, and when I tried to play sick, to get out of going uptown to see Jay, he insisted on our going. I felt good, but when I left him to go into the bathroom and get ready a sense of apartness and dislocation swept over me. Order, I thought. Examining the tiles on the walls, the smaller pieces that formed the mosaic on the floor, the angle of the towels hanging from the rods, drawing the shower curtain so that it extended exactly half the length of the tub, studying all the minutiae and their arrangements, anything but the face in the mirror and the room as a whole, which would have admitted of larger things, an entire world, beyond my power. This stopped working, soon enough, each element of the bathroom, seemingly reduced and distilled to its essence, began to stand for something else. Each tile, a meal. Each bottle and jar on the toilet tank, a golden hour with Jay. Better I should look at an apple, its whole and recondite form. So what if working parts lay within? Smooth and round and firm, blemished here and there, but an apple. Outside, I heard Sean banging into the walls, nervous and tense for me. I hurriedly put on my makeup, slipped into the golden dress I'd bought one day with Jay on Orchard Street. Sean waited by the door while I put my things in my purse, and we left. It had grown bitter cold outside, Sean stood on the sidewalk as I locked the door and shut the gate behind us. The picket I grasped to pull it to was ice. On Sixth Avenue we tried to hail a cab, but none would stop for us, so we took the subway. The station was equally cold, and nearly empty, and I watched my breath, standing near the edge of the platform, my weight resting on my left leg, the toe of my right shoe extending slightly over the edge. Sean leaned against a stanchion, facing me, one leg bent at the knee and the other thrust out at an angle designed to compensate and keep him on balance. "You're looking off into a future that seems populous with unknowns," he said. Somebody walked by, smirking, and Sean said, "Fuckin cold, hah?" The man laughed as he passed Sean, who looked back at me. "Christ turned water into wine via rhetorical means. It was a trick: his gift to us. In seven loaves he envisioned soup kitchens, a future of vast poverty, physical and spiritual. As a thing shows its scaffolding, we may hold it in contempt or exalt it to a pinnacle of harmlessness. 'Prescience' is an educated sorting from amongst a finite number of variables. My gift. To you. Limit your variables. Select." He was quiet for a moment, staring at something near my protruding toe. "Don't worry about . . . the Eater." Sean's sermon was mercifully cut short by the arrival of the train, but this deus ex machina did nothing to alleviate my need to make sense of what he had said. We both drew back from the edge of the platform as the train sped into the station, raising hot metallic wind in its wake. We boarded and sat down, and I thought of Jay, engulfing everything, with his corresponding need to eliminate, a bulimic mechanism, nourishment and sustenance exiting along with rank waste. Is that what he meant when he called me a "pile of shit"? Or anything? An old Jamaican woman began to yell as the doors closed and the train entered the tunnel, its din swallowing hers. I thought of myself, layers of numbing routine, stupefying lists of flaws and weaknesses, torrents of malicious opinion, raw voices raised in strident opposition to "the facts," experiences sullied by the interpolations of memory. To eliminate all this, start fresh—bright party colors—? Sean's oblique, untenable wisdom had, indeed, reached its mark. Closing the windows could serve the same purpose as razing the surrounding neighborhood. Jay! God, even the silhouette of that name, hook-shaped, drawing everything toward him. I was borne uptown, his cud. We arrived late to find Maureen, Miles, and Richard Poindexter lingering together in a doorway a little down the block from the club. Maureen seemed slightly uncomfortable about our having seen them together, made nervous conversation, but Miles ignored us except to make a point of caressing her thighs and breasts, rubbing his face in her hair, as she squirmed, grabbing his hands, trying to stop him. Richard laughed at this spectacle, encouraging Miles to continue. Slimy bastard. I asked him why he wasn't inside and he replied that he'd been thrown out, "Thanks to her," as he said this he reached out with his thumb and forefinger and tweaked Maureen's erect nipple, visible through her brassiere and blouse, so that she raised her hand from where it had been occupied fending off Miles to swat at him, enabling Miles to lift her skirt and grab at her crotch. I could hear the band from where I stood, jumping through hoops for Jay. On Maureen's guilty face I saw the map of forecast misery. We left them to go inside, gave my name to the man at the door. Of course Jay had "forgotten" to put down a plus-one, so Sean and I split the $2.00 between us. I had to pee, so I went to the bathroom. There was a tiny trace of blood in my urine. I felt very bad. I had come—for what? Even that was obscure now. Fragments of a broken mirror lay on the tile floor. Shattered. I thought of praying, but could only imitate Sean. When I came out of the bathroom, Sean was waiting for me. We walked down the aisle leading toward the stage together, greeting friends in passing. Jay leered at me as we approached, and as we seated ourselves at one of the tables in the front he said, into the microphone, "Well, if it isn't the slut and the nut." Dave broke into hysterics, and the drummer, some stranger who looked as if he belonged on 8th Street, did a little flourish. Nat didn't respond, staring into the audience, the anguish and desperation thick off him. *I* knew what he was looking for. Mimi shook her head: "What a scumbag." "Who?" I asked. "Jay?" He kept walking in little circles on the stage, glancing at me, smirking. He was up to something. Or maybe I saw him plain, for once, there had always been some morsel between us, and now I saw centered in all of those nervous mannerisms, the way he held the microphone in one hand and ran the fingers of the other along the length of cord trailing from it, energies with unclear sources, more accustomed to exhausting their potential in the assault on some mundane provender. Preferably prepared by my loving hands. The jaws, working. "No, not—" Just then Jay turned suddenly and punched Nat in the shoulder forcefully enough to cause him to stagger. "Hang onto your grief and troubles, Natula! This one's for all our loving help-meets out there!" A slight ripple of laughter passed through the audience. "Oh, God, I hate this one," said Girl, rolling her eyes and drumming her fingers on the tabletop. Jay belched as he counted off the song, "Now I'm Laughin' at You, Girl." I hoped my sandwich was iron in his stomach. I thought it was poetry once, to listen to him speak and sing, the sounds and shapes of the words only lightly burdened by the information they carried. Now they bowed under the weight of it: a message of hate. "Read in the Bible that the future's pretty bleak/you cut my hair off cause you thought to make me weak/one of your miscalculations/you made me go and lose my patience!" All that I had truly believed in, since answering his ad in the *Voice*, had been him, and now he turned it against me. His behavior onstage had become manic, frightening, he jounced violently back and forth, banging again and again into Nat, working his way to the corner of the stage where Dave stood and pulling at his guitar strap until Dave kicked at him, his eyes shone brightly as he sang the lyric and then he turned toward our table, looking directly at me and pointing as he sang the idiot chorus, "Now I'm laughin' at you girl. *Now* I'm laughin' at you, girl. *Now* I'm laughin' at *you*, girl. Now I'm *laughin'* at you, *Girl!*" Dave began to play, tortured sustained notes emerging from the amplifier—I suddenly realized that the solo was a reworking of "Pop Goes the Weasel"—"Asshole!" said Mimi, Jay held the mike by its cord and began to swing it in a circle over his head, feeding the circle from the slack length of cord he held so that it grew and grew, until it was passing dangerously close to my head, and as Dave played the final "Pop!" I purposely leaned into the path of the microphone, allowing it to strike my right cheek. A loud thump, slightly reverberant, could be heard throughout the club and the taut length of cord suddenly slackened into several undulant waves as the microphone fell into my lap and then to the floor. I leaned back in my chair and closed my eyes, slowly raised my hand to my cheek to feel the tender swelling and then dropped the hand back into my lap. I said, "Oh," and then the tears began to run down my face. I sobbed softly at first and then more strongly until finally I was shaking, my head in my hands, wave after seismic wave of pain cresting and flattening and receding and I became aware of a flashing white light outside of myself; I opened my eyes to peer through my fingers and I saw Miles kneeling on the floor beside me, photographing me. "This is great," he said. "Jesus, *everybody's* crying tonight!" "You really are an asshole, Miles!" said Mimi. Sean was shielding his eyes with his hand, blinking rapidly and uncontrollably, and as he rose to approach the stage Miles slipped behind him to take his seat. "Saw what happened, Suze," he said, shaking me by the shoulder. "you should pay attention, not be so careless. Rock and roll's a contact sport now." He removed the roll of film from his camera and put it in a black container, which he slipped into his shirt pocket. Patting the pocket, he smirked at

me. "For my private collection of heartwarming memories."
"Prick," said Mimi. She grabbed my hand. "Come on, let's get you
cleaned up." As we began to walk back up the aisle I heard Jay:
"A request? A *request?* The Stutter King has a request, everybody!" I turned to see Sean submitting to the indignity of being
patted—slapped, actually—on the head by Jay. "We *all* wish you
were someone else, jerk." When we entered the bathroom's tiny
space we found Maureen brushing her hair before the mirror over
the sink. She looked at our images in the glass. "God, I hate this
one." Nat was singing. "Where've you been, Mo?" Mimi asked. I
said nothing. "Your brother *already* thinks he owns me. I'm going
to have to lay my cards on the table with him. With them. With
both of the motherfuckers!" She leaned on her arms against the
sink, head down, and I saw her eerie doubled image: sad Maureen,
shoulders shaking expressively from behind, a portrait of misery;
and her gleeful, cackling face in the mirror. She stood, wiped her
nose. "I'm sorry," she said. "I'm very sorry. *I* do what *I* want.
Nobody has to put up with this kind of crazy shit. Why live out
some stupid, fucking romance novel?" She reached out to touch the
welt on my face. I winced and pulled back, but she did not recoil
from her sudden act. "It's just a stinking hole they want."

After Mimi and Maureen had left me to get a drink or to go to
a club or on some other adventure in the intractable night, abolish-
ing with an insouciance I could not countenance the solid reality
of recent events—as if they were beyond their control, and not
worth reworking, worth dying again and again in the imagination
to emerge from the wellspring of some newness—I sat alone in the
bathroom, rocking on the toilet in the stall, knowing what I was,
and knowing that I was at the center of an island which had once
blossomed with all the feral tangled bounty inherent in the earth.
This stifled old land spoke to me now; to deny its voice from
beneath the strata of metal, glass and concrete would be disingen-
uous. The planet dies in pieces, but all things leave traces of their
greatness for posterity to gape at in awe and wonder . . . there was
silence . . . my face hurt. . . .

The barroom was deserted and a man wiping the tables until
they gave off a golden radiance paused to unlock the door and
expel me into the polar void. I drew my coat tightly around me and
took a few uncertain steps, proceeding with abnormal care along
the icy sidewalk. I noticed a figure sitting motionless on the sidewalk, left leg protruding over the edge of the curb and the other

crossed beneath it, his back to me, and though I suspected it was a vagrant or derelict it filled me with worry. As I passed I saw that it was Nat, he looked into my eyes and unearthly sounds began to come out of his mouth. In the golden illumination of the streetlight I could see that his face was glazed with frozen tears, and as these cracked and began peeling in shreds a new face emerged, in the image of the old, and I knelt, putting my arms around him, we remained that way for a few moments, his sounds had begun to assume the recognizable configurations of words, but I did not hear him. Together we walked to the corner and hailed one of the golden taxicabs. Inside, Nat said sadly, "I'm not one hundred percent." I kissed him, we kissed. Pure gold. Everything working itself out, assuming its proper place without guidance, no need to take a position or draw a line. The world is what I make it. At Seventh Avenue and Perry Street, the taxi suddenly pulled over. "Please get from cab. This it." I looked at the driver's eyes in the rearview mirror. It *was* it, I could see that. No need to approve or disapprove. Another, making his own sense of the insurmountable grid. My house was two blocks away, we paid and walked, passing the fruit stand and its banks and banks of golden oranges.

Where Are They Now?

Jay Lustig has become a prostitute and lives in the vicinity of West and Bethune Streets in New York City. Dave is a leader in the Men's Movement. Nat Phenomenon disappeared on August 29, 1982. Richard Poindexter won the Montana State Lottery and lives in retirement in Bayonne, New Jersey. Hi-Fi, after several personnel changes, became world famous, and then broke up. Don McOral is a copy machine operator, and claims to be working on an "insider" novel. Mona Barron renamed herself Barni Floodgate and makes pornographic movies for a highly specialized market. Paul Marzio is a pyromaniac whose tendencies are frequently exploited by real estate developers. Maureen Ferret died after neglecting to treat what was posthumously diagnosed as alcoholic hepatitis. Miles Miller resides with his mother on West 40th Street and reputedly "takes classes." Jed Solowicz has sixteen letters to the editor, each of which embraces some aspect of conservative philosophy with which he is in agreement, posted on his refrigerator. Girl Bovary is lead vocalist with a local rap group, Kore-Us Grrrlz. Mimi Miller spontaneously combusted on Easter Sunday, 1986. I took the rap for my boyfriend on cocaine smuggling charges and am currently incarcerated at the Women's House of Detention while awaiting trial. Sean Dennis believes that he is being photographed at all times. Cheaters became quite successful, moved to a new and larger location, and was shortly thereafter burned to the ground by a psychotic optometrist. Opinions matter only when they cause pain.

We've been talking about the Simple Expedient, Vertical Madness, the Ruling Class, and some other bands. What about Hi-Fi? When was the first time that you saw them?

It was during one of my sleepless periods. I often go through times during which I feel so full of energy that sleep seems quite unnecessary, often for days at a time, although I wouldn't characterize myself as a highly strung person. I realize, of course, that "highly strung" is, of needs, a comparative expression and as such all but useless now. Except within the framework of empty rhetoric, where words echo familiarly and even assume the guise of meaning without actually having any. Under the circumstances, I am quite highly strung, I would have to say. An old riddle asks, "Who is both best and worst at what he attempts?" The answer being, the first to attempt it. I submit that it is also true for the last person to attempt anything, or to assume a particular state of being, such as high-strungness. I have little doubt, though, that my unique situation would leave some at a total loss. For example, those people who have made it a habit to arrange their lives in such a way that credit for all good that happens accrues to them, but that the blame for errors is shifted to others: they would doubtless go mad, or create phantom scapegoats. Straw men, to knock over, as it were. Many artists were accused of this sort of thing. I believe that it's a matter of perspective. For example, I have always thought that my sense of smell is as good as other people's, that is, average. Despite the fact that I have both the best and worst sense of smell in the world, I still consider myself to have an average sense of smell. On the other hand, a feeling of relief or depression can eliminate any sense of perspective. I am relieved, for example, of any of the burdens attendant upon being passive and reserved since I am quite assertive enough to go unimpeded about my daily business. Passivity such as mine rarely extends to inanimate objects; that is, I never feel as if I have to stick up for my rights with them. Occasionally, I will spend hours mustering the will to tackle what I consider to be an unpleasant task—dirt, for example, frightens and disgusts me.

But I rarely think of myself as being "passive" in the face of dirt. Phobic, perhaps.

Hi-Fi?

A perfect case in point, really. Their willingness and ability to perform in front of large crowds of people fascinated and enraged me. It won them both acclaim and prestige, as well as more tangible rewards, while I was obliged to content myself with a daydream life I never felt the courage even to discuss, let alone act to bring into being. Now, of course, embarrassment and chagrin are alien to me, except, of course, in the case of my problem with dirt. And theirs were problems I do not now have to face—so much had to do with perception, with what others thought of and expected from them. Coiffed, attired, scripted lines gushing from their mealy mouths. Looking at old videotapes of them I am struck by the look of fear on their faces, as if one misstep could bring the whole thing crashing down. It did and it didn't, of course. I have no such worries. If I don't feel like bathing, I don't. My opinions are inevitably deferred to. The other day I called for presidential elections, nominating Lincoln. "The party of Reagan deserves no less!" I argued, at the convention. Lincoln trounced George Washington in the general election and I am at present quite contentedly guiding his presidency. No worries, none of the apprehensions that the mannish women and effeminate men at Little Red Schoolhouse and Elizabeth Irwin had hoped to instill in me for life. Arguably, the stakes were higher for Hi-Fi. Yet I was always made to feel that the very availability of the most ordinary necessities was dependent upon my yielding up of part of myself in exchange. "I thought Lincoln freed the slaves" was a popular expression. Perhaps that's why I favored him. Even if I had had the proper character to defend myself, a quick temper, I would have had to give something up. Jay Lustig was one of the most assertive people I have ever met, and he is dust like the rest. And even if you have been made to believe that you must give your best in order to deserve food, clothing, and shelter you are simultaneously taught that you can do nothing well. And even if you accept the duality that demands that you obsequiously and with great thanks submit that which you have done poorly in order to receive that which you require to continue to do things as poorly as you have been taught you are incapable of doing better than, you must simultaneously pretend to feel tremendous sorrow over your poor offerings. And even if you humbly offer your very worst as tribute to those who would feed you inadequately, clothe you in rags, and house you in a shack so that you may survive another day to err, and make a great show of feeling sorry about the paucity of what you offer, you must simultaneously feel guilt over your failure to sincerely experience the sorrow you display. And if you have rejected all of this, are true to yourself at any cost, you are rejected by members of the opposite sex as surely as if your gonads were coated with disease. They've got you covered. You'll note my judicious use of the second person in this entire respect. *I have no such worries.* I now strongly defend my own opinions, as a rule. And if it were possible for me to be called upon to give an opinion about something I know well, I wouldn't be embarrassed at all, especially since, as I have said, I am most knowledgeable about all subjects. As well as least knowledgeable. And, of course, I do bear that sense of perspective I mentioned in mind.

What happened the night that Hi-Fi performed at Cheaters?

That was a very interesting evening, occurring as it did at a very pivotal moment in history. I say that without irony. What I found interesting about it, interesting perhaps being an understated way of putting it, was the way in which everything was laid bare, or rather stripped to its essence. This may have been my impression alone—although that is of no consequence now—and is of course affected by memory and the passage of time. Although as the evening recedes its events become indistinct and even, theoretically at least, subject to debate—although, of course, my own interpretation is the final one—certain *things* remain constant and thus reinforce my conviction that the evening was pared-down and can perhaps be distilled into a litany of some two dozen or so *objects*. Whether any of these has any deeper import, in a semiotic sense, is something I have not yet developed an opinion about. On the plane of the actual, these objects certainly have import since in a physical sense each of them is related to and had an effect upon the others. For this reason I will decline to give the litany since the relationships would necessarily be obscured by a presentation in that fashion. This is often the case; I recall taking several standardized tests toward the end of my tenure at Elizabeth Irwin that requested one to identify such relationships via analogy, i.e., "Spiders are to flies what . . ." and then the choice you would have been drilled to make would be "bleach is to stains," although even at that time I saw no reason why the correct selection could not be "a gin and tonic mixed in a tall, slender tumbler and garnished with two minuscule wedges of lime is to a look of disgust crossing *someone's* face," although that's probably not the best example.

Are you talking about Nat?

At one point, yes. Although I recall that what tended to cross Nat's face most frequently were blushes. That swerves somewhat far afield, however, having nothing to do with the evening in question. To put it to rest, though, I happen to recall this because it was something that I had in common with Nat, and so Nat was the one I identified with in the daydream existence I have mentioned earlier, although I had no use for this particular trait when I was actually being him, or, rather, thinking about being him. Nat had many salient characteristics for which I had no use. Some of them would have been redundant, such as his fear of contracting disease from doorknobs, and others were merely unattractive, such as his nervousness around certain kinds of livestock. Now, if I so choose, I am free to be Nat at all times, and to jettison not only those aspects of his personality that I do not like but to add those of my own that I do, although there's a question as to whether this would actually constitute an additive process, if that's clear.

Who is in control?

Speaking from a rather narrow standpoint, that is, assuming that what is being referred to are the events as we relate to them today, in their present form, I was, and am, and will be. The future, its pattern and order, seems very bright to me.

What kind of "pattern" and "order"?

The reinhabitation of the world is dependent upon the establishment of cohesive, interlocking sets of complementary data to the exclusion of all other sets of data. To fall back on the analogous way of putting things so dear to my former mentors, a world structured in this fashion will be much like a family that gets along together quite well, which stands in stark contrast to the way that things were before. And, naturally, if the criteria of needs and superfluities are established a priori, then I will be able to truthfully claim, for example, that I no longer blush, whether I am Nat or I am me, although it is unlikely that I would make such a claim since blushing will most probably no longer exist. Along these lines, any desire I may once have had to wear expensive clothing, also for example, will no longer exist since the concept of expensiveness, or even of expense, may no longer exist, may be dispensed with, in a world devoted to harmonious interaction, as unnecessary. I *am* often afraid that I am going to blush; it will be a pleasure when this is no longer possible. Although a paradox does exist: if we are to accept what I have previously mentioned about many of the disagreeable aspects of my personality depending for their very existence upon the perspective of others, then it is possible that my decision to eliminate the existence of such things is equally dependent upon my primacy in the world. One such disagreeable aspect being that people, once, could pretty easily change me even when I thought I had made my mind up on a particular subject, although I suppose that this would logically make this an agreeable aspect. Again, this semantic point is dependent upon the perspective of others.

Are you telling the truth?
I can stand as much pain as others can.

Did anything significant happen after Hi-Fi began to play?
Certain substitutions and absences became apparent. I place the two in different categories although in the case of some of the absences a substitution was quickly, although perhaps not consciously, made. Likewise one could say the same about the endless movements, ending in stillness; the voids inviting occupation, the actions unavoidably resulting in reactions, the causes underlying inevitable effects. Which is why, as I have also explained, I avoid any attempt to characterize the evening in such a manner as the question "Did anything significant happen, etc.?" demands. It tends to give me gas. What I prefer, again, is a pure litany of *things*. I am the last to work on this problem and this is the methodology which I have determined to be most useful. All by itself, the litany would probably make you drool. But you have annoyed me by hurrying me, pressing me on this particular point. I hope that you're enjoying your little scavenger hunt; I know that you're the one who is usually pressed for answers to those monolithic unknowables. *Sartor resartus.* Although I would guess that by all appearances these would not seem to be monolithic questions. On the other hand, sometimes everything depends upon its smaller components. It's a matter of one's perspective, I suppose. Much can depend

upon a black suit jacket, glazed with chalk dust. Or the sight of a new lover's familiar clothing, hanging unoccupied in the closet. Or a tabletop on which sits a cigarette, smoking in an ashtray, beside a gold lamé handbag. Or a note placed on an elegant mahogany sideboard. These are all diminutive things, the mice of ideas, but one's face can become paralyzed just in the attempt to speak of them.

All right, what happened after *the performance?*

Skin, sensitive to the wind. Black, tarry bowel movements. Dreadful premonitions. Chronic fatigue syndrome. Repeated, haunting imagery in dreams. Attempts to lay bare the thin strands of history. Parties, socials. Live sex acts. Avoided responsibilities. Repaired door latches. Paranoid suspicions. Scientific studies. Agoraphobic incidents. Child pornography. Feelings of dissociation. Careful grooming and dressing. Personalized services. Sexual misconduct. Sudden, terrifying, awakenings in the middle of the night. Chronic forgetfulness. Equestrianism. Incestuous desire. Mindless diversion. Deferential behavior. Suicide. Spectatorism.

Where Are They Now?

Everyone and everything on the face of the earth has been dead for the past ten years.

Coda: Playback

Sunday, January 20, 1991

A couple and two solitary drinkers remain in the lounge with Marzio and together the five of them obey the flight attendant's electronic command to return to their seats as the airliner begins its final approach. He descends the spiral staircase with abnormal care, fingers white-knuckled gripping the narrow handrail, the others behind him waiting in various stages of impatience, the rhythm of their steps broken by his painful and overwrought search for purchase. Moving down the narrow aisle between two columns of seatrows, he reaches his seat just as the jet lurches suddenly to port and throws himself into it, gasping, vaguely embarrassed, his chin slightly doubled, cheeks puffed, lips separated. He hurriedly adjusts the equipment that will strap him in. The flight has been a sustained agoraphobic incident, the continent's barren fissures and ridges of all shapes, sizes, and deformities elegant and motionless in the winter sun bespeaking epochal intractability. Now he refuses to look out of the window, stares straight ahead at the geometry of faded color on the headrest before him. The aircraft swoons again —a gentler sensation, here in his seat, but no less nauseating—and he surrenders to morbid desire and turns his head to look briefly through the greasy window, its shade half-pulled against the sun, to see acres and acres of aluminum siding glinting and gleaming in it, brickface affected with a dull sheen. Once more the stewardess demands his attention, he listens (eyes again on pastel squares, triangles, circles) as she advises him that the plane will circle for a half-hour or so, and invites him to watch, for the second time, *America in Action!*, a sports highlight film. As a hockey player with stick raised in triumph glides across the ice, he turns to survey his neighbors, left and right: across the aisle a middle-aged businessman studies the contents of a file folder, and from the headphones clamped over his ears comes an attenuated "A Hard Day's Night," all cymbals and rhythm guitar. Beside him a woman reading a thick paperback novel, *All About H.*, starts a chapter entitled

"Mary Sweet," her long and painted thumbnail obscuring the back-cover blurb, his eyes moving, inevitably, to the posed photograph of the author, to some truly astonishing information, set in large red type, about hardcover sales figures. He monitors the movement of the plane through the air, opening his central nervous system to the ancient reflexes which in happier primitive times would have permitted numerous frenzied alternatives denied him by the politesse and technology to which he is captive. The plane banks abruptly, angling steeply toward a bridge; through the window he can see that it is visibly losing altitude now, and he starts, taut and tense as if an electrical current is passing through his body. The cabin is quiet, except for the rush of air through the ventilation system and the droning mechanical noises the jet makes as it prepares to meet the planet. All passengers seem to occupy the same quiescent vacuum within the enveloping sound and motion—either in anticipation or in dreamy contemplation of the forms coming into kinetic resolution from beneath the patchy cloud cover or, like him, in a kind of reasoned statistical terror. He opens the metal lid covering the obsolescent ashtray, a coffin now for chewing gum wrappers and viscous childish debris, snaps it shut, *All About H.* has turned over a new leaf, this chapter is named "Twisted Labyrinth," the businessman across the way listens to the Zombies now, tinny "She's Not There," file folder tucked into the briefcase stowed securely beneath the seat in front of him. On-screen a newscaster jaws silently for a few moments, the picture changes to an image of hundreds of pairs of uninhabited amphibious combat boots spread across a small patch of desert, to the reassuring and cartoonish grainy shot of a "government building" exploding from the inside out, to prolonged comical shots, both contemporary and archival, of soldiers and marines grimacing over their rations—and then, following the newscaster's close, returning to the exploding building. This is followed by a brief round of applause in the cabin. He loosens his tie, slumps back in his seat, thinks of feigning sleep or unconsciousness. Across the aisle, a squeaky arpeggio signals the beginning of a new song. He *is* exhausted: this joyless cross-country trip, the pounds of words spoken and transcribed that he carries—the fictional possibilities of it all! He bends to retrieve his canvas carryon bag, removes from it several magazines, the top one announcing F. X. ROLAND—SELLOUT!, proud prostitute thus yclept pictured holding in one hand a crudely lettered sign, "F U CN RD THS ➡," trained at a hardcover book, *False Endings.* In nascent fantasy had pictured himself much as Comrade Roland; now his racing mind tracks the movements of a figure, hands thrust deep into the pockets of his jacket, walking among weeds sprouting thickly between railroad ties; measures a gin and tonic mixed in a tall, slender tumbler, counts the wedges of lime garnishing it; recalls the phrases of sixteen letters to editors read and reread; fleshes out the details of a flat, sharp-edged world awaiting the placement of a template over its precise contours. Marzio is under contract to write an authorized biography of Hi-Fi, idolized gimmick of many years' duration. He is nine months into his work, full human gestation, and today is the anniversary he had been hired to celebrate. It is a decade since "Jay Lustig made the mistake of asking the decidedly thuggish crowd at Cheaters, a third-rate nightclub, whether any of its members cared to sit in for then-bassist Nathaniel Speilvogel [*sic*], who had been ejected from the premises for some obscure reason. The boys disagree on the nature of his infraction: Dave seems to remember that it had to do with setting a fire in the dressing room, while Jay claims that Nat stormed out after an argument with his girlfriend at the time, Girl Bovary (now Mrs. David McCall). Richard, for his part, insists that it was he who was thrown out." Marzio has injected himself into this black night, thinking to make the best of it all that he can, putting it on a plane wholly and spookily separate from life, as artificial as any fiction: what else to manufacture from the stark and contradictory facts? He asserts the historian's arrogant familiarity with the unknowable, has catalogues of the (probable) contents of pockets and purses, of clothing, of furnishings and decor, weather reports and television listings; reconstructive means of attack, holding in abeyance his suspicion that he might be wrong about any one inference because it could cause him to doubt everything he has come to accept. He has learned to let events fall next to one another like dice, challenging the relevancy of their correspondence but not the unambiguous sum, yet he has been unable to generate an acceptable draft for his meeting with the Sponsor tomorrow: doubts *have* surfaced as he follows the spoke of the present back to the hub from which it radiates, ending up at this defunct nightclub on an evening precisely ten years before the one now approaching from the east; two dates conjoining at a distance, vinculum that brackets a decade's worth of fading remembrance. He replaces the magazines, withdraws a thin file containing his scant manuscript. Working title, *Where They Are Now*.

* * *

They passed through a gallery, white-painted walls, white tiled floor, white pedestals supporting white plaster objects, through a pair of doors leading to the roof garden, lush urban arcadia, heavy-smelling, red clay underfoot dark from the evening's watering. The summer heat hit Marzio immediately and he began to sweat beneath his shirt and jacket, grabbed the damp cool frond of some overhanging growth and pressed it against his cheek, his forehead, peered into the green veiny network that tapered to the brown point held close to his face while listening to the path being beaten to a patio hewn out of undergrowth, edenic redoubt pushed to the edge of the parapet wall, on which Dave McCall sat to smooth a joint between his fingers and wait as Marzio followed, shedding jacket and loosening tie, looking down into the street where a group of girls waited for a glimpse of golden hair. Dave gripped the wall with both hands and reclined, lifting his legs so that they pointed stiffly skyward, and a small indignant commotion rose from the street below. He righted himself, laughing, then lit the joint to draw on it meditatively.

"You'd think the bitches would have something better to do with their lives."

Marzio had first seen them as he approached the house, inchoate womanhood gathered on car hoods, under the trees, smelling of Juicy Fruit and Dippity Doo, banal and serene but increasingly unwholesome to him as he had drawn near, sensed their fixation on the house before which they congregated. They had engaged in casual and overt acts of vandalism—with house keys applied to painted metal, with colored chalks on the sidewalk—scrawled signs meaningful and notorious only to them. Stared at the house: three stories and penthouse, stoop bordered on one side by a basement suite, dark behind grated windows, on the other by a garage; he had felt the hush, the eyes on him, as he joined with the house, became part of it, ascended, rang the doorbell, disappeared inside. While waiting in a front room, he had watched them through the windows, the house under their brooding surveillance reflected in their rapt gaze.

"Really weirds me out, here every day from like morning till night. Not that I wouldn't mind boning one of the skanks."

Marzio said nothing, looking on as Dave dragged on the joint, held the smoking nub out to examine it, dragged again, torso swollen with held vapor.

"Never shit in your own house though—I save it for the road."
He put the roach out on his tongue, tucked it into a small painted
box he removed from his trousers, came down off the wall and
crossed to remove a guitar from a stand next to a patio chair, gold-
plated hardware flashing, percussive open A string followed by
ringing E, A, C#, E sounded as one. Singing, hesitant, mistakes
punctuated by "wait . . ."; strumming, naked sound of the
unamplified solid body baring where left fingertips depressed
strings an instant after rigid right arm dropped, falling back on the
faithful tic of first plucking the tonic note as the three other fingers
of the left hand rushed to catch up (he called it a style); Dave
demonstrated a new song, "Like a Doll's House." To Marzio, the
moment seemed, like its maker, utterly prefabricated; he struggled
in his notebook (ancillary tape machine whirling simultaneously)
to lay the burden of a past, of a supple relationship to other parts
of the world, on this strangely mechanical creature. The lyrics and
accompaniment flowed on, smooth as syrup, despite the incompe-
tence and hesitancy, discord forming sharp right angles in the air
as the arm dropped like dead weight, the lips wavered—all a matter
of choreography. Margins gradually filled with idiot faces, cross-
hatching, speech balloons containing top row capital symbols,
framing the clean unmarked page.

"What do you think?"

Startled out of his reverie, Marzio looked up to see Dave carefully replacing the guitar in its stand—he jotted, @#!*%&!, red
flags waving madly in his brain, but still, $$$$, to be considered—
"It's different . . . interesting."

"Samsara. I mean, I'm really no better off than them," gesture
panned to encompass rooftops, esplanade, BQE, darkening water,
Manhattan "tried to get that into the song, like we're all on the
wheel? *'Read in the Bible as you sow so shall you reap/I got a
million miles to go before I sleep'*—I mean there's no like equality
or inequality. Why I'm not into charity, like, they're where they
are for a reason? You know? Every now and then we have some
benefit thing and I go along with it because I like have to but I
can't help, you know thinking, like maybe we're even delaying
them? We all move toward a godlike state, why we're here. Delaying that? I mean that's what I mean, everything I have now, Hi-
Fi and all, was like waiting for me on a plate. Karma."

Dave stood in hiatus for a long moment, eyes roving nervously, hands traveling up the length of his body, past his waist, his chest, above his shoulders. "How's my hair?" he turned to look directly into Marzio's eyes, his face tight with pain and uncertainty "I mean, how is it?"

Dave led Marzio into the third-floor studio. It was decorated to Dave's own peculiar taste, untouched by professionalism and its attendant frigid grace yet no less processed than what Marzio had seen of the house so far. The broken sofa and dented folding chairs spoke and sang in devotional tribute to the rebel. These stood in contrast to the banks of expensive equipment. Dave gestured at boxes of reel-to-reel tapes stacked on a table.

"Working on the outtake album. Like, nitch marketing to our core fans; B. J. says it'll shore up their support to reinforce against their potential loss after the EMP-TV thing is made public."

"EMP-TV thing?"

"Just something we're kicking around. Anyway, much more creative than another greatest hits collection."

"About as cheap too, I guess."

"You kidding? This is about the biggest pain in the ass in the world. We gotta take all this old shit, remix it, re-record parts of the songs, write total new parts in some cases, dub in ad-libs. . . ."

"Why not just use the outtakes?"

Dave halted his why-me gesticulations to look at him strangely. "Because they fuckin *sound* like outtakes. We make mistakes. We say stupid shit. Plus half the time there isn't more than one or two of us in the studio at the same time. Jay's been phoning his vocals in for two years. The idea is to like make it sound as if we're a working band, coming up with the big new ideas as we go. We even hired some guy to write our fuckin lines for us."

"Who? I mean, out of professional curiosity."

"Just some jerk B. J. unearthed out in Frisco, where nobody'll ever find him. City fuckin weirds me out, man."

Marzio found his way to a bathroom papered with hundreds of varnished *Rolling Stone* covers. While urinating, he studied the walls: one, two, a total of nine covers featured Hi-Fi. On one a heavy black line had been drawn next to Dave's head; he leaned closer and made out, to his delight, a small speech balloon within which a feminine hand had written "I eat scum" still faintly visible beneath the eclipsing streak. He finished, giggled through his ablutions, and emerged.Unsure of his ability to return straight-faced to the studio—the little cocksucker!, giving away at last to his dislike—he made for the double doors, moved through the dark tendrils of flora toward the patio, deserted now save for the three empty beer bottles, his tape recorder and notebook, and the glossy brochures spread out on the table: What Would You Pay To Keep Him Out? Recommended By Big City Police Chiefs Across America, Centurion® Armed Driver & Escort Services, Instant Response Links Your Home To Police, Fire, Emergency! Cerberus® Professional Security Systems *meeting the security needs of VIPs since 1969.* Beyond the roof the towers of lower Manhattan loomed, carved out of western sunlight. Marzio began to feel as if his presence in this setting was somehow counterfeit, engineered—the shabby suit, the cheap haircut, his scuffed loafers surfacing from the depths of the patio mosaic, its elegant muted pattern, as twin focal points—something out of a police melo-drama: "Just the facts" (tape spooling hypnotically toward its terminus through the transparent cassette). He gathered his belong-ings, wandered back through the wilderness of Dave's world, through the white room, down the spiral staircase, through the hallway lined with thousands of exiled LPs, pausing at the studio door, which gave forth the smell of marijuana and the sound of high-pitched noodling, down one, two flights of stairs. In a kitchen he recognized vaguely from magazines and Sunday rotogravures, its imprint of generic individualism, Girl sat at a butcherblock counter, legs entwined around those of her high stool, a plate of greens pushed away and defaced by a clove cigarette butt, live one smoking in her hand, boredom incarnate, from book (*How to Get Out of a Losing Relationship National Bestseller 40th Big Print-ing*) to magazine (*Chi!* Pizza Big City Styles Girl McCall not just "mrs. hi-fi" "Wok" A New Story By The Author Of Big Bright Zero His/Hers: Oral Sex *great new designer looks!* TAMPONS: PASSÉ?) to television ("Like to get *your* Contractor's License?") to tape (Up From Neva Tony Award Winner Original Cast Record-ing RUSSKY MAN · SAMOVAR QUEEN · A WISH FOR ANATOLY · SAMIZDAT NITESPOT 8 OTHER HITS FROM THE TONY AWARD WINNING SCORE). Her skin glistened with a light coat of sweat, leotards dark with it; she had revealed in greeting him two hours earlier that she had promised herself a workout, woman of her word, the television: "1-900-TRU HEAT for live conversation *now*" equally glossy woman on-screen dialing a telephone, lifeline into the abyss

of Saturday night isolation, Girl turned her eyes from Multimedia
Spread With Cuisine, "Good hunting?" exposed one ear from beneath headset; Marzio moved in, shyly approaching the butcherblock altar, but Girl's eyes shifted, inevitably, to the more colorful
and vibrant offerings with which she had purposefully surrounded
herself, replacing the headset and shrugging, humming, "Disap-
pointments are for the books, da dum, da dum, just like your
looks—" There was a screech of feedback from outside the
room, Dave entered wearing an Epiphone semihollow body rigged
with a wireless transmitter, pale blond wood obscured beneath
a collage of floral decals, photographs, contact paper banderole
reading FREE BEER, Girl gritted her teeth, persevered in song,
"*Pe*restroika, springtime again!," but was overpowered by

, scowled and raised her hands to her ears, at which Dave removed
the guitar and draped himself over her back, arms hanging limply
over her shoulders, rubbing his face in her hair "Aw, I'm just havin a
little fun. . . ." "God, I hate this" caressing her thighs and breasts,
giggling—she slid off the stool to move from beneath his embrace,
then cautiously resumed her place at the butcherblock. "You're a
real sweet bitch, you know that? A real sweet bitch." He sat in a
vacant stool opposite hers, reached for the plate, found ash, withdrew. Drummed his fingers on the butcherblock, stopped to return
a baleful stare, waited until it had turned back to the television,
then resumed, Girl doggedly ignoring him throughout, moving
only to adjust the volume of her tape player "Fag show tunes," to
operate the television's remote control "hockey? It's summer. You
don't even fuckin *like* hockey," to flip the pages of *How to Get Out
of a Losing Relationship National Bestseller* "that's a stupid book.
A stupid book for stupid little girls." She began again to hum and
Dave addressed the room at large, "What a fuckin waste of space.
Fuckin magazines and clothes and cars and toys and bullshit and
won't even *fuckin* talk to me." Girl silently began to collect *How
to Get Out of a Losing Relationship National Bestseller, Chi!* <u>Pizza</u>
Big City Styles, Up From Neva Tony Award Winner Original Cast
Recording as Dave stared at her and Marzio shifted from foot to
foot. The three of them turned toward the sound of the guitar
hitting the floor, landing first on one of the cutaways and then flat,
fretboard down, to see the daughter, Cora, moving backwards

toward the doorway, an expression of terror on her face as she regarded first the guitar, and then her father, who rose, reaching out to grab the little girl by the wrist and pulling her "And how many *fuckin* times do I have to tell you not to touch the *fuckin* guitars?" "I'm sorry, Daddy. I'm real sorry." Dave shook his head slowly, muttering, "*Nobody* has to put up with this kind of crazy shit," released her. Girl took her by the hand. "Come on, you. Let's get you cleaned up and off to bed." She reached to touch the bruise taking shape on Cora's arm and, wincing, recoiled from her own act. They left the room and Dave gazed at his distorted reflection in the toaster, malevolent twin face rippling across the rounded chrome surface as he moved to examine it in three-quarter profile, clenching his jaw and flaring his nostrils.

In the nursery, Girl watched as Cora smiled and bowed at her image in the mirror on the wall, spinning, a strip of sheer golden fabric she had wrapped around her rising and snapping stiffly, then dropping as her body came to rest. She lost her footing, fell, giggled, then was up again in front of the mirror, standing sideways, looking coyly over her left shoulder at herself, holding out the shining cloth at arm's length toward the mirror, running one hand over the wrinkled length of the glove covering the other, smoothing it with eerily mature finesse.

"Who are you tonight?" asked Girl, wearily.

"The Fairy Princess! I'm going to the nighttime ball and I'm going to meet a rockin roll star like Daddy and he meets me backstage and he asks me whether I want to hear a very beautiful song and I tell him I'm the Fairy Princess."

"Yes? And does he sing it for you?"

"Well, I tell *him* that the song has to come from me because I'm the most beautiful girl in the *whole world*."

"What did he do?"

"I told him I would like to hear a song all about the Fairy Princess!"

Girl laughed, and reached to embrace the child, lifted her and carried her to the sarcophagus of molded plastic in which she slept, as she continued, "Then he told me he wanted me to come with him and he put me in his big car and we drove around the *whole world*!"

"But didn't you miss your Mommy?"

"Uh uh."

"You didn't miss Mommy one little bit?"

"Well, we stopped and picked her up and she came with us so it was OK."

Girl adjusted the sheets over Cora's body.

"I want a story!"

"No more stories. You already had a story."

"I *told* that one. I want *you* to tell *me* one!"

"I'll tell her a story." Dave said this to his wife from the doorway, Marzio standing in the hallway beyond, and in the mute instant that they stared at one another, as the child froze beneath the covers her mother had placed over her, Marzio saw what appeared to be a look of contempt cross Girl's face—a slight curl of the lip, the subtlest suggestion of a rolled eyeball. Whatever it was it passed swiftly as Dave entered the room, neared the bed, and Girl kissed the child on the forehead and left. In a moment Marzio heard coughing from beneath the sound of running water. The little girl looked at her father and then hid her face from him, and he burst into laughter, retreating to sink into a chair across the room from her, leaning forward, his elbows resting on his knees. He grinned up at Marzio.

"We have a really good one tonight."

The child burrowed beneath the stifling covers, burying herself completely. "Don't wanna story," she said, her voice muffled.

"What was that?" Dave's voice wavered slightly, and he turned again to Marzio, his eyes shining.

"Don't *want* a story."

"Why sure you do. I *heard* you tell Mommy. Now, come out of there. It's so *hot*." Cora complied, exhuming herself to lean on an elbow, sweeping the hair out of her eyes with her still-gloved hand. "And take that silly—" The girl cringed, appeared about to conceal herself once more, and Dave stopped, then continued in a honeyed monotone. "Don't you want to take the glove off? *Real* princesses don't go to bed with their gloves on." Cora rolled onto her back to pull the glove off. "Hand it to Daddy," leaning forward "Hand it to me!" He took the glove from her, yanking it so that it made a slapping noise as it left her hand. "Now, where were we? Oh, yes! And try to look, you know, a little happy, for Chrissake." His fingers found a slight rip in the glove's seam, and he worked it as he spoke, tearing the glove along its length.

"Once upon a time there were three people, a man, a woman, and a little girl, and they all lived together in a house a lot like this one. The man and woman went about their business and the little girl played, and laughed, and hated little boys, and went to school and painted pictures, and did all sorts of things, some of which she told the man and woman about and some of which she, you know, like didn't."

Cora stared at the glove, a smile arrested on her face.

"One night the man and woman and the little girl had all finished playing together and the little girl had brushed her teeth and washed her face and was in bed, when the woman heard a very strange noise coming from the back stairs, behind the kitchen." He inclined his head slightly in the direction of the kitchen. "The man was in his studio and the little girl lay in bed, waiting for her . . . kiss. And the woman went down the back stairs, to see where that strange noise was coming from!"

"Maybe, Daddy, maybe it was the haws."

Dave looked at her curiously, balling the glove up in his hand. "What do you mean, the haws?"

"The haws Mommy says are always hanging around."

Dave clenched both fists, laughed tonelessly. "It wasn't the haws. It wasn't, you know, *here* anyway. Anyhow, she was down there, the back stairs place, for quite a while, so the man got curious about what was taking her so long, and he got up to see where she'd gone. And do you know what he finds?"

No response. Dave shrugged slightly, sighed, turned to Marzio. "Do you know?"

"What?"

"He finds the back door half open, and a breeze blowing in from outside. And he calls out, Mommy, Mommy, where are you? But there's no answer. And then, the family cat walks back in from outside, and it's shivering, and its fur's all *white!* And you know what? Huh? Do you?"

"No-o-o."

"It had been all *black* before. So the man got very frightened and he ran all the way down the back stairs"—Cora flinched as Dave loudly stamped his feet in simulation—"leaving the little girl *all alone* in the house. And she waited and waited in her bed, feeling that cold, damp, howling wind blowing in from the back door."

"No."

Dave rose now, bending over to retrieve a flashlight from under the bureau before moving over to the lamp on one nightstand.

"And then . . ."

"No, *don't!*"

"... all the lights ..." Clicked it off.

"Please!"

"... suddenly started ..."

"DON'T!"

He crept up to snap off the lamp on the other. "TO GO *OUT!*"

"DON'T TURN OFF THE LIGHTS! DON'T TURN OFF THE LIIIIIIII—!"

He extinguished the remaining light, near the bookshelf, as the little girl's last word broke free of the phrase in which it was rooted, rising and peaking in an earsplitting scream, sustained, then dropped, and then resumed again. Shaking with suppressed laughter, Dave shone the beam of the flashlight directly into the hysterical, contorted face; watching her as her frenzy mounted until finally he switched the flashlight off, the terrified screams piercing the blackness into which the room had been plunged.

Allowing himself the slightest sense of regret that his intuition has once again been proven wrong as the aircraft lands, taxies, and comes to rest without incident, Marzio deplanes and makes for the smoker's area, a narrow crammed corridor between GIFT SHOPPE and GIFTE SHOP, line of molded plastic chairs faced on either side by banks of sinister-looking telephones bristling with screens, switches, knobs, magnetic-card strips, chiming and warbling with their warm-throated calls. An assortment of drawings provided by the second grade class of Miss Eileen Rosenberg, Joseph Clifton Elementary School, Oradell, are on display and Marzio lights up beneath rectangles of butcher paper covered with the children's verdant, smeary undulations, gigantic blotchy suns, and jagged animals and houses. The smoke irritates his throat and he bends slightly at the waist, the hard cough rising from within him and shaking his body, and he puts the cigarette out in the filthy urn beside him, rises and walks through the gateway leading to the main terminal, passing beneath a yellow ribbon flanked by a wreath and a menorah; passing lines of people submitting to hand-held metal detection, a bored cop wearing a flak jacket detaining a group of unhappy dark complected men; past duty-free counter, bookstore, cocktail lounge, WOMEN Changing Table; past a depressing multitude of F. X. Rolands at the NEWSSTAND; down an escalator; past the baggage carousel, the surface transportation counter; finds himself in a taxicab, PLEASE NOT TO SMOKE—DRIVERS ALERGIC of course affixed to the open partition, finds himself giving the driver careful instructions, a SoHo address. Marzio worries vaguely that his continued lack of productivity will have legal repercussions—his Sponsor is familiar with litigation as an inevitable part of public life; he has seen him flip expertly through summons, caption, preliminary allegations, causes of action, prayer, exhibits, proof of service; pausing over bold, capitalized proper nouns and elongated trains of zeros—but is truly concerned that he will be asked to surrender the keys to the Prince Street offices and abandon these peopled events, which he feels belong to him now. What belongs to history will be up to the Sponsor, he knows this, has always known it: the Sponsor is expert at pushing the counters around, understands the systemic nature of throwaway communications that accrete beneath the current until the stipulations of legend have been met. He reaches into his bag for a padded envelope forwarded to his Los Angeles motel by a service located deep in the bunker of the nation. He now receives these on a weekly basis—wherever he is—filled with clippings culled from newspapers and magazines all over the English-speaking world: reviews, news stories, analyses, interviews, three-dot items; each interesting in that while directly connected to his subject, in the most painfully specific terms, it momentarily rides the surface in naked candor, illuminated by the luster bound to the events in which the famous participate, and then disappears into the larger category that is its fate, where its unique facts dissolve. Part of Marzio's job is to assist in such disappearances, to create the categories and then to stock them, REBELLION, DECADENCE, SCATHING WIT, OUTRAGE. Et cetera. In a "bizarre incident" Richard Poindexter is arrested at Bergdorf-Goodman on the charge of having shoplifted two plastic wallet inserts, priced at seventy-nine cents each. A young woman, apparently under the influence of a mixture of alcohol and sedatives, falls to her death from the roof of a townhouse on MacDougal Street "reportedly owned by Jay Lustig." Dave McCall's Brooklyn Heights brownstone is broken into and vandalized, the words SHOE'S ON OTHER FOOT NOW scrawled on the wall "in blood." A CPA with a Big Six firm in Chicago claims that a "largely incoherent" Jay Lustig had burst into his office and demanded of the "startled auditor" that he strip and surrender his clothing. A twelve-year-old girl is found dead of a heroin overdose in the men's room of Los Timadores, an "illegal Washington Heights nightlub" in which it is alleged that Richard Poindexter holds partial ownership interest. Dave McCall makes an unscheduled appearance onstage with a band performing in Flushing Meadow Park and twenty-four people are injured, eight seriously, in the "resulting crush." "Shocked dinner guests" report that Jay Lustig sets a place at his table for a small white grape, which he introduces as "Zoe" and then engages in intimate conversation. Dave McCall, in "widely reproduced" comments first published in the German weekly *Täuschen!*, declares that nothing soothes his chronic indigestion more than the consumption of Herco guitar picks, Gleem toothpaste tube caps, and other small items manufactured from plastic. A "noted subliminologist" avers that in a recent magazine ad for Seagram's whiskey featuring Richard Poindexter standing before an elegant mahogany pool table, the precise arrangement of the balls on the felt skeletally suggests the face of Satan. Dave McCall is served with a "massive lawsuit" after a scuffle at Petardista's, a homosexual nightclub outside of Dallas. A photograph is published depicting Jay Lustig recoiling from the outstretched, deformed hand of a hideous dwarf, wheelchair-bound with some sort of grotesque feeding device around its neck. Caption: "Hi-Fi High-Five?" The New York offices of Cronus Records are "picketed by a coalition" of minority, gay, and women's groups protesting that *XLN SandWhich*, Richard Poindexter's current solo album, is racist, homophobic, and sexist. Filtered through him, doubling back attired as PR, the assault refreshed. He remembers the comment of a waitress attacked by Jay Lustig for serving him small portions: "It's not the pain that hurts, it's finding out that one of your idols is a real asshole." Filtered through him, the soft tissue injuries become mere abstractions; fully healed, they endow their maker with a subtle aroma of danger and allure, sheerest voodoo.

Doorman stiffly erect and unsmiling in pearl grey uniform with gold brocade, security console behind which he withdrew Brazilian teakwood, in which was recessed Koberna® telecommunications panel topped with four Dunleavy® seven-inch closed-circuit monitors. He spoke into a telephone receiver, nodded, permitted Marzio to pass the console.

. . . Floor of flawless Italian granite with alabaster inlay, glazed terra-cotta urns lined carpeted path leading to elevator bank, where handwoven tapestries hanging from a wall of translucent marble moved in gentle currents of air from behind a Grecian water bearer pallid and naked dead center of a fountain. . . .

Marzio waited in front of the private elevator as a video camera overhead swung around and paused to scrutinize before the brushed steel doors parted to allow entry. The car was finished in reflective polished brass, with rosewood handrails and Holzer™ heat-sensitive control panel. It ascended silently and without turbulence, sense of motion digitized and conveyed via the numbers which, each in their turn, appeared, softly faded, appeared on the LED readout. The doors glided open, his sallow reflection yielding to one more distant (but no more robust) in the Henken® twisted rope mirror hanging directly opposite the elevator, from a wall painted with elaborate trompe l'œil effect to depict mouldings and cornices (cyma recta, pellet, ogee, cyma reversa), their interstices affected with the illusion of shadow and shine as if in anticipation of the soft light cast by the Grant-Wolpa® table lamp on the Bax® cherrywood stand. Treading lightly on Oertel™ carpet below, Marzio traced the distant voices he heard to the rear of the apartment, followed the sound.

Drumbeats, whines. Montage of frescoed stations of the cross. An altar, before which a figure genuflected: profound as a ziggurat, head's shaved lines of sigla denoting little more than the pink scalp below, thin shoulders hunched in effort of raising empty chalice, fringed epaulets shimmering in golden motion, "Bring some mo this shit, bitch. *Cold!*" Corpulent mass of the base, concealed beneath extravagantly colored textile. "Bitch come in here, hair all in her face again, not look at me, I be slappin her shit down. Word." Female hands clutched at a rosary, crucifix beneath swinging wildly. A huge gold-plated dollar sign eased its way on its chain out of his shirtfront, "S" bisected by a miniature drumstick—this frozen on Trinitron™ screen as Richard Poindexter remotely paused the VCR, turned from his bosom's wavering image to Marzio, "Come in, sit down. Just got the rough cut of my new video, for the solo album."

. . . Vergara® Maple Natural™ flooring covered by Gonella® faux-Tibetan rug depicting traditional design of "eight auspicious symbols," early Ching Dynasty® vase set atop Ju® wood cabinet, Ludwig® bass drum, with aerial toms attached, in a corner, the name Hi-Fi℠ emblazoned across its skin; on the wall above it a Fender® Precision Bass® guitar, pickguard indecipherably inscribed, next to this a quartet of Miles Miller™ photographs beside Kotara® standing lamp, Devlin-Roche® sectional sofa fronted by Hochstein® Krystal-Top™ coffee table on which were arranged new paperback editions of works by Dunlop®, Hofner®, Marshall®, Roland®, and Shure® (each, curiously, inscribed by its author "couldn't have done it without you!"); copies of *Details®*, *The Face®*, *Spy®*, *Conjunctions 14®*, *Sunshower II®*; a small brass figurine of the Hindu® goddess Kali^{SM}; a colored Wurlitzer® jukebox of early-Eisenhower^{SM} vintage resting with darkened potential against the wall opposite the windows. . . .

> She got a fine fine ass—ass her fo the time
> She got a fine fine ass—ass her fo the time
> She got a fine fine ass—ass her fo the time
> She got a fine fine ass—ass her fo the time

Poindexter nervously squeezed a loaf of Supremes® White Bread™ in both hands as he watched the screen, Florence Ballard's® face on the glossy wrapper expanding and contracting as if preparatory to flashback to happier days, Marzio peered past his shoulder into Bobby Sherman™ mirror next to Partridge Family® schoolbus, hand surfing lightly over moussed waves of hair, glanced at the Beatles® clock, whose hands reached for but had not yet caught twelve o'clock.

"Should we get started?"

. . . Crawford® turntable, CD player, cassette deck, reel-to-reel, amplifier, graphic equalizer, and tuner stacked in Mock & Bartenhagen® maple cabinet, on which CDs by Snowman®, the Tumblers®, Paste-Up®, Double Exposure®, Endnote®, MMPI®, Ten-Year Plan®, Shaggy Dog®, and Vertical Madness® are piled beneath a Dead Kennedys® poster depicting Jesus^{SM} nailed to a crucifix of dollar bills. . . .

> Caught her inna confessional an all her shit froze
> Bowed her in de head an den I rip offer close
> "Donoffer no resisance putta nine up yo cunt"
> Eat me like a pig an while she do it she grunt

. . . Hand-colored eighteenth-century French vegetable prints from the Desher Archives®, Worthing® wet bar concealed within the Tomita® grand piano, Precher® New Heritage™ silver candleholders on both Ryan® oak trestle table and adjacent Fairley® Honduras Mahogany™ sideboard, on the sideboard the following document:

NAME: Mr. RICHARD POINDEXTER
DATE: October 26, 1990
ADDRESS: 51 WEST 81st ST., NYC

FOR INSURANCE PURPOSES

ARTICLE
1)   LADY'S CHARM BRACELET: CLASSIC   CURB   LINK
STYLE, ROUND SHAPE SOLID LINKS, EACH MEASURING
APPROXIMATELY 5 MILLIMETERS IN WIDTH, BRIGHT POLISH
FINISH FOURTEEN KARAT YELLOW GOLD, BRACELET MEASUR-
ING APPROX. 7 INCHES IN OVERALL LENGTH, ATTACHED
WITH THE FOLLOWING THREE-DIMENSIONAL LARGE FINE
QUALITY SCULPTED AND TEXTURED FINISH CHARMS:

A) "House Trailer" - measuring approximately 35 mm.
   in length by 15 mm in width.
B) "Straitjacket" - measuring approx. 25 mm. in
   length by 20 mm. in width.
C) "Prescription Jar" - measuring approx. 34 mm. in
   length by 12 mm. in width, with four spherical
   shape cultured pearl "capsules", each measuring
   approx. 2 mm. in average diameter.
D) "Android" - measuring approx 34 mm. in length by
   15 mm. in width.
E) "Guillotine", with one polished peridot pebble,
   measuring approximately 28 mm. in length by 20
   mm. in width.
F) "Drink Ticket" - measuring approximately 20 mm.
   in length by 18 mm. in width.
G) "Death's Head", with flexible link "Mardi Gras
   Beads", measuring approx. 30 mm. in length by
   20 mm. in width.
H) "Round Table" - measuring approx. 15 mm. in
   circumference, 5 mm. in width.
I) "Manuscript" - measuring approx. 33 mm. in length
   by 25 mm. in width.
J) "Pitchfork" - measuring approx. 35 mm. in length
   by 15 mm. in width.
K) "Wrapped Condom" - measuring approximately 25
   mm. by 25 mm.
L) "Hammer and Sickle" - each measuring approx. 15
   mm. length by 12 mm. width.

All charms are stamped 14k, bracelet attached with a
spring ring clasp.

$12,500.00

"You want something to drink? Beer? Wine? Sangria?" Marzio looked again at the Beatles® clock, where noon had just broken loose from the hands' embrace, declined, "An orange drink, or something?", assented to this.

rapin a nun
rapin a nun
rapin a nun

. . . Facchino® granite countertops, Griswold® range oven, Marley® dishwasher, Klein-Freeze™ refrigerator, Finney-Griffin® cabinetry, Revland® sink and fixtures, Knauss® cast iron rack suspended from ceiling holding LaLande® cookware, on a wall a snack rack from some forgotten bar and grill, one lonely bag each of Quinlan® pretzels and Wise® potato chips dangling; Dodsworth® wicker picnic hamper, opened as if to display the two partridges, two mallard ducks, Dungeness crab (twenty-four hours out of the Pacific) and two live-frozen trout (from Denmark) within, California Chardonnay (Monge® '89) beside it. . . .

The telephone on the Vasquez® desk, a sleek Ekdall® multi-line device, had as its counterweight an ancient Western Electric® Bakelite™ rotary dial phone. One of these rang and Richard emerged from the kitchen to lift a receiver to his ear, "Yes, uh huh, that's a no-brainer. To, what, talk?" Concern and horror spread across his face. "Depression *Strip*? You're kidding . . . right?"

Sittin on her monkeh wif my pope hat all big
Jewnose bitch she eatin me like a pig
Gaver soul to Jesus butta body's fa sin
Puter back in da booth yall wo know where to begin

. . . Golding® ornamental bone and chrome hatrack, Goetz® automatic sill warmer, Jean-Paul Coffee℠ triptych (title conveniently written across the three panels, "Brooklyn-Berlin Paradigm"), Persiani® Ceramic Orchard™ on Gill® Plexiglass™ and cowhide display table. . . .

"Nah, nah—I'll tell you the real deal. My friend Scooter—right, him—he *knows* the Peruvians and he says that's bullshit, you have to go out to Lorimer Street if you *really* want the lowdown on the tattoo thing. When? Sunday? Sunday, Sunday . . . I don't know. At . . . Great *Truth's*? How mirth-provoking."

rapin a nun
rapin a nun
rapin a nun

... set of Toleikis® hand-tinted postcards depicting Midwestern motel rooms, original Krazy Kat™ daily panel strip, Knox® leaded glass umbrella stand, Ewing-Thomas® recessed halogen illumination system, Wheeler® tournament class billiard table, Everbrite™ neon sign reading "Copies 4¹/₂¢," unopened pack of Lucky Strike™ green. . . .
"Nah, nopenopenopenope—the *Norfolk* Street property's where we're removing all the old medicine chests from. Right, yeah, right. Listen, I—no, listen, these dumb spicks've been renting the place below market value for *years* . . . tell them it's a carry-forward."

> Don diss me wit yo piety—my plunge it need variety
> Yo slit it look so tight—beneat da black an white
> Better pray fa absolution cuz tonight I'm gonna fill ya
> with some seminal pollution

. . . McQuiston® painted steel mock joists, Fielhauer® Oxygem™ dehumidifier and air-purification system, Booker-Moran® heated towel stand, Peasley® VerbaTross™ Talking Scale, Milton-Bradley® Twister™ bathmat, Eduardo Marx℠ handpainted shower curtain, Ferrando™ marble sink, Jacuzzi™ tub, and pneumatic toilet (with Albe® heated seat), Hsu℠ excelsior and corrugated tin heat lamp, Sawin™ medicated genital soap, Bargé® shampoo for dyed hair, Carson of Beverly Hills® pore-opening deep-cleansing body bar, four mounted Collier® Grotesques™, Dunbar-Cox® straight razor, Sanders™ cowhide strop, Cote® medicated shaving soap, Guest® Capillex™ electronic noseclipper. . . .
"Tell them to buy fucking blankets. Tell them to wear sweaters. I'm being *patriotic*, for Christ's sake! What? *Housewrecker's*? You're, like, joking? Hmmm?"

> Maybefy blow yo muthuhfuckin haid off yall lay back an
> keep still—
> Maybefy bust a cap up ya ass yall bend ta my
> nigga will

. . . Empi® wicker hamper, Whalen® brass bed, Stark® Normandy Down™ comforter, Melendez℠ limited edition lithograph (Kokane Seriez), 3/50, *Spirit of the Times*, Weiland™ gypsum board and sheepskin airport environment, Pearson® white oak bureau and armoire, Astrid Kirscherr™ print depicting the

Beatles® standing at a Hamburg railroad siding, Fresques® valet, Franz Kline® "phone book" brush and ink drawing. . . .

"These are like twenty-five units that are not getting warehoused or torched, so, like, what the judge has to say about reasonable upkeep or whatnot is of little relevance since I'm already doing everybody a big fuckin favor. We must have a bad connection, did you—you didn't—suggest Los Tramposos?"

> She got a fine fine ass—ass her fo the time
> She got a fine fine ass—ass her fo the time
> She got a fine fine ass—ass her fo the time
> She got a fine fine ass—ass her fo the time

. . . Aerial photograph of Ebbets Field®, taken prior to the third game of the 1947 World Series™, Winters® zinc blinds, Van Gorp® antique washstand, John Holmstrom™ *Pedophilia* drawing, Fiester-Martin™ copper lunch bucket, Chia Pet™, John Chamberlain® *Tiny Piece* on Badarak™ plaster of Paris pedestal. . . .

"A friend of mine—you don't have to know who—he's got a place out near La Tourette park—no, like the disease, near the Henry Kaufman Campgrounds—he'll take the copper pipes, no problem. So take the ferry, do I give a shit? Hilarity is overcoming me at this moment since I believe I heard you say the *Nova EboraCafe*. . .?"

> Like ya hippie-lookin hero yall ah gonna get hammered
> ho down da bitch, ho dat shit down, god dammer
> I'm thrashin, I'm wildin, I'm poundin like a brute
> Been a long time since dis home wore da grey suit

. . . Whitelock® transdermal atomizer Cahalan® keratin strengthener Heubach® topiary cockroaches Shockey® crushed velour coasters Walters-Jones® Nostrumatic™ pharmaceutical inventory software Riggs® holographic display screen framed photograph of Charlie Parker® at the Royal Roost ca. 1948 Tanner™ stressed aluminum in-out basket set Jeannie M® Roadkill Calendar™ Zelaya® wormwood scrub apothecary case Collins-St. Charles® stackable chrome Minutemaster™. . . .

> rapin a nun
> rapin a nun
> rapin a nun

"Look, can you . . . ? I've got someone here, he's, well, he's a Samsonite® vinyl attaché case, Bostonian® slip-ons, Gold Toe®

argyle socks, Robert Hall® single-breasted grey flannel suit, Lands' End® $19.50 Oxford button-down, Neil Martin® bar sinister repp stripe tie. What can you do? Oh, that's good, right, Apocalypse 9, now I know you're kidding. . . ."

> I'm down wif da penguin, not askin yo puhmission
> I'm bustin loose from the hood an I gotta sense a mission
> Sicka Charlie an his god allus sayina me "NO"

. . . Bustamante® Portalux™ door hardware Belina® hurricane lamps *Rock'n'Roll High School*™ poster Ralph Bakshi® hand-painted cells Yves Klein® announcement with original cobalt blue brushstroke by the artist framed Chesterfield™ print ad featuring Ronald Reagan℠ Coleman® full-size rocking horse photograph of Richard Nixon℠ with Elvis Presley® sepia tone photograph of Zachary Taylor® Murai® ergonomic recliner chair. . . .

MEET DA PENT UP RAGE A DA GHETTO!

Christmas trees, brown, partially decorticated, surrounded by needle-droppings, tinsel, fragments of colored glass, are stacked at each corner; the air redolent of pine and desire long since palled; here and there are the cartons that once held toys and electronics but most of these have gone with the first wave, weeks ago; he descends deeper and deeper into the fashionable bowels of the island, moves past various signs of the times offering hints, boasts, advice, warnings; each asserting its epigrammatic preeminence, DYKEBITCHWHORESLUTCUNT emasculating **MEAT IS MURDER** killing off first four letters of **PROPERTY = THEFT** owning corner of building near **IGNORE THE WHITE CULTURE** paling beside **WE WILL NOT ACT CIVILIZED IN THIS FUCKIN' CITY** politely making room for **SOCIETYS A PARADE OF GARBAGE** detouring around **YOU ARE THE YOU ARE THE YOU ARE THE YOU ARE THE** stuttering on its own existential truth in overlap, breaking free on fifth and top layer **YOU ARE THE PRODUCT SOLD BY POPULAR CULTURE.** The cab pulls to the curb blocks shy of Marzio's destination. "Get from cab, please. This it." No mood to argue, Marzio pays the driver and steps out, barely having removed his belongings and closed the door before the car sweeps into an illegal U-turn near bent and twisted metal rail set in conical bases of concrete painted with broad diagonal yellow and black stripes, crunch of tires on broken glass, lusterless red sun stenciled on its door now traveling east toward its matutinal point of origin.

Spilling off the well-kept cusp of West Broadway onto Houston, Prince, Spring, Broome; gathered around the reefs of commerce fingering their way up past torpid schools of consumers and lustrous bait; ragged men hover motionless on the street, Styrofoam begging cups outthrust to display the greasy sugary coins collected therein, lining the sidewalk at respectful intervals, unmistakable even in silhouette as the late-afternoon sun obscures the dour expressions and blunt features. Outside the building at 144 Prince Street where the small suite of offices is maintained—carpeted, plush bud, tightly closed against the outside world—he pushes his way past one supplicant, billed as BLIND/but/FOR thE/ GracE/OF/GOD, the punchline implicit, and enters the vestibule, the locked stairwell, climbs the steep flights framed by the diminishing perspective of the latticework of unpainted Sheetrock, stopping on the correct landing and again using the borrowed key, pausing before the ten thousand dollar double doors (poorly hung) to retrieve a different key from the chaos of wrappers, slips of paper, and cash in his pocket. Penetration, the void realized. Inside, he lights a cigarette, the coal glowing brightly and flaring as it scorches a jagged path down the white cylinder, looks around in the growing darkness without turning on the lights. There are chairs and a receptionist's desk and industrial art on the walls. He raises the cigarette to his lips and inhales, limply drops the arm down at his side. On the receptionist's desk a Federal Express envelope awaits him, dot matrix return address LEBOEUFPESCI &FOWLER, he gathers it up along with the laptop and overnight bag and attaché left by the doors, carries them all into the conference room he has commandeered. Sullen quiet: revelation's pace has decelerated to that of glacial thawing, but never ceased, the room a crystal chamber of ice, concatenation of phenomena mounting—drifting smoke defines column of light extending from window and assuming angles of objects it falls upon; cloying odors from flowers banked atop long table; building's renovated service core shuddering as city's interred machinery grinds on; energized crackle of white noise; acrid, acrid taste in mouth—peaking, each then ebbing and resuming its proper status as background irritant. All the metonymic gravity of a crime scene. The enhancements his specific occupation has added to the room have lost their workmanlike appeal—are, in short, a mess: two file cabinets in the corner contain meticulously organized results of his first few months' labors and what has come after has simply grown, expanded, chronologically arranged by default (the bottom of a pile necessarily older than its top), but beyond that simply a collage with a single unifying theme: file folders; diskettes; notebooks, dusty in disuse (all titled, half in jest, "Marzio's Folly"); cassettes; the bulletin boards on which are hung endless photographs, a devotion for hopeless cases—

> O Holy Saint Jude, Apostle and Martyr
> Great in virtue and Rich in miracles,
> to you I have recourse in my hour of need . . .

—and yellowed fliers. Things drive him to distraction as they appear, unexpectedly, as if to skew the latest theory or interpretation, rigidly official things ("**COMES NOW, PLAINTIFF, THOMAS J. ECKLEBURG . . .**"), typeset things ("Appearing the 16th at the I-Beam, the Hi-Fi's . . ."), tangential things (". . . it is our finding that demolition of said elevated tracks could compromise the integrity of surrounding structures inasmuch as said tracks bear much of the weight of said structures. Since the post-renovation and residential development value of structures is well-known, it is suggested that demolition proceed after maximum coverage under existing A&E liability policies has been secured . . ."), evidence of pioneering predating his own ("A year ago Hi-Fi was known only to patrons of New York clubs. Today there isn't an American who doesn't know their names, and their fame has spread quickly around the world . . ."), submissions to be called into question, ultimately to be dispensed with, even in a chronicle devoted to outrage and rebellion, as "unnecessary" (although this too is mere rationalization). Their very resistance to taxonomy perhaps marks the encroachment of chaos, willful breakdown of order, leading to this room stifled in its aura of dust and wood pulp, keen chemical smells. How to explain the Short List of statements (very specifically designated as such in the anonymous note accompanying it) with which he is invited to agree or disagree—"I have had periods of days, weeks, or months when I couldn't take care of things because I couldn't 'get going.' " "I have met problems so full of possibilities that I have been unable to make up my mind about them." "I can read a long while without tiring my eyes." "If I were a reporter I would very much like to report news of the theater." "I have difficulty in starting to do things." "I have a habit of counting things that are not important such as bulbs on electric signs, and so forth." "It makes me feel like a failure when I hear of the success of someone I know well." "I have never seen things doubled (that is, an object never looks like two objects to me without my being able to make it look like one object)." "People can pretty easily change me even though I thought that my mind was already made up on a subject."—? Each seems to mock him, its asserted truth taking on dangerously polemical proportions within the context of the work he assiduously avoids, even as he logs thousands of miles of jet travel, feet of magnetic tape, kilobytes of disk space. He feels the fading oscillations of the table beneath his fingertips as the building trembles again, is still, the room in near-total darkness, piles of material assuming fantastic, disturbing shapes in the gloom, whole weight of the shadowy tableau taking on more significance under the influence of this mundane optical event and his imagination than any effort he's made to hammer out cohesive, interlocking sets of complementary data from it. He turns on the light, catches sight of himself in the mirror, greyly luminous in the humming fluorescence. He is the compiler, he lists things, finding in the letters representing their true and palpable existence an easy substitute for deeper meaning, or perhaps meaning itself. "What I prefer, again, is a pure litany of things. I am the last to work on this problem and this is the methodology which I have determined to be most useful." Hadn't he said that? He picks up a volume of Marzio's Folly, opens to see where his natural cramped hand had yielded to a freer, more whimsical style of notation—short entries sprawl across facing pages, handbook of desperate confusion right down to picturesque glass-rings and perfectly round cigarette burns, EXPERIENCE+THEME+EMOTION=BANALITY (for some), tied to nothing, insignificant flotsam. He realizes that he is moving through events which the manuscript will one day encompass, nothing is safe.

"Right, right this way." B. J. Hornbeck's gentle grip on Marzio's elbow tightened momentarily as he guided him into the courtyard, words punctuated by the rhythmic crashing noise which grew louder with each step, emerging from beneath the shedding screen of deciduous vegetation into mean January sunlight, where at the sight of them a young man paused in his labor of bending and unbending his knees, bending slightly forward at the waist while arching his back, bringing a sledgehammer up over his head while throwing out his chest, and then reversing the procedure, the sledgehammer striking the fender of one of four new BMWs grouped in a semicircle. Two of the cars had already been subjected to the treatment. Three cameras were mounted on tripods in strategic locations, three others hand-held by men who circled, all capturing the destruction. The young man stood, slightly pigeon-toed, hands planted in the small of his back, smiling and then laughing, the handle of the hammer leaning against a thigh. Hornbeck's hand now yanked uneasily at cloth, as if willing the two slowly advancing bodies through the door at the far end of the courtyard, still yards distant.

"$160,021.00 for props, fleet prices, the twenty-one bucks is the hammer, the overhead, Jesus. Well, it's big money, you know, it's a thing now, I shouldn't, shouldn't complain, but God knows, imagine what'd happen if you laid a hand on one of *their* cars, that one, he, he has parking privileges—this is New York, I say, who listens?—privileges written into his . . . what?" The door, gained now, proved recalcitrant, Hornbeck sadly relinquished the elbow, pulled violently at the door, the Universal Buck giving slightly, more so than the portal it framed, crumbs of brick tumbling onto Hornbeck's arm, and he fished in a pocket, found a key, continued, "I usually *like* taking the courtyard, why I took you, spring and summer it gets some green in there," looking back at the battered automobiles as the hammering resumed, "you meet too many people in the walkway," nutating toward the structure overhead which spanned the width of the courtyard, linking two sides of the building, "they *want* things, you know, but on clear days you can see the river, Jersey, from there, now they've torn down the tracks," entering, proceeding down a baffling series of broad corridors, their jagged shifts thoroughly disorienting to Marzio, who followed close at Hornbeck's heels, gripping the wall like a blind newborn animal, turning yet another corner and descending a ramp which declined at an angle of approximately forty-five degrees, "Watch, here, it's not for people, I don't know why. . . ." At bottom, the ramp opened onto a large square room, a freight elevator recessed in one of its walls. Hornbeck ceased talking for a moment to jab at the button. "Listen, Paul, sorry, I don't mean to be, to be babbling like a bag lady here, it's just property, destruction of valuable property on that level, in the name of social justice, it bothers me, they come to me, I OK it, but still, I said, 'Why not show the kid *building* a car, working as part of a harmonious team, black, white, chinks, whatever?' A Christmas kind of thing. My big mouth: they said I was denying them their artistic freedom. Did I ask for 'We, We Are the World'?"

The elevator arrived, an open cage. Progressing, passing levels painted varying dirty shades of black, white, black, gray, and finally white, stopping on this pale tier and stepping into a corridor, moving toward the white door, marked PRIVATE, at its slightly less moribund end, through it, into a dim, bluepainted, thickly carpeted hallway, framed posters and photographs lining the walls, the Blonde Waitresses, Big Effin' Hammers from Hell, Brave Lobsters, Blaiza Glori, others from the stable, past and present, all beset and dominated by the regular, recurring image of Hi-Fi, its component faces: at the Grammys, in hysterics over a partially obscured newspaper headline, at Cannes, backstage at the Nassau Coliseum; the overall effect that of a shrine or memorial. Hornbeck stalled on the threshold of the room to which the hallway inevitably led, Marzio colliding with him while taking his penultimate carpeted step before treading on the wide polished boards of the room. Hornbeck turned to lay both hands on Marzio's lapels, adjusting the knot in his tie, Marzio stepped back, fingers nervously seconding whatever imperceptible alteration Hornbeck had made to the cravat, as Hornbeck fiercely whispered: "He's, he's still *resting*."

The room was filled with grey daylight trickling through the huge and hazy windows, the wire mesh set within the panes of glass illuminating the building's industrial origins, and with two battered steel desks, a four-drawer file cabinet, a swivel chair, a straight chair, a portable lectern, two wastepaper baskets, a cork bulletin board, two tensor lamps, a metal storage cabinet, a drafting table on which curled and yellowing blueprints detailing a massive stage set were unfurled and pinned, and a portable black and white television set, which was turned on, the volume low. Seated in the swivel chair behind one of the desks a figure ate grapes from a white porcelain bowl in the shape of a toilet.

"Yoo, yoo-hoo . . . anybody home?"

"Just Jay 'Wool Hat' Lustig."

"Jay, good to have you, you don't know, you look, it's so *good*."

Jay rose to extend a tentative hand toward the lacuna between Hornbeck's outstretched arms, withdrawing even the hand and retreating a step as Hornbeck persisted in his synthetic enthusiasm, grimacing, "Take it easy," as hug encircled, climaxed, and resolved into mutual backslapping. Flushed, smiling, Hornbeck took two suits in tow as he made introductions, and then all sat, Hornbeck lingering on his feet for a moment before turning one of the wastepaper baskets upside down to use as a chair, sheets of discarded vellum tumbling to the floor. Lustig reached out to further expose the stem. Taut skin, sweet juice. Marzio watched the grapes disappear, gnarled stem taking shape from beneath the moist fruit, skeletal against the white of the bowl. Lustig plucked another grape, examined it momentarily prior to ingestion.

"Out of season. Maybe. You know I don't know. You know I don't know what the fucking street outside my house looks like?"

"He's kidding. Kidding. Jay is very, *very* active in the—"

"Now, who *is* this guy? One of Dimitri's sanitized hacks? He's hungry, I see it in his face, I remember what it's like. More dangerous than Albert Goldman. You're out in some fucking literary firetrap in Brooklyn, in Williamsburg, right? Watching the plaster crack, listening for those urchin footsteps on the stairs, no wonder you're such a poor hungry motherfucker, driving those rents up in search of the pure, your cathartic goddamn hand and a white page, alchemy, right! Why not type out some old *Tiger Beat* article and triple space it, add your own interpolations. Make sure each one is as Juicy, Chewy, and Yummy as what it's embellishing. Why even talk to me? Deal with this beautiful man. This is a beautiful guy. You know that? The lies, the sheerest bullshit. Shameless! Did you know he tried to lean on the Nobel Committee to consider us for the peace thing after *Live from Club Auschwitz?*"

"A tack, tactical move, Geldof was coming on strong."

Hornbeck stretched to daintily grasp one of Marzio's neglected lapels.

"Once we all had a perfect, coherent, all of us, them on the creative end and me not so much but still, on the business end, and we all knew, knew what we needed, were looking for—"

"Too scatological for Stockholm. . ."

"Ah, perfect coherent vision of the perfect rock and roll band, what it would consist of . . . and it was *good!*"

". . . they'd rather take the prize money and quietly invest it in DeBeers."

"I listened, listen, speaking of, I was listening to *Club Auschwitz*—"

Lustig's face collapsed in on itself, muscles moving in imitation "'Oh the power, the pain, I felt the pain of six, six million'—you hypocritical little fuck—now he hypes Nation of Rage and 'Evil, Evil Jew.' I am of course obligated to be a party to this, *all* of this."

"That's, that's business Jay, one thing I've learned—"

"Dead Jews sell records? Good business is where you find it? Just Do It?"

"I, I was going to say—my conduct is controlled by the customs of those around, in the business, it's not what I necessarily want, but certain rules, you expand or you, well, die, perish, sink. It's something you might, might want to consider."

"Fuck it."

Hornbeck exhaled heavily, hit chest with fist in cardiac feint (tired gambit).

"Jay, we, we want, need, to present a united front, here, now more than ever, it's, it's not . . ." he made conciliatory gestures, churning motions with open palms, "the point is, there's a real America, thataway—"

"'Thataway'?" Jay's wet fingers flailed toward the Hudson, sticky precipitation landing on Marzio's jacket.

"Yes, ah, thataway, and, and it wants real American words, words about condoms and crack babies and little girls getting caught in wells, the 'suburb sound,' the 'suburb feel.' "

"Nothing I know shit-all about, pardner."

"This, it isn't *news*, Jay. Five, five million units shipped, four and a half million returned, and he wonders, you wonder, people wonder—no wonder I have the acid stomach, the blackie, black tarry, bowel movements. I have the greatest respect for you, as an artist and a person, but what is this, this, this 'Canal Street'? this 'Cinema Village Balcony of Manhattan'? It doesn't, doesn't take a, you don't have to be a rocket scientist to figure out that nobody's interested in your 'Me and My Cheez Doodles,' except maybe Borden, who we don't *don't* have a contract with. So we find, find ourselves . . . ah. . . ."

"'Now we have a crisis situation.'"

"Now yes we *do* have a critical crisis situation, thank you very much, it transcends, it intensifies, everyday business. A united front, we have to close ranks here. I don't want to get, go into a big thing about this EMP-TV deal, but Jay, Jay, the beauty part—*no* out-of-pocket touring or promotional expenses. *No* merchant's right of unlimited returns to be, be exercised. All, *all* rebroadcasting and publishing rights revert after the first airing. Two sponsors who we *already* got endorsement deals going with, like a double dip. I, we all, understand, this is a frustrating situation, you're not happy with the, with all the, but the details, nothing is etched in—"

"Not happy? Me? Some asshole writing our songs for us? Like the fuckin Monkees?"

"Now, when we first, first proposed the, ah, proposition, you and David especially both, both seemed very amenable to the—"

"My old friend Dave's had writer's block since he started ordering Trojans by the gross. Either that or someone swiped his rhyming dictionary."

"—and then *you* took your little, little break up at, whatchamacallit, Greystoke?"

"*Moor.*"

"The . . . what?"

"Grey*moor*, Iago."

"I, I don't—but, in any rate, negotiations had to, to be negotiated, time is a, a time-sensitive issue."

Jay sighed. He turned to look at the television screen, on which Richard Poindexter shattered stained-glass windows. "Good old Richie," he said. "Is it true that O'Connor let him use St. Patrick's in return for a cut of the gross?"

"Jay, we can postpone, do this later, you should—did you take your medicine today?"

"*Every* day." He laughed.

"I, I'm sorry Maul, Paul, I should have, he's really very very tired still. When do you get back from the Coast?"

"Sunday."

"Well, maybe next, next week maybe—"

Jay reached to increase the volume of the television.

> . . . levision series concept is apparently the latest element of an aggressive marketing strategy developed by Cronus executives, led by CEO B.J. Hornbeck in tandem with senior representatives at Hi-Fidelicatessen Management Services in response to Cronus' declining market share. The small, nationally dist . . .

"—What?"

> . . . bel's downward spiral has been exemplified by the sagging fortunes of Hi-Fi, the company's erstwhile mainstay . . .

"Huh how did the little bastard find out about—?"

"*I* told him."

> . . . uching bottom with the band's most recent
> release, *Lambs to the Slaughter*, which experi-
> enced disappointing sales despite having been
> timed to exploit the Christm . . .

"Jay, you don't know, you could have, this could, it's all privileged, insider, tip-top secret—"

> . . . lieved that the two companies have been
> involved in discussions about the project with
> Empire Communications' Vice President for
> Creative Development, Peter Dimitri, since
> early fall . . .

"This is, it's foolish, it's spiteful and selfish—"

> . . . lthough early reports of the deal, long
> rumored to be in the offing but consistently
> denied by representatives of both companies,
> sent Cronus stock soaring to a record high of
> $21.125 at closing yesterday, attention is now
> focusing on the propriety of the negotia . . .

"Oh my god. Oh my god. Oh my god."

> . . . pecially the apparent partnership between
> Cronus and Hi-Fidelicatessen, which is highly
> irregular . . .

"Strange bedfellows indeed."

> . . .ccording to one prominent entertainment
> attorney, Jeff Solowicz, probably tortious. . .

"You, you *are* crazy. The money, the money—do you know
how much *money* is involved here. The money."

> . . . rsistent rumors that unnamed members of
> the band are reportedly unhappy with the
> prospect of appearing on weekly televisi . . .

Jay cackled, "That's me!"

"You, you're not being fair, not being fair at all—"

> . . . culation is further fueled by reports that
> songs composed for the series would be cred-
> ited to band leaders Jay Lustig and Dave
> McCall while actually being written by outsid-
> ers. From New York, this is J Cheuse . . .

"Fuck fair, *motherfucker!* Ten years of this shit, I want a di-
vorce. Sitting there at that goddamn bar, making nice to that Nazi
bouncer so we could go on, and I thanked you for it! And now you

want me to be Mike Nesmith with the wool hat and the kooky fast-motion jump cuts and on EMP-TV yet."

With unexpected resolve: "And you will be." Hornbeck waved Marzio out of his chair, snapped, "Interview's over," coming around to gather a pendulous fold of textile in his hand, steering him toward the hallway, Marzio turning to look at the figure who toyed with the thoroughly denuded stem, half hearing ". . . tickets, I've got, you want? tickets? Really, very, *very* hard to get, *Stately Wayne Mania!*, Not The Real Thing But An Incredible Simulation, you'll enjoy . . . ," and then leaving him to the blackness of the world suspended within him, for the broad streets and the buzz of indifferent conversation.

Marzio awakens on the conference room table, stiff-necked and cold-footed. His pathetic manuscript awaits him. He stands, looking out the window at this bright cold morning, a slight scowl on his face. Tense anger ratchets up in him as he dresses, the seats behind him, unoccupied, reminiscent of all the reluctant depositions he has pulled, like festering teeth, variations on the same questions over and over, innumerable sadnesses all fueling some greater good that even he is ignorant of; the principals (of course) brushing it off, recalling nothing—just another night—but the peculiar insistence of the wronged, the injured, upon holding to memories of bitter clarity disturbs and moves him. "Black flies rose from it as I passed." What has he seen, scrutinizing ten years' worth of scrutiny, that arouses him like these iridescent minutiae? Of course such obfuscations are related to outright dismissal, one painting fact over the nucleus of an agenda while the other reverses the process, brazenly concealing truth within the privileged core. Yet, this glistening kinesis around decayed matter—the stories do enthrall.

He stands before the chalkboard sign outside of the bistro, reading daily specials written in lurid color beneath a nictitating eye formed from one of two letters O in the restaurant name, the other wide and staring out at him as his own pass blindly over the unappetizing list—Ham and Egg Pizza à Matin, Lone Star Barbecue Chicken Pizza, Mauna Loa Pineapple Pizza—faintest stirrings of hunger from within; he shifts the attaché case from hand to bare hand, considers his pride, considers the cold, opens the door.

Those at the bar when he enters take no discernible notice of his arrival; he lingers at the threshold allowing his eyes to grow used to the dazzling light under which public house amity withers, the antiseptic cleanliness that exterminates any chance at intimacy, before moving forward as white-oxford-shirt-and-black-skirt approaches, speech breaking silence as she edges past him to slip behind a lectern he has left in back of him (a perimeter violated); he instinctively turns to follow the sound of her voice and sees her open a leather book embossed in gold, *Hoodwink's*, he mentions the Sponsor's name; her responding voice testy? (he is early), friendly? (she moves out in front of him, dactylologically bidding him to follow), he walks behind her through the dining room, past tiny portions laid out like advanced continental drift on enormous white porcelain plates, past inflated rubber lobsters, past velvet Elvis paintings, past huge sombreros, past a large plastic snowman in Wayfarers and with brightly colored jams covering its sexless naked body, past fish embedded in clear Lucite blocks, past scores of underweight women, past Stanislavskian busboys chiseled beneath their uniforms, past three papier-mâché Corinthian columns supporting nothing, capitals and astragals well short of the ceiling, past a space divider constructed entirely from cases of Brooklyn Lager beer, into a secluded rendezvous overlooking not so much as simply overlooked, its single table unoccupied. He is left alone to sit, brood, snap breadsticks in half. Eventually, he opens the briefcase to remove the manuscript, discovers the urgently colored Federal Express envelope there, breaks the seal, begins to read.

VIA FEDERAL EXPRESS

January 18, 1991
Mr. Paul Marzio
144 Prince Street, Ste. 300
New York, NY 10012

Dear Paul:

Just wanted to make sure my side of things is represented accurately. I know only too well how these things can go if left unchecked—there is a kind of event that can be made manifest only through the creation of an artifact that substitutes for memory. Through this, the moment itself is made incandescent, reinforced in its ability to withstand recall. I had been amazed by the first trial I attended. Banker's box after banker's box rolled into the courtroom on handtrucks, exhibits numbered well into the thousands. Although the volume of paper initially staggered me, I gradually realized, while watching the subtle pattern of interaction that had evolved between judge, jury, witness, and attorney, that a mere sheaf of documents somehow served to convey the pressure in the air on the evening that the events which had brought us all together in court had occurred; the breezy smell of eucalyptus and surf; the hum of the refrigerator in the plaintiff's kitchen, which had exploded when he opened it, tearing him into pieces. The law had seized me then, its desultory appeal replaced by something more purposeful. Although the man's body had not blown apart along any recognizable anatomical lines, his plight had been summarized and presented to twelve ashen-faced jurors as neatly as a puzzle. This is the sort of past with which our civilization is most comfortable, I think. It is established by consensus, which proves nothing, since unanimity of opinion only demonstrates people's willingness to rely on the specious. Any information posited becomes "fact" simply by dint of its existence. The truth lies somewhere between fact and propaganda, and can be assembled, piece by piece, from the raw materials at my disposal. My skill with the manipulation of such data has won me acclaim and a certain amount of prestige in the community, no members of which ever question the sinuous practice of tinkering with history's recondite shape. And why should they? Henry Ford had insisted that history is bunk and then had gone on to prove it by transforming the nation into its own bloated myth. Henry Ford is the reason why I live in a house at the edge of the desert, in the center of the only truly great metropolis to spring full-blown from the American psyche. Three hundred years ago a houseplant wouldn't have survived here, yet now it is Paradise, bounded by the peaceful ocean which swallows men, ships, and airplanes. In coming here after Cardozo, I had escaped from the wreckage of my youth, leaving it behind along with the greater part of the continent. I knew that, from then on, there would be constant conditions to maintain, nebulous standards that served as the bedrock of this unstable land and concrete objectives that hovered tantalizingly above them. I knew that there were secret desires, clotted with filth and degradation, but that there were appearances which could legitimize and bury them. Gigantic segments of my life were thus banished to that ghetto of things I "used to do," things I could refer to with a sort of chuckling nostalgia or feigned horror, as if discussing the youthful theft of hubcaps: processed food, canvas hi-tops, blended whiskey, tub-in-kitchen railroad flats, tobacco, domestic lager. There was a substantial period of time during which I made many mistakes— the first time I'd referred to the "L.A. Times" I hadn't realized that "L.A." served as a pejorative, and there was a starchy silence around the conference room table that even my wise selection of a bran muffin instead of a glazed doughnut could not dispel—but the lessons were learned easily enough and I don't believe that any permanent damage resulted from my faux pas. Even the glazed doughnut slid effortlessly into the past. What is it about illustrating my concern for the future of my bowels that indicates to the Partners that I'm able to handle increased responsibility? Who cares? It's all related, in some way, to low-cholesterol foods and caffeine-free diet colas, to health club memberships and utter indifference in the face of incipient melanoma, to the controlled ire I'm expected to express at the theft of the BMW emblem from the hood of the 325i and the careful, careful nursing of that single glass of chardonnay at lunch.

The fact of my life as Nat Phenomenon rests much more uneasily in that area of past regrets. I have done everything I possibly can to conceal it, a task which has been made no less difficult by Hi-Fi's rise to fame. Fortunately, almost as if by mutual agreement, all of the official histories that have been disseminated carefully omit any mention of the fact that I was one of the original members of the band. I'm sure that this hasn't been done in order to spare me from embarrassment or a sense of loss that, oddly, was most acutely felt while the band still endured obscurity, but rather to preserve some illusion of fluid continuity, a sense that everything is as it had been in the beginning, that it will always be that way. Even the old photographs have somehow been altered so that my image is excised entirely! You must understand that my reluctance to "cooperate" with you is based on my sincere and empirically supported belief that the Hi-Fi "phenomenon" (please pardon the pun) is due to come to an end, that ultimately, and very soon, the time will come for the legend to begin feeding on its own darker side. The indications of this are irrefutable and are surely obvious to you. I am convinced that when this does occur, the ugliness people will seek at the heart of the band will be traced to me. This sends a shock through me so profound that for hours (*billable* hours) I am reduced to straightening piles of papers into even rectangular stacks, or walking from my office to the elevators touching each surface that lies to my right, or methodically multiplying numbers in an effort to grasp the relationships between the sums of the digits of the products and their progenitors. I have no time for the good old days. Yet, I have some of the materials you provided me at the office now; they're spread out on my desk and overflowing onto the floor and the visitors' chairs. Photographs, fliers, tapes, documents. Fifteen hours of not looking at them has sharpened them, rid me of the compulsion to view them in purely formal terms—I can refer to the images in the past tense, instead of as present abstractions. But still, there's a certain disconnectedness, a sense that it's all remote from my life. Mostly there's a fear that somehow these ghosts, long since laid, will infiltrate and disrupt whatever it is I've built, not because I feel that my entire present can be wiped clean by the revelation of the excessive behavior that I'm certain can and will be imputed to my past (although I'm convinced that it could have *precisely* that effect), but because the sudden disclosure that I was once one of them, the actual confirmation of their flesh-and-blood status, might upset the balance of things. Pete Best, you'll recall, was a suitably tragic figure—to be one step from attaining that kind of total fame and then to plunge to the mindbending reality of a lifetime spent slicing bread seems appropriate, if not just. But even in my anonymity, I'm the personification of what America plugs away toward, even as it keeps a wistful eye on the four figures descending from an airplane, mounting a stage, delivering perfect ripostes to reporters' questions at eagerly awaited press conferences: an excellent education, a six-figure income— I've even been approached by the local Republican Club as a potential candidate for the state assembly. You can see that the newspapers would adore the discovery of the "former Hi-Fi" flipping burgers at a McDonald's—but to find me in an Armani suit on my way to the Toastmasters meeting could create nothing short of a panic.

I enjoyed the photographs, though. Unlike the others, I can remember the circumstances surrounding each of them. I can imagine the boring routine they endure now, entire days set aside for photo sessions, photographers constantly in the recording studio while they attempt to work. The sustenance of the image seems to be much more grueling than its creation. Back then it had been exciting, and the tension and self-consciousness we brought to what we perceived as immortality is evident in all of those flared nostrils and flexed quadriceps, awaiting our transformation in the pan of developer from four boys on a railroad track (shadowy alley, debris-strewn lot, tenement stoop) into a Rock Band. Even the feel of the instrument against my abdomen, its neck under my thumb, failed to do that—there was little fun in any of that, too much work was involved, afterwards we had to load the equipment into a cab or carry it through the streets, the hot lights blinded you and made you sweat, strings broke, microphones went dead, tiny audiences sat mute at the conclusion of a song, or an entire set, God. Rock and roll's promise had never seemed to lie in the deafening chaos of its execution, where everything, finally, was indistinguishable. Of course there were no nuances, no shades—what else could we do but slam head-on into everything? It's All Right! I Like It! I Love You! "Baby!" I'd shout, singing the sixth above Jay's lead vocal. These raving sentiments were utterly appropriate no matter what their inspiration. But what do *you* want with these pictures? I can just see you poring over them, attaching significance to this one or that one or, worse, letting them speak for themselves. Disaster. I must know what they say or can be made to say. Looking now at my reflection in the sheet of plate glass that overlooks the evening traffic on Santa Monica and the reflective Mylar facades of its buildings; the lamp behind me obscures my expression, my features, the very color of my clothing. It doesn't matter. Take my word for it, since then I've gained a little weight, two diagonal lines have begun to form, framing my upper lip. It's part of my job description to be aware of such things; to stand in the men's room, listening to the rude eliminative noises of the high and the mighty, complaining sotto voce but audibly about some nonexistent receding hairline. Do you think you're going to do me a favor of some kind by "setting the record straight"? Do you really believe that I feel I'm missing out on something by having been denied the privilege of becoming a prime target or inspiration for every vengeful maniac in America? (I can imagine someone gunning down Bush in the next couple of months for the love of Dave McCall!) By having been denied the privilege of having twisted cripples reach out to me for sustenance? I realize the difficulties inherent in attempting to impose the perspective of old perceptions upon the clean lines of the present. I've often wondered, Where Are They Now? Objects of affection, objects of scorn—no real way to view them as individual human beings, to understand them as people who breath air, walk the earth, fart, piss in the sink— although I realize that this is precisely the sort of trivia that the fans dote on, can't you see that it has the effect of distancing them even further? Instead of taking this arcane data and *comparing* it to normative behavior, it instead becomes the *model* for normative behavior. Fact: When *Tractor Law* appeared in 1987, Jay was pictured on its sleeve wearing a sweatshirt from the University of Illinois at Urbana-Champaign. The admissions office later reported that inquiries had more than doubled!

One paradox has haunted me throughout the years, the fact that in avoiding all of that madness I also lost the opportunity to shrink and vanish, to lose myself within the rock and roll hero's shell. Nobody ever understood that I'd sought to lose myself in that band; that my interest in rock and roll was not based on some preening exhibitionism but instead on a shyness that sought a kind of public non-identity. The very name I took then suggested the sort of remote persona through which I sought recognition. What else is a natural phenomenon other than some mundane law of physics raised to the level of spectacle? Not that I wanted personally to be associated with this condition. Frankly, I would have preferred that the band itself be named "Nat Phenomenon." Yet Hi-Fi was, and is, sufficient, suggests perhaps that the band is merely the faithful agent of some higher truth. They riveted the planet's attention to a certain image, a certain sound, a few memorable anecdotes, and thereafter ceased to exist.

Today I left the office early, went to the beach near my house, parking adjacent to the broad esplanade overlooking the ocean and then descending to the beach itself, barefoot, my pants rolled at the cuff and billowing gently in the wind, my jacket thrown over my shoulder, mimicking an image I had seen hundreds, if not thousands, of times. I stood in the surf staring at the improbably large sun as it slowly set, its light hanging at the rim of the earth, darker high and gradually darkening lower in the sky, as if I were waiting for the world to pass through me, changing to meet my pain and indecisiveness and then, rotating slowly, disappear into darkness. I knew this wouldn't happen. I turned and walked back toward the stairs climbing to the esplanade, watching my shadow undulate as it moved across the broken surface of the beach. My wife has given me a needlepoint motto for my office, "He Who Works With His Back To The Sun Never Gets As Far As His Shadow." She is a Protestant and I have come to expect such things from her, just as I expected the home-cooked meal she would ambush me with: burnt chicken breast, boiled potatoes, mineral water, a spinach salad piled high with the dripping flesh of vegetables. Listen to the details of her day, virtually indistinguishable from those of any other, only the faces of the aerobics instructor and the pool man change. The thought of the pool man disturbed me, for some reason, and I sagged to my knees, just yards shy of the stairs climbing to the esplanade, and began to caress the rough sand that had been sloppily applied to a child's castle or other "structure," smiling grimly to myself. At home, I reasserted control, attempted to catch her unaware. I slunk into the back yard, peering through the kitchen window at her, a figure mechanically performing chores in a warm and brightly lit room. I watched as she swept debris from the counter into the palm of her hand and took a sponge and began to methodically wipe its surface, her arm working in a big, regular motion. She stopped, leaning on her arms on the counter, exhaling or sighing (who could blame her?), bringing a hand up to her forehead and sweeping the hair from it, dragging her hand slowly back over her scalp and allowing the strands to fall into place, then tossing the sponge into the sink and wiping her hands on a dishtowel. Her secret life, mundane as it may be, is something I try to penetrate as often as possible, partially out of the

wild desire to catch her at something, but mostly out of my pleasure in the inequity of it; the idea that I violate her more deeply
than the brittle circumstances of our marriage would seem to allow.
She knows nothing of me beyond what little I have allowed her to
know. Her acceptance of my reinvention of myself seems complete
and satisfactory to her, and I remain convinced that she could use
the discovery of what remains concealed to tease dead things back
to life. Your call, of course, had disturbed her. I put her off, but I
could tell she wasn't mollified. The curiosity you aroused, simply
by making a bell ring in my home, speaking a few vague words to
her. Intolerable. At dinner I went on for as long as I could with my
limping conversation regarding the beauty of Monopoly and the
game's "relentless, implacable logic." We then had a brief argument arising from my innocuous referral to her as "big." She
demurred to this on grounds too predictable to enumerate here.
Bone structure, etc. I stared deeply into her cornflower blue eyes
searching for signs of any neural activity whatsoever. Panic. No
pad to multiply numbers on—are interrogatories really only a
means to generate more client fees, or are they a valid and constructive method of discovery? Is the patio door locked? Was there
a period during the early sixties when working-class Brooklyn was
mercilessly canvassed by aluminum siding salesmen? What is the
self-myth that lies at the heart of my aspirations? Is it possible for a
toilet to explode, and, if so, is the likelihood of such explosion
increased if one is sitting upon it? What is the latent heat of fusion?
Can it occur in a bucket, in Mormon Utah? Why do chainsaws and
airports have precisely the same visceral effect on me? What is it
that occasionally makes me feel sympathetic toward Hitler? Pete
Best, Signe Anderson, Mick Taylor, Glenn Matlock. Ringo Starr,
Grace Slick, Ron Wood, Sid Vicious. Michael Bachmann. Our
kitchen table is constructed of imperfectly matched pieces of pine,
which rest unevenly on the floor and rock whenever an attempt is
made to cut food. Still, I looked affectionately around the house at
the things I'd accumulated, the volume of them, the way that the
purchase or acquisition of each had negated a void that I hadn't
known existed until the precise moment at which it was filled, and
the way the item then disappeared into the whole as if it had never
been absent. I began to feel the disorder begin to edge its way in,
was aware of the tenuousness of it all, the delicacy with which
things are sustained, the probability that in spite of all efforts and
attempts to achieve knowledge and understanding life itself is a

meaningless interval in which one tries to keep occupied as painlessly as possible. Eventually, the skin will fall from my bones, my achievements lost and uncelebrated, and I will simply become another thing rotting into sameness with the earth. Until then you'd merely been a threat, but at that moment I sincerely loathed you, thought of you sitting in Brooklyn as if your conspicuous bohemian life was somehow a glorious sacrifice, as if you were sanctified by each waterbug you had to kill with your shoddy, 14th Street zori. All of your delusions of grandeur, all of your prattle about "truth," and you still couldn't rise above the clichés you comfortably spouted, trying to wheedle an invitation to drop by, trite lines about the beauty of the sky, the land, the ocean. Stupid idiot! Overhead, a helicopter speeds by to drop its payload of (nontoxic, the "Times" and county authorities stress) defoliant, executing the scorched-earth policy recently adopted against unvanquishable foreign insects. No doubt when the completion of the process once again leaves the tattered acreage in repose, it will emerge with the intent of its maker restored; as barren, inhospitable desolation. Or so God's agitpropagandists seem to suggest. I've seen them several times lately, on the esplanade, sandwich-boarded to the tune of the usual exhausted clichés, to wit, "THE END OF THE WORLD IS COMING," although they surely know that the planet itself will abideth forever, regardless of the status of its inhabitants. I think of all those beet-red American faces, quietly blackening where they've been left to rot. You think of yourself as a sharpshooter ensconced in an aerie high above life's stately procession; I'll show you what happens to miscreants. A mere corrective, one of life's little modifiers. Not that you'll necessarily register the lesson. But still, I wonder how it is that you can be so stupid as not to realize that Hi-Fi, that I, that you yourself, regardless of the descending order of our respective means (sorry about that), are all locked into the same rhythm—"Our music is just—well, *our music*." Swallowing Jay's bullshit whole and then proceeding as if there's actually anything palpable to debunk. Thirty seconds' worth of concerted thought would have led you to the inescapable conclusion that every square inch of Hi-Fi's territory—its image, its music, its fame—was surveyed, mapped, parceled out and sold while Jay was still in diapers, perhaps even longer ago than that. Like all idols of the marketplace, Hi-Fi dominated, but never outgrew, the original open-air souk which created and then clamored for it. An infinite amount of "product" is available for consumption, but in the end it's only four men that everybody seeks, four men existing according to the same limitless rules and the same finite boundaries as the rest of us, irrepressible id of adorer and adored notwithstanding. Dolls. Lunchboxes. Saturday morning cartoon shows. Bedsheets cut into thousands of square-inch sections. As if the wearying idea of confronting one's self in the clothing and hairstyles of the kids on the street isn't enough, there are still the records, videos, and concerts to be dealt with. Lost children, all of them, surrendering their dreams and reposing them in these four dimming lights. I'll tell you something: the Aztecs took the bravest and handsomest prisoner of war and for one year turned him into a demigod. He was given beautiful women and fine clothing, permitted to study with the priests, and taught to play the flute. At the end of the year he walked to a pyramid topped by an altar, accompanied by his consorts, who sang mournful songs of grief. Ascending, he broke the clay flute he had mastered into pieces on the stone steps as he went. Then he was laid upon the altar, given a perfunctory dose of cocaine, and had his heart ripped out with an obsidian blade. No doubt that at the base of the pyramid there were always watchful Aztec Marzios, wisely kept in a state of expressionless illiteracy by the ruling classes. Not that rodents like you ever fail to do anything but stutter on the truth when it would seem to be yours to impart. The contradiction lies in the way that your fluency seems to extend only to those things that are self-evident (your rapture over the sea! surf! sun! sand!—I'm going to be *sick*). Nevertheless, the placid orthodoxies according to which I, too, have constructed my life are loaded with the restrained energies that can never achieve their potential through the specific outlets provided for their venting. You and I are of a kind, all right: we both opted for the pound of feathers over the pound of coal, and we both have paid the terrible price of self-inflicted obscurity. Whatever it is that has prompted you to conceive of this book, and has prompted me to do anything within my power to preserve the whiteness of the page, can not have been succored by either of our rash acts, and will ultimately seek an exit. I calm myself with my belief that both of us will, in the end, have our due; that both of us, eventually, will at last rejoin Hi-Fi onstage, at the center of the spectacle which has for so long engaged the attention of the world. Everything else: the prevailing avatars of state, commerce, letters, sport, cinema—mere peripheral squiggles. That is because they smack of the continuum, I think, of civilization's inexorable dragging of itself forward. Rock and roll, rock and roll. Its very transience enhances the impalpable now, capturing fragments of it and carrying them against the flow of time. If you click, soar to the summit, capture an era, it is impossible later to contemplate that era without believing that every event held you at its core. It's a shame that it is not possible for upheaval in this case to come about through death and exile, through blasphemous denunciation of the hallowed corpse lying in state; the revolutionary photographer's study of overturned Chippendales and cups half full of cold tea—that sudden rupture in the facade. It occurs to me that revisionism has a double edge, that it is not necessarily upheaval but a kind of fastness that is sometimes sought, an anchor to which a nebulous future can be secured. Why do you want to toy with the natural order of things? It'll end, soon enough, but of its own accord. When a moment reaches its apogee, the shadow of the calm which is inevitably to follow should never be permitted to cross the stunned, blinded faces of its architects and participants—worse times *are* a-comin'! (the words, my credo; the knowledge, my cross)—but if you listen very carefully, you can hear it as the fat lady begins to sing.

Very Truly Yours,
NATHANAEL SPIELVOGEL, ESQ.

NS:vsf
cc: File

h   10/2014 S